—Diana Gabaldon, author of the Outlander series

'In Gortner's skillful hands, plots and counterplots come to seething life . . . . Lovers of Tudor history and suspense fiction will be riveted by this swift-paced, sexy, enthralling novel.'

—Nancy Bilyeau, author of *The Crown*

'Gortner has done it again! Intrigue at the Tudor court never looked more lethal than in his capable hands, as forbidden desires and deadly rivalries turn sister against sister and plunge our bold hero into a labyrinth of deceit. Full of breathtaking action, dark twists, and unexpected revelations, this is an unputdownable read!'

—Michelle Moran, author of *Nefertiti*

Praise for THE TUDOR SECRET

'Gortner handles action with aplomb, adding a riveting, fast-paced thriller to the crowded genre of Tudor fiction.'

—*Publishers Weekly*

'Even Tudor fans who know the main players and historical backdrop will be captivated by Gortner's storytelling and his engaging hero . . . Grabbing reader interest [with] the quick pace and lush historical references. This novel is both entertaining and thoughtful.'

—*Romantic Times*

'Brilliantly executed plot and three-dimensional characters . . . highly recommended.'   —*Historical Novels Review*

'An exciting, vividly rendered story of intrigue and espionage.'

—*Book List*

'If you're looking for a book that will pull you back into the Tudors, this one is a good choice.'   —*Bookreporter.com*

Also by Christopher Gortner

The Tudor Conspiracy
The Tudor Secret

Writing as C.W. Gortner

The Last Queen
The Confessions of Catherine de Medici
The Queen's Vow

The
Tudor
Vendetta

Christopher Gortner

HODDER

First published in Great Britain in 2014 by Hodder & Stoughton
An Hachette UK company

First published in paperback in 2015

1

A CIP catalogue record for this title is available from the British Library

Paperback ISBN 978 1 444 72092 1
eBook ISBN 978 1 444 72104 1

Printed and bound by CPI Group (UK) Ltd, Croydon, CR0 4YY

Hodder & Stoughton policy is to use papers that are natural,
renewable and recyclable products and made from wood grown in
sustainable forests. The logging and manufacturing processes are expected
to conform to the environmental regulations of the country of origin.

Hodder & Stoughton Ltd
Carmelite House
50 Victoria Embankment
London EC4Y 0DZ

www.hodder.co.uk

For Erik

The past cannot be cured.
—ELIZABETH I

The
Tudor
Vendetta

Chapter One

She stood before me, clad in black velvet, her mane of blond hair tangled about her face. Shadows embraced her; as she moved toward the cot where I lay as if paralyzed, her long hands reached up to the lacings of her bodice and she began to undo them, one by one.

I could not move; I could barely breathe. Desire raged through me. I heard myself moan; that one, weak sound crumbled my resistance. She was so close, I already anticipated raveling my hands in her lush hair, feeling the warmth of her tongue in the whirlpool of our mouths and the current of her touch as she yanked at my clothes, pulling down my hose to grasp my hardness.

"I want to know something other than fear," I heard her whisper. "I want to feel desire, if only this once." Her gown was now unlaced. I watched with my heart in my throat, knowing in some dark part of my soul that if I did this, I would never forget or escape it. I must live with the remorse until the end of my days with the betrayal of the woman I truly loved, who waited for me even now, far away and unaware.

But as the dark velvet of her gown pooled at her feet and I

beheld her flawless skin, her rose-tipped breasts, and ribs woven like lyre strings under her pallor, I couldn't think anymore. She lowered herself upon me and I pushed inside her roughly, in fury, feeling myself engorge even more as I coaxed pleasure from her, until she bucked her hips to meet my stride.

My seed gushed forth with breath-shattering suddenness. She clenched herself about me, making me cry out. And as I shuddered, our heat subsiding like smoke from a doused fire, I felt her cold hand pressed upon my chest and looked up to meet her eyes as she lifted her hidden knife swiftly, its edge gleaming, before she brought it down, plunging into my heart—

"Nooo!"

With my shout still on my lips, I bolted upright in my narrow bed. Gasping, struggling for reality as it opened around me in jagged pieces, I kicked my covers aside and pulled myself to the edge of the bed, lowering my face and cradling it for a moment in my hands.

"Breathe," I told myself. "It's not real. It was a dream. She is gone. Dead." Coming to my feet, the remnants of the nightmare sticking to me like cobwebs, I realized my nightshirt was drenched, soaked in sweat. I yanked it off and padded naked to the low table with its copper basin and pitcher, not feeling the pervasive cold until I tipped the pitcher over my mouth and drank, the icy water hitting my belly and making me tremble.

Turning to the bed, I pulled the scratchy wool blanket off it and wrapped it around me, hunching my shoulders as I gazed past the garret's narrow confines to the small, warped-glass window set like a lopsided eye in the wall. Outside, it was still dark, the spires and peaked rooftops of this foreign city a spiked silhouette against the night sky. As I sat there, huddled, the memory of my betrayal fading back into the depths where I had consigned it so I could keep on living, the indigo night began to lighten, a creeping pink-gold flush announcing dawn's arrival.

How long had it been? Sometimes, I almost forgot. Now, as I wrestled with the memory of what I had done, I forced myself to remember. Almost four years. Four long years since I had fled from my enemies, leaving everyone and everything I knew behind.

I had not left England willingly. Following my last harrowing assignment at court, where I had lost my cherished squire and nearly my own life, I managed to safeguard Elizabeth, but not enough to persuade her half sister Mary from sending her to the Tower. After two months of terrifying imprisonment, Elizabeth was released and sent under guard to a remote manor. My beloved Kate stayed by her side but I had not been able to get near them. The queen had ordered me from court and I'd taken refuge in the country home of my mentor, William Cecil, whose informants kept us apprised of Elizabeth's circumstances even as Mary embarked on a horrific persecution of her Protestant subjects in her zeal to please God and her husband, Philip of Spain. When word came that Mary believed herself with child, the noose tightened again around me. Her trusted adviser, the Imperial ambassador Simon Renard, whom I had previously outwitted, sent men on the hunt for me, and Cecil secretly arranged to send me here, to Calvinist-dominated Switzerland, where an agent of his, Francis Walsingham, resided after having fled England upon Mary's accession.

I let out a shivering breath, the knot in my chest starting to dissolve. Why now? Why, after all this time, had I once again dreamed of Sybilla Darrier? I had barely thought of her in so many months, even as I lived every hour of every day with the consequences of her actions.

Why did she haunt me still?

The minutes slipped past. I could not return to sleep. Once I heard our housekeeper, Gerthe, rattling about downstairs, stoking the fires and preparing the table for breakfast, I set aside the blanket to wash hastily with the water that remained in the pitcher. Freezing once more, I clambered into my nondescript uniform of black hose, breeches, and simple doublet—the garb of a Calvinist merchant-apprentice, my disguise.

"Up already?" asked Gerthe brightly in German, when she saw me enter the small chamber that served as our hall. She was a plump, industrious woman of indeterminate age, not remarkable in any way. I had seen a hundred like her every day in the streets, servants to a hundred households that appeared, at least on the surface, exactly like ours. Walsingham had chosen her because of it, I suspected, just as he no doubt ensured her loyalty by taking her occasionally to his bed. She had that warm, slept-in look about her this morning.

I gave her a smile, sitting on the stool at the table as she served me fresh goat cheese, brown bread, and a cup of mulled beer. "Is Master Thorsten awake?" I asked her, between mouthfuls, using Walsingham's alias.

She nodded, occupying herself at the hearth. "He went out early. He said you were to wait for him in his study." She glanced over her shoulder. "Go on. Eat more. You look pale, Master Johann. You must keep up your strength. Winter is here and I've a feeling it's going to be a hard one. It snowed a little last night already."

My alias was ridiculous, but Walsingham had insisted that

John was such a common name, no one would doubt it. As my command of German and Swiss was poor at best, he had to pass me off as a cousin's son, obliged to leave my native land because of the Catholic persecution. Those who fled Rome's depredations were welcome in Basel and, for the most part, went unquestioned. By now, every Protestant in Europe was aware of the horrors perpetuated by Mary Tudor against their brethren in England.

"In his study" was Walsingham's code for the chamber where he had taken to teaching me the intricacies of our craft. Finishing my meal, I thanked Gerthe and climbed back upstairs, past my room and down the hall, to the last door. I took the key from the inner pocket of my doublet and unlocked it. When I stepped inside, I found Walsingham waiting.

"Gerthe said . . ." I began, and he nodded. "I know. Close the door. I came back while she was fetching water from the well. Come and sit. It's time to begin."

His eyes, cold as onyx, stared at me. It never failed to unnerve me, that piercing look of his, like a coiled serpent about to strike. His spidery hands hung from the unlaced sleeves of his black doublet. Small-boned, with stark, angular features, permanently shadowed eyes, and a manicured beard, he appeared ageless, though he was not yet thirty. To those who did not know him, he would have seemed innocuous in his unrelieved black and skullcap perched upon his prematurely balding head—garb better suited to a Huguenot pastor than a man in secret service to Cecil, making me wonder why I had ever feared him. I first met Walsingham when I was still a callow squire to Robert Dudley, newly come to court. He had acted as go-between during my first assignment and I had found him a catlike and untrustworthy menace. Yet when I arrived after my voyage across the Channel and ride across the Low Countries, Walsingham had received me politely, if not with overt warmth.

I soon realized my mistake. He might not pose a threat to me, but he was dangerous, nonetheless. Once I had settled into his narrow gabled house, located in the merchant section of the city where international gossip was rife, he proceeded to impart a chilling mastery of death and survival. He had traveled extensively in the years since he had left England, into the courts of Italy and other, more distant lands, where intrigue was endemic and methods for disposing of one's foes both plentiful and imaginative.

He had no patience for error. I was there to learn, he said, and he challenged me almost at once with obscure texts and puzzles that required feats of calculation and memory. He taught me to write with both my left and right hands, including writing backward so that my message could be read only in a mirror. He set me to daily sessions to hone my skills with the sword and poniard, making me undergo grueling hours of practice that left my thighs and arms burning with exhaustion. Even more exacting was the mysterious art of how to empty myself of sensation through practices employed, according to him, by assassins in the Far East. He taught me to how to count each breath until I slowed my blood to a crawl in my veins, then had me sit naked and immobile before an open window exposed to winter's snowy blast, with only my breath to kindle heat in my limbs. He made me walk barefoot over strewn glass without acknowledging pain and conquer warrens of obstacles he prepared at night in the lanes outside to build my stamina. My body was his machine, which he set to stalking strangers and uncovering their secrets without them ever knowing I was there. I was astonished by how much I could learn about a person when they believed they weren't being watched, and appalled by the acts of cruelty and vice I witnessed—all of which, Walsingham assured me, were necessary fodder for blackmail.

Only once did I refuse him, when he ordered me to swim the width of the Rhine, insisting I overcome my aversion to water. Narrowing his eyes at me as I shook my head, he intoned: "Any weakness could be your undoing."

"I'll take my chances," I retorted. Because no matter how much he lectured on the importance of subduing our emotional frailties while conquering the inherent resistance of our bodies, I would never willingly brave another plunge into deep water.

Despite his lack of praise or encouragement, in time I began to realize he was impressed with me. I'd come to a land where the language gargled in my ears, a city where I knew nothing and no one; though only twenty-five, I was already a veteran of two missions in Elizabeth's defense and had relinquished any hope of having a normal existence. I had nothing to lose and everything to gain. I would excel no matter the cost. I had been at the mercy of those who would see me dead. When the time came, I must be ready.

As Cecil had told me, to be a spy was my fate.

Now, I saw on the table before Walsingham a plain wood casket, its lid open to reveal rows of identical cork-stoppered vials. I suppressed the urge to roll my eyes. This was his latest lesson in torment, which he had been subjecting me to for several weeks now. Taking my seat, I waited as he extracted a bottle, uncorked it, and set it before me.

I picked it up, brought it to my nostrils. Taking a deep inhale, but not so deep that anything could enter my lungs, I focused my entire being on what my sense of smell revealed.

"Lemon," I said at length. "And musk. . . ." I hesitated, trying to decipher something murky within the other smells, tantalizing yet elusive. What *was* it? I knew this scent. I had smelled it before. Was it part of a perfume? Or was it the sign of something venomous?

Walsingham's voice broke into my thoughts. "Poison or perfume? You don't have all day to deduce its contents. In most cases, if it's poison, you'll have less than a minute before the intended victim dies."

I lifted my eyes, staring hard at him. I had experienced the horror of his statement all too vividly. I had held a boy, my friend and squire, Peregrine, in my arms as he perished because I had not acted fast enough. Walsingham knew it, of course. He used it to his advantage to prod me into an emotional reaction.

"You shove this at me and expect me to decipher it in— what? Five seconds?" I said, knowing as I spoke that I was doing precisely what he intended. "It's perfume."

"It is not. And you must decipher it in less than five seconds." His bony finger tapped the sample before me. "Almond," he stated and I sagged in my chair. "Yes," he went on, with that insufferable superiority I'd come to dislike even more than his blank slate of a face, "most common poisons will smell faintly of almond, if you train yourself sufficiently to detect it. Though, of course, there are exceptions."

"But this wasn't one of them," I said.

He pursed his lips, retrieving the sample and returning it to the wooden casket. His hand hovered over the rows in search of his next selection. Poison or perfume?

Abruptly, I pushed back from the table. "Enough. I can't do this. My nose is still clogged from all the smells you had me work on yesterday."

Though he had perfect control over his expression, so that he often appeared more stone than flesh, I discerned mordant amusement in his gaze. Finally, he said, "Will you feel thus, I wonder, on the day you're called upon to defend our queen? This is what we *do*, Prescott. We are intelligencers. We cannot concede defeat even when we are weary, because our life is nothing compared to the one we must protect. You almost failed her last time and she barely survived it. Now, you must sacrifice everything you feel and think, if you're to become her weapon."

I gritted my teeth. Loathe as I was to admit it, he was right. I had nearly failed, and in the process been obliged to shed the last illusion I had that I might retain any semblance of the man I had been. Too much had happened. I'd been the cause of too much loss. The memory of Sybilla naked in my chamber, a siren of deceit, returned to grip me in a vise.

If I had been better prepared, she would never have destroyed as much as she had.

Peregrine might still be alive.

Tugging at my doublet, I turned to the narrow window of this bare room where I'd spent so many hours in sweltering heat or frigid cold, with this man for whom I bore no affection. As I gazed out onto the city, a sudden pang overcame me. I missed England. I missed it with everything I had inside me, though my life there had been rife with lies and sorrow, though I was as much a stranger in my own country as I was here. I missed the green of the hills, the majestic oaks, and the silver rain. Most of all, I missed Kate, even if I knew I could hold no claim on her anymore, not after what I had done.

"We bring our regrets with us wherever we go," Walsingham said from behind me, with that uncanny ability he had of discerning my thoughts. When he first did it, I had thought it an eerie coincidence. By the fifth time, I began to think he was a seer. Now, I knew it was but another of his sleights of hand, a trick he had perfected after years of studying the unspoken turmoil in those around him, while he stayed aloof.

I chuckled. "Am I still so obvious? I must be such a disappointment."

"Only to me," he said dryly. I heard the rustling of paper. Drawing a breath, I turned around, bracing myself for another endless day of unintelligible inscriptions I'd be expected to unravel. Besides the detection of poison, it was my most persistent challenge, the decoding of ciphers, and he knew it. He told me that educated men like me had a much harder time training their eye to see past the haphazard randomness of a cipher to the inevitable structure underneath.

"Every code has a flaw," he said. "None is invincible. But we allow its chaos to confuse and overwhelm us, just as its creator intended. We forget that if one man devised it, so can another man undo it."

I found it hardly reassuring, not when I faced a page that looked as if a rat had scampered over it with ink-stained paws, but I had nothing else to do and resigned myself to this next task, at which I would labor all day until supper, followed by—

My heart leapt. Walsingham held a paper with a broken seal.

"A letter," he said. "From my lord Cecil." When he saw my frozen stance, his lips twitched as if he found himself on the verge of a rare smile. "I thought to wait until we finished for the day. Evidently, we have."

He extended the paper. Snatching it from him, I devoured its contents with my eyes, then, realizing it was composed in Cecil's habitual cipher, made myself slow down and read again, carefully unpicking the code that I had by now committed to memory.

I looked up. "This says . . ." My voice turned harsh with incredulity. "You've waited all this time to tell me?"

"I hardly see how it makes a difference. We can't leave at a moment's notice."

"But, Elizabeth—this letter says she's already establishing her court at Whitehall!" Indignation exploded from me. "Queen Mary has been dead over a week!"

He shrugged. "I obey Cecil's instructions. He wrote first to advise me of the queen's illness, after it was discovered that her pregnancy was actually a malignant tumor in her belly. He relayed he would make the necessary arrangements when the time came. Passage had to be booked, passports obtained; I had to oversee the closure of this safe house and transfer of its contents. There are papist spies here, watching for us as surely as we watch for them. We must leave without rousing notice, part of the crowd of English Protestants who went into exile and now return at Elizabeth's behest. Secrecy remains of the utmost importance." He flipped the lid of his box shut. "We'll depart the day after tomorrow at first light. You can start packing."

I glared at him. I had nothing to pack, save for my clothes

and a few books. "I can be ready in under an hour," I said through my teeth.

His brow lifted. "Then I suggest you cultivate patience. The very fact that I have to remind you of it proves you're far from ready." He turned to the doorway, his coffer tucked under his arm. "We'll take an hour and then go over that cipher you couldn't break last night." His tone hardened as I began to lift protest. "Until we are back at court, Master Prescott, you remain under my charge. Is that understood?"

I gave terse assent, the letter announcing Elizabeth Tudor's accession crunched in my fist. If I could have, I would have swum back to England that very hour, my fear of deep water and his charge over me be damned.

Walsingham's snort as he walked out indicated he knew it, too.

Chapter Two

$\mathfrak{B}$y the time we landed in Dover four days later, waited for our luggage to be unloaded from the hold, and shoved our way through hordes of travelers to find the inn where the mounts Cecil had arranged for us were waiting, I almost wished I'd opted to swim instead. Crossing the Channel at any time of year was arduous enough, its currents and sudden tempests unpredictable as a vicious child, but in mid-November, with winter clamping down, the journey had been a purgatory that emptied my very guts.

I must have looked as terrible as I felt, for Walsingham arched his brow at me. "I trust you can ride? We've still a long journey ahead to reach the city and I'd rather not pay an exorbitant price for some lousy room in one of these overcrowded dockside inns."

"I can ride," I muttered, though I staggered like a newborn foal and could still taste the rot of sea-churned bile in my mouth. Coming upon the forlorn mares awaiting us, I realized I couldn't wait to reclaim my Cinnabar, whom I'd had to leave behind in Cecil's manor, and hoped someone had thought to bring my horse to court. "Though I hardly see how we'll get far on these," I said, as we strapped our bags to the saddles and sidestepped the muck of the yard to mount. "They look half-dead on their feet."

"Messengers have been racing back and forth across the Channel since Elizabeth took the throne," said Walsingham, as he fastidiously arranged his cloak over his saddle. "There probably aren't enough of these nags to satisfy the needs of those who send and receive intelligence. We're lucky to have obtained horses at all. We could have found ourselves crammed into public transport with the rest of this mob." As he spoke, he passed disdainful eyes over the city, its white-stone royal fortress brooding on the chalk cliff that overlooked the cluster of winding streets and crooked buildings, punctuated by a multitude calling, cursing, and shouting at each other. Squalling gulls and rooks wheeled overhead. Walsingham's nostrils flared as if he could detect individual smells within the general miasma of ordure, unwashed skin, and garbage.

"We'll be overwhelmed at this rate," he said, "all these exiles returning; there are too many of them and too few of us. I daresay, nobody's passport is even being checked. Anyone with a purse and able tongue can bribe their way in."

I paused. A chill went through me. His countenance had darkened. With another appraising stare at the city, he said to me, "Mark it well. This is how chaos sneaks in."

Yanking his mare about, he led us onto the road.

He proved as taciturn on horseback as he had on the ship, conveying only what was necessary to advance our progress. Still, we had no choice but to halt for the night. While our horses had proven hardier than their dejected attitudes suggested, we needed rest, and Walsingham chose a roadside inn after we'd gone far enough to outpace the multitude of carts and carriages departing Dover for the four corners of the realm.

Our room was a mean affair, containing a dirty mattress and rickety stool. We opted to sleep on the floor instead, wrapped in our cloaks with our bags as pillows, as neither of us was of a mood to be infested by vermin. Nevertheless, I ended up squashing numerous fleas and was scratching welts on my neck and arms in the morning. By the time we took to the road again after a breakfast of stale bread, flat beer, and moldy cheese served by a scowling wench with a boil on her lip, I was beginning to realize Basel's astringent Protestant air and scrubbed cobblestones had much to commend them.

Walsingham made no comment, though he too must have marked the contrast. We'd vacated a tidy home in a tidy Reformed city for a three-day ride through the Low Countries and along the coast to Calais, where we'd boarded a vessel to be tossed about like a child's toy, only to arrive unceremoniously back in our homeland along with hundreds of other refugees, who cluttered Dover like cattle. What did he make of it, this upheaval that had overtaken our existence? Even as we rode past the copses of oak trees on the side of the road, avoiding waterlogged ditches that reflected a leaden sky threatening rain, all around us the foundation of our world was shifting.

Yet Walsingham rode as if he were impervious, and soon the bite of the wind sinking its teeth in my neck subsumed my own ruminations. Muffled in my doublet and cloak, my cap pulled low on my brow, I anticipated the proverbial crack of thunder and gushing release of icy rain. Other travelers began to appear, walking in groups and riding on mules or carts, some driving livestock, shepherd dogs barking at their ankles. The road grew wider and more crowded, so that we had to slow our pace. I sensed a quickening in my nag's gait. Peering ahead through the dusk, I discerned a smoky haze hanging over the glittering breadth of the Thames. The river coiled like a dragon's tail, spanned by the great Bridge on its twenty stone piers. Beyond it clustered the city, having outgrown its ancient lichen-spotted walls—a patchwork of orchards, gardens, and affluent suburbs spilling beyond the main gates.

My chest tightened. Every time I had been in London, I'd ended up risking my life; this city was never safe for me, and as if he sensed my trepidation, Walsingham gave me a pensive glance. I thought he would merely rebuke me with his stare. Instead, he said quietly, with more consideration than he had thus far ever shown me, "Returning home is never easy, unless one is a fool. But here is where you belong. It is what—"

"We do," I interrupted, with a taut smile.

He nodded. "Indeed. Never forget it. On us now depends everything."

We left our horses in Southwark at the designated return stable, Walsingham muttering that he was in no temper to contend with the crowds lining up at the Great Stone Gate to traverse the Bridge. Night was falling, along with curfew, and a tide of impatient, tired travelers queued up for public wherries at the landing jetty of St. Mary Overy. The stench of churned-up leavings and the dirt in the streets were just as I recalled. I also detected, even here in this pleasure-loving district across from the City, where brothels, gaming dens, taverns, and baiting pits abounded, a tangible air of suspicion and impoverished fear. Gaunt figures hustled to various assignations without so much as a glance at each other, when in the past I'd noticed that Londoners, while invariably wary of visitors or foreigners, were usually pleasant to their fellow citizens. A lone gibbet near the Great Stone Gate revealed a potential cause: the rotting carcass of a Protestant, headless and limbless, so decayed its crow-gnawed ribs showed through tattered shreds of skin. I had no doubt that the rest of whoever this poor soul had been was hung on other gates, as was the habit with traitors, and averted my eyes as I had to force myself to look away from the many beggars, crawling on gangrenous stumps into doorways for the night. Emaciated dogs snarled and competed with feral urchins for leavings in the trash heaps.

A tribe of these orphans assaulted us as Walsingham whistled and called out for a private boat, thrusting out grubby hands to implore us for alms, their pitiful eyes and scrawny faces unable to hide a pack-like cunning as they circled us, angling to filch whatever they could. I'd contended with these Southwark wildlings before and tucked my purse, dagger sheath, and anything else that could be stolen into my clothing; with a disgusted moue, Walsingham yanked out a groat and tossed it as far as he could.

The children scattered to pursue it, snarling like curs. A wherry arrived just in time. Shouldering our bags, we boarded and I took my seat square in the middle of the bench, gripping it as Walsingham gave me a long look.

"To Westminster," he told the boatman. "And quickly, before the tide turns."

He wiped clotted dirt from his cloak as the vessel swirled into the Thames, the lights of Southwark winking behind us like distant stars. The boatman's lantern bobbed on its hook and cast erratic shadows over Walsingham's face, deepening the hollows of his cheeks. "Order and control," he said, as if to himself, "must be her first order of business. All that"—he sniffed, as if to rid himself of a distasteful smell—"evidence of papist savagery must be removed."

I heard an unusual undertone of fury in his normally reserved voice, but before I could remark on it, the boatman said, "Aye, Bloody Mary would've burned every last one of us, no matter that she gained her throne with our support. Good riddance to the bitch, I say; she might have been queen but no one's sorry she's dead."

His words plunged me into my last memory of the queen who'd been dubbed Bloody Mary by her own subjects, glaring at me in her chamber at Whitehall with her soiled gown gaping at her thin breast, ravaged by the knowledge that nothing she did or said could ever overcome her sister's magnetic appeal.

"She'd have seen our Bess dead, too," the boatman added, hawking phlegm over the side. "Mark my words: She'd have taken the princess's head sure as we sit here."

"Yes, well," said Walsingham tersely, "she's gone to judgment now, my good man."

"Hellfire's all she deserves. Let her get a taste of what she served up. Some might pray to the saints to see her through Purgatory but I hope she's headed straight to the Devil."

Walsingham grimaced. A staunch Protestant, he eschewed both the concept of salvation through Purgatory and the cult of saints; the boatman's declaration must have been an uncomfortable reminder of how religious unease still held sway over England. For many, the old faith and the reformed one had coalesced into a barely understood construct that people adapted to their particular needs. To Walsingham, this very idea was anathema. I could almost hear him making a mental note to address the issue of religious uniformity as soon as he had opportunity for audience with our queen.

Thoughts of Elizabeth quickened my blood as we reached the public water stairs at Westminster. We disembarked for the short walk to Whitehall. Night pressed in around us, inky cold; cresset torches in brackets shed soot as we came to a halt at the Holbein clock tower. Here, Walsingham produced documents, sent by Cecil, I assumed, to ensure our entry. While the guards inspected our safe conducts, I let my gaze pass over the imposing brick façade of this palace that I'd left in disgrace.

The mullioned casements were blazing with candles, the silhouettes of passing courtiers wavering behind the flame-lit glass. Faint laughter reached me; gazing into the enclosed great courtyard past the gates, I espied a couple muffled in sable and velvet, entering the palace through an archway. Whitehall was less a cohesive structure than a bewildering warren of interconnected buildings, an elephantine and still-unfinished pastiche. It had consumed the old palace of the archbishops of York, which King Henry confiscated from Cardinal Wolsey after he failed to bring about the annulment the king needed to marry Anne Boleyn. Wolsey had died for his failure, on his way to the Tower; six years later, Queen Anne, Elizabeth's mother, met her own fate at Henry's hands. I wondered how Elizabeth must feel, knowing that she was now ruler of the very palace that had seen her mother's rise and fall and nearly her own demise.

I started at the press of Walsingham's fingers on my elbow. "Come," he said. "We'll have to find our own way to the hall. It seems Her Majesty holds a reception tonight and there are no available pages about to bring word to Cecil of our arrival."

The jolt of life we encountered upon entering the palace presented vivid contrast to the last time I'd been here, when every access had been shuttered and guarded following an aborted rebel attempt to depose Mary. Now, Whitehall's wide tapestried corridors and numerous galleries shimmered with glamour, jewels winking and laughter echoing as courtiers moved in satiny stampede toward the great hall. I'd resided in Whitehall, experienced life-altering and heartbreaking events within its walls, but never had I seen as many people as I did at this moment, so that I fretted over my disheveled appearance until I realized no one paid us the slightest mind. At my side, Walsingham moved with soundless stealth, his black-clad figure a feline shadow among the peacock herd. His jaw clenched under his beard; he did not need to say a word for me to know he disapproved of such uncontrolled access to the queen's very person.

At the great double doors leading into the hall, we paused to check our cloaks but weren't given time. Behind us, courtiers pressed like an unstoppable tide, sweeping us into the expanse, the hammer-beamed painted ceiling suffused in smoke high above us, a fogbound sky; the black-and-white tile floor strewn with trampled rushes, which formed a slippery meadow under our feet.

The cacophony was deafening; the air was suffused with the heat of dripping wax from the many candelabras in corners and hanging on chains overhead, of musk and perfume splashed on bare skin, of sweat, grease, and spilt wine. A posse of ladies sauntered past us; one of them, pretty enough in her dark blue satins, shot an unmistakable look at me. As unexpected heat kindled in my groin, I recalled with a start that I'd not been with a woman since—

I looked away, banishing the memory, even as my admirer's companions tugged her away into the crowd, one of them whispering loud enough to ensure she was overheard: "Comely enough, I suppose, but did you *smell* him? I warrant he hasn't bathed in weeks! Only a papist would dare come to court bearing such a stench."

Walsingham commented dryly, "So, we're papists now, are we?" Even as he spoke he searched the crowd, devising a path to the raised platform, where a cluster of privileged, bejeweled figures could be glimpsed. Having navigated crowds in this hall before, I appreciated the challenge. I doubted we could approach the dais without being detained, given our unkempt persons.

"Perhaps we can take a drink first," I said, eyeing a page as he hustled by with a decanter. I was suddenly parched and had my goblet in my bag.

Walsingham said sharply, "Drink?" as if I'd suggested we swim across the Thames. Thrusting his bag at me, he marched forth, carving his way like a blade, his determination causing those in his path to shift aside, scowling and grumbling. I followed in his wake, carrying our luggage, and caught a fleeting glimpse of my admirer to my left. She winked at me. Her friends nudged her, giggling.

Then, all of a sudden, yeomen in green-and-white livery barred our passage with their pikestaffs. Behind them stood the wide dais with its empty throne, situated by one of Whitehall's famed Caen-stone hearths. The privileged nobles gathered about it turned to stare. I had a discomfiting impression of hawkish noses, trim beards, and contemptuous eyes before they parted, revealing another man, his hand casually poised on the throne's upholstered armrest.

It was none other than my former master, Lord Robert Dudley.

Chapter Three

He looked better than expected, though in truth I hadn't been expecting him at all. I cursed under my breath at my lack of foresight. He wore rich, ash-gray velvet slashed with ivory silk, a profusion of seed pearls picking out his family emblem of bear and ragged staff on his sleeves. His broad shoulders offset the muscular legs he was so vain of; he looked nothing like the gaunt prisoner I had last seen in the Tower, and without warning all the pent-up rage inside me surged. Ever since I had been a foundling in his family's care, Dudley had delighted in tormenting me. I could tell by the hatred igniting his dark eyes that he had not forgotten it, either.

He took a step forward. "What," he hissed, "are *you* doing here?"

I met his stare. I too had shed all vestiges of the youth he had known. Hardened by my training, confident that in a fight I could more than match him, I was no longer afraid of his bark. Before I could react, Walsingham said with appropriate deference, "Begging my lord's forgiveness, but I was summoned by my lord Secretary Cecil. This is my manservant and—"

Dudley snarled, "Manservant? Since when was this cur anyone's servant? He's incapable of it; he bites every hand that feeds him. And by God, I've a mind to tie him in a sack and drown him myself." He was actually starting to step down, fists curled at his sides, when an authoritative voice called out, "My lord, if you please! These men are here at my invitation."

Relief overcame me as I turned to see Cecil coming toward us. I was in no mood to contend with Robert Dudley now, though judging by his frozen stance and the glare he directed at Cecil I had no doubt that I'd have to deal with him later.

Cecil was somewhat out of breath from his brisk walk across the hall. He quickly assessed us with that expert ease that made everything he did seem perfectly timed. He looked tired. Having reached his thirty-eighth year, he'd started to display a middle-age paunch, no doubt from all the hearty fare he enjoyed at his country manor with his devoted wife Lady Cecil, but his russet beard remained free of telltale gray and he still retained a keen air.

"Master Walsingham, we did not expect you so soon." Cecil did not greet me and I lowered my eyes, feigning subservience. Evidently, I was indeed to act the role of manservant, as Walsingham confirmed with his next words: "I apologize for the inconvenience. The trip took less time than expected and I hired a wherry to avoid the Bridge. But, my man and I are clearly not fit company. If a room could be made available . . . ?"

Dudley guffawed, swiveling with aristocratic bonhomie to his fellow nobles. "Do you hear that, my lords? They would like a room! Perhaps we can equip it with fine linen and a hot bath, as well, eh?" His derisive laughter faded abruptly. As he swerved back to us, he said, "Lest you had not heard, Her Majesty has only just assumed her throne. I'm afraid we are full at this time, unless you'd care to bed in one of the kennels." He fixed his taunting gaze on me. "I'm sure your manservant is acquainted with such, having lain with dogs all his life."

I kept my face averted, lest my disgust for him showed. I noticed Cecil was adept at hiding his own distaste, well acquainted with Dudley's preemptory manner. He also knew how deep the rift ran between my former master and me; but Dudley was still a childhood friend and intimate of the queen's, and Cecil managed to display the appropriate level of respect when he replied, "My lord, we are of course fully aware of how little space there is at court. However, I'm sure Her Majesty would wish us to find suitable lodgings for our guests."

Rage darkened Dudley's countenance but before he could retort, a sudden hush fell over the hall, followed by a susurration that rippled through the courtiers like wind. At the dais, the nobles tugged at their doublets and hastened to bow. Dudley himself did not move, staring at me with a violent promise that seemed to empty the hall around us, so that we stood alone. He mouthed, "You are mine, Prescott," and then he swept into practiced obeisance, leaving me to whirl about as Elizabeth made her entrance.

The effect she had on the assembly was immediate. Everyone seemed to hold their breath as her slim figure passed through a flutter of curtsies and bows. She held a jeweled pomander, and a slight flush on her angular cheekbones enhanced her pallor. She wore sienna damask, her fiery hair twined in an agate-studded net to expose the length of her alabaster throat. She was not beautiful—her forehead too high and features too narrow, her nose an aquiline thrust—but she conveyed such a consummate illusion of beauty that most believed her to be. Her dark amber eyes glittered, capturing me with that leonine intensity that first made me hers from the moment she had directed their power at me five years ago. Now, after having survived numerous attempts to either imprison or execute her, she had finally attained the seemingly impossible feat of becoming queen. I had been one of those who had fought to see her to this moment, and my heart swelled at the sight of her, so that I couldn't move until one of her thin red-gold brows arched.

Lurching to one knee, my awkward obeisance brought forth a covert smile on her lips that vanished as soon as it appeared. She swept past me to mount the dais, her women bustling behind her to arrange themselves on upholstered cushions at her feet.

I glanced up at these women, my breath catching in my throat as I braced to find Kate among them; to my simultaneous relief and disappointment, the woman I loved and had forsaken was not present.

Elizabeth waved her hand, bringing the entire hall to its feet; on her finger, she wore the signet ring I had last seen adorning her sister, Mary. "Carry on," she said in a slightly hoarse voice. "I'll receive everyone shortly." As the courtiers returned to various activities while maintaining covetous watch on her, she shifted her attention to us.

"Well?" she said. "I sense tension. Would anyone care to explain?"

Dudley shoved forward. "Your Majesty, I was just informing my lord Secretary Cecil that given the quantity and rank of those already seeking lodgings at court, we cannot possibly accommodate these . . . new arrivals of his."

His tone, to my revulsion, had turned acquiescent, almost servile, but it did not fool me. I knew his history. I had lived it. His family's machinations had cost both his father and younger brother their heads, but Dudley had survived, though he was as guilty of past treason as they were. He had always relied on his charm and long-time association with Elizabeth, and as past experience had shown, she was not immune to him even when fully apprised of his guile. In my opinion, he had always been her greatest threat, his ambition overriding all other considerations, including his own unfortunate marriage to a Norfolk gentleman's daughter. He kept his wife far from court, forever scheming to find a way to end the marriage so he could wed Elizabeth instead. Elizabeth had kept him dancing on the end of a long string, alluding at promises she had thus far failed to deliver, but I had seen how much it cost her, and I was not reassured to witness the reciprocal warmth in her eyes as she contemplated him. Theirs was a lifelong bond, forged since childhood by the volatile arena of the court; their magnetic attraction now seemed to burnish the air between them like invisible flame.

Then she said with a touch of dry mirth, "I created you Master of my Horse, my lord Robert, not steward of my palace. I would see all my guests lodged as befits their station. We have this entire city at our disposal; surely, not every nook is taken? And if my lord Secretary holds these new arrivals of his in such esteem, then surely so must we."

She was playing by the rules of the game she had long established, the implicit warning in her tone indicating she would tolerate only so many liberties from him in public. Humiliation darkened Dudley's face. Unlike the other nobles, he remained defiantly clean-shaven, doubtless because a beard would have detracted from the taut virility of his youth. I tended to forget he was still a young man, only twenty-six, in fact, a year older than both Elizabeth and me.

Cecil said, "We are honored, Majesty, by your gracious consideration. Master Walsingham has been abroad these past six years, as you know, and serves in my employ. I assure you, he shall prove a valuable asset to your reign."

"I have no doubt." Elizabeth accepted the goblet a page brought her. Before the page could pour from his decanter, Dudley burst up the dais to take charge of it and serve the queen himself. "You are welcome to our court, Master Walsingham," she went on, with a grateful nod at Dudley. Save for the one brief glance we had exchanged, she had not looked at me again. I wasn't certain how to interpret it. Was she pleased I was here or had my presence brought with it uncomfortable reminders of everything I knew about her?

"Alas," she went on, "I regret we cannot talk more at length, for as you can see"—she motioned to the row of courtiers already queuing up to greet her—"I'm going to be occupied most of this night and, I'm afraid, for the next few days. Have Cecil arrange a convenient time. He now oversees my council and," she said with pointed emphasis, "my daily schedule."

Still, her expansive smile after this speech conveyed more delight than I'd ever seen her display, clear proof that after years of sidestepping those who yearned to see her fall, including her own sister, our late queen, she was enjoying her newfound power. Cecil had always been her most stalwart champion, as dedicated to his own self-preservation as hers. He had worked tirelessly to steer her past the scaffold that loomed over her during the past reigns, recruiting informants like me to ensure her safety. She could not have chosen a more capable man to rely upon, as I had good cause to know. When it came to protecting Elizabeth, no one was more lethal than Cecil.

"Your Majesty, it would be my privilege." Walsingham bowed again. Elizabeth nodded and beckoned Cecil to the dais, obliging Dudley to step aside as she and her secretary took a few moments to converse. Dudley scowled. He and Cecil had never been friends; Dudley may not have known exactly how deep Cecil's hatred of him ran, but he knew enough to suspect that the man who had once served his own father could never be trusted, and I took a moment to savor his discomfort before I reached for our bags.

Then I felt his attention fixate on me once more. Looking up, I saw his mouth twisting into a malignant smile. I had seen that same look on his face throughout my childhood, whenever he decided to make my existence unbearable by waylaying and thrashing me or chase me into the stable loft so he and his hellion brothers could strew my belongings in the hog sty. Again, I schooled my expression until Cecil left the queen and bustled back to Walsingham and me. "Her Majesty has allocated a room for you in the lower part of the palace," Cecil murmured. "It is not spacious, but private enough. I'll take you there."

As we departed from the hall and the courtiers surged forward eagerly to receive their favor from the queen, I did not look around.

We moved through the galleries, where tapestries and smoke-stained paintings hung on the walls, the light of tapers in sconces ebbing into patches of darkness that brought out the glow of the icy moon outside. Much here remained unchanged, portions of the palace still raw and bunted in scaffolding, an ever-evolving transformation that had begun under Henry's reign. When I had first come here, I'd found it a bewildering labyrinth designed to trap the unwary. Now, I easily recognized certain turns and isolated courtyards beyond the bays, having spent enough time racing its passages that I would never get lost again.

Cecil's voice brought me to attention. "I'm relieved you are both here at last. I trust the voyage wasn't too difficult, given the hasty nature of my summons?"

"Not at all," replied Walsingham. "And lest it be of concern, I had my papers crated and shipped separately as requested. They should arrive at the assigned warehouse in a few days. The rest of it was destroyed."

"Good, good." Cecil nodded. "I've no reason to think you were marked abroad as one of my agents, or indeed that anyone outside my immediate circle knows what kind of work you do, but one can never be too cautious these days, especially with Her Majesty about to declare herself. I needn't remind you that as a Protestant queen, whom Rome and Europe's Catholic princes believe to be illegitimate, she is in a vulnerable position until she can prove her strength." He paused, grimacing. I found it strange he'd yet to direct himself to me, behaving as though I truly were Walsingham's servant. "Indeed, we have Catholic nobles in this very realm who, if I know them at all, will seek to resist Elizabeth's rule and even undermine it. We mustn't let our guard down now that she has the throne but rather ensure she does not lose it."

Walsingham frowned, though Cecil's report did not come as a surprise. Since I had known Elizabeth, she had been in the midst of peril. However, I had hoped she would find relief now that she was queen, and I finally ventured to make my opinion known. "Surely, she can count on some measure of safety?"

"Safety?" Cecil regarded me in astonishment. "She's less safe now than she ever was. We face entire nations of would-be assassins." He ticked off each menace on his fingers. "First, we have France, where her cousin Mary of Scots resides and already claims to hold superior right to England by virtue of her own Tudor blood. Then we have Spain, where our late queen's widower Philip II holds out hope that he may yet win Elizabeth's hand, yet his sole true desire is to make this kingdom his. Last but not least, we have His Holiness the pope in Rome, who would muster every Catholic force he can to depose Elizabeth." He paused again. "Does any of this sound safe to you?"

I resisted the urge to scowl. Cecil always had the ability to make me feel like a gauche squire, easily duped. "No, it does not," I said. "But does she not also have the entire realm and treasury at her command, not to mention the fact that we sit on an isle—"

"The realm is divided," interrupted Cecil, "and our treasury near bankrupt. Between Mary's catastrophic reign and the exodus of our tradesmen because of her persecution, she has left us on the brink of ruin. Our coinage is debased, revenue in arrears, and religious and political stability most uncertain. We have much work to do if we are to shore up our defenses. In the meantime, Her Majesty's sole protection lies in our intelligence and her royal person, which we must offer in marriage as soon as possible, so she can provide the realm with an heir—and not become an international scandal because of her dalliance with Dudley."

The moment I heard his pronouncement, I understood he was about to thrust me into another unpleasant assignation. When I saw him exchange a meaningful look with Walsingham, I could not contain my anger any longer.

"God's teeth!" I swore, coming to a halt. I had to hold my tongue as a cadre of courtiers hurried past, late for the festivities in the hall and trailing cloying perfume. As soon as they were gone, I said, "Have I been brought all this way to be your fishmonger?"

Cecil said coldly, "I believe it is treason to compare our sovereign to a bawd."

"Aren't you doing just that?" I said, eyeing Walsingham, who remained impervious. "Did you know about this?" I demanded. "Is that what all my training was about, all those days and nights of memorizing ciphers and waving a sword until my shoulders bled? I thought I was to be an intelligencer, not some common lackey brought to court to—" I returned my glare to Cecil. "To stand guard over the queen's bed like a eunuch."

Cecil pursed his lips. As the tension between us thickened, he motioned Walsingham to a nearby window seat. Taking a moment to collect his thoughts, Cecil said, "I believe we struck a pact: I protect you and you protect her. I expect you to abide by it."

"I have abided by it," I retorted. "Indeed, I've done nothing but abide. Lest you forget, I gave up everything to do your bidding. I nearly died for it. I had to go into exile and leave Kate"—my voice quavered, despite my efforts to control it—"without explanation, because it was safer for her to think I had abandoned her than risk her falling prey to those who would do me harm. All of this I have done for you without question."

"Oh, I wouldn't say that," he said, with some asperity. "On the contrary, if memory serves, you have done nothing but question me from the hour we met."

"Because you were never fully honest with me!" I had to pause, draw in a ragged breath. I was tired and out of sorts. Seeing Dudley in the hall had rattled my nerves and fatigue dragged on me like wet wool. This was not the time or place for a confrontation, and still I could not help myself. The last thing I wanted was to be a pawn in another gambit against Dudley, with my own life at stake. Taking Cecil by the arm, I drew him further away from Walsingham.

"You saw how Dudley reacted when he saw me," I went on in a low voice. "He's hell-bent on vengeance because I thwarted him. I helped Elizabeth escape when his father ruled in her brother's stead; I brought his family down by working to see her sister Mary to the throne. And the last time I went up against him, when he was imprisoned in the Tower, I coerced letters from him that would have incriminated Elizabeth in his plot to depose her sister. Dudley hates me. He always has. He also has the cunning, if he sets his mind to it, to realize we keep a secret from her—about me. If he discovers I am part Tudor myself, the last-born son of her own aunt, Mary of Suffolk, it will be my doom. He knows Elizabeth will not take kindly to any threat to her throne. Her own father King Henry had men beheaded for less."

"Your imagination runs away with you," said Cecil. "Dudley will never find out the truth of who you are. Moreover, even if he did, no one would believe him, much less Elizabeth. His enmity toward you is so overt, it makes him look desperate." He stepped closer. "The threat to your well-being is less pressing than the threat he poses to this entire realm. He may wish to see you ruined, but he is far more committed to his own aggrandizement. Need I remind you that he has always sought the crown of king-consort?" When I did not answer, Cecil nodded. "No, I see that I do not. You know as well as I do how high Dudley aims, and once a woman loses her virtue, regardless of her rank, she has lost it forever. One moment of weakness on her part, and Dudley could win the biggest prize of all. If he does, then we will all indeed be at his mercy."

The gravity in his tone gave me pause. "You talk as if you believe she would actually marry him. Have you any proof that she . . . that they have . . ." The words stuck in my throat. The very thought of Dudley and Elizabeth becoming lovers sickened me.

"No, I have no proof," admitted Cecil, to my relief. "But you also know there has always been that possibility. She cannot see, or doesn't want to see, how dangerous he is. Now, for the first time in her life, everything is hers for the taking—or so she believes. Becoming queen has clouded her judgment. Like most inexperienced new monarchs, she gives no credence to the wolves waiting to devour her. And we both know that Dudley is the worst wolf of all."

I had to agree. Nevertheless, I still thought he discounted Elizabeth's capability. She might love Dudley but after having fought so long to obtain her throne, I did not think she was about to surrender power to anyone. Still, the very fact that Cecil had reason to doubt sent a chill through me. I was not sure I wanted to hear all the reasons why he harbored such a fear.

"He's still married, isn't he?" I countered. "She'll never consent to be his mistress."

"For now, yes, but it is the only obstacle that impedes him, and I've reason to believe that obstacle may soon disappear. His wife is gravely ill. My informants report she has a malignant growth in her breast. Should she die . . ."

"Does Elizabeth know?" I said, dreading his response.

"Yes. I told her. Indeed, I warned her that to show favor to a man like Dudley can only blacken her reputation. She would not heed me, saying that while she may have made me her secretary of state, my purview does not extend to her private affairs. One of her first official acts was to grant Dudley a title. She has also appointed apartments for him close to hers, where they can be seen daily, practicing the latest dances, playing the lute, sharing books and God knows what else. He's even invited his so-called astrologer, Dr. Dee, to devise a propitious date for her coronation. It's an outrage: the queen of England consulting that madman who believes himself a conduit for spirits—and all because Dudley whispers ceaselessly in her ear."

"I . . . I had no idea it had gone so far." My stomach knotted. The last thing I wanted was to once more find myself thrust as a wedge between Dudley and his ambitions.

Cecil said, "It's gone further than even that. Even as she dallies with him, the papists fling doubts of her legitimacy against her, citing Rome never sanctioned King Henry's union with her mother. Not to mention that any prince who cares to pursue her will think twice if they learn they must compete with her Master of Horse. Already gossip spreads abroad, making my job even more impossible. Dudley is a blight. He must be excised, eliminated as a threat."

"And you expect me to do it?" I exclaimed. "His former

squire, who helped ruin his family? You want me to—what? Stab him through the heart in a duel over her honor?"

Cecil sniffed. "I hardly think killing him is necessary, much as the idea might appeal. Dudley cannot be other than who he is; in time, given enough incentive, he will show his hand. Until then, however, we need someone to distract her. She requested that I bring you to court. After Dudley, I daresay there isn't a man in all of England she likes more, nor one better suited to remind her of it."

I stared at him. "Are you asking me to . . . seduce her?" He regarded me in silence, until I hissed, "God's teeth, man, are you mad? We are kin! Her father was my mother's brother."

Cecil tugged fastidiously at his sleeve. "Again, your imagination runs wild. There are many ways to seduce a woman, and crown notwithstanding, Elizabeth is still very much a woman, and a young one, at that. She trusts you. It is a powerful weapon, if you learn to use it."

I might have burst out laughing had the entire conversation not been so outrageous. "So, what is your plan, exactly? To wield me as an instrument of envy? To stoke Robert Dudley's already burning hatred of me to such a fury that he'll afford you the means to discredit him?"

"Have you a better plan?" he replied. "She values you highly. Dudley is aware of it; already, he seethes at the very sight of you. He does not know you share her blood. Your presence at her side is all that is required. Let Dudley dig his own grave."

"Or mine," I said through my teeth. "Because that is what he'll try."

"Let him. I will be ready. Until then, however, you will watch over her, keep her occupied until I see to her coronation and other tasks on my plate. She must be steered away from further entanglement with Dudley. I do not want"—he exhaled a terse breath—"*we* cannot afford any more rumors where he is concerned. I must present her as a suitable royal bride."

As distasteful as the scenario was, I had only to recall Dudley's mouthed threat to me in the hall to concede Cecil's point. Besides, it would not be long, I wagered, before Dudley devised some means to attack me. I might as well prepare.

"Fine," I said curtly. "But you'd best be ready to safeguard me, should Dudley get out of hand."

"You have Elizabeth to do that," he replied. "But, yes, naturally; should the situation become unmanageable, I will intervene. In the meantime, I shall supply everything you need, the necessary coin for your expenses and apparel, as well as—"

"Is my horse here?" I interrupted.

He blinked. "I believe so. Once I heard you were on your way, I sent a groom to fetch it from my manor of Theobalds so it could be housed in the royal stables."

"*He*," I corrected him. Turning about, I retrieved my saddle-bag. "His name is Cinnabar." I started walking in the opposite direction, passing Walsingham as he frowned and rose from his perch by the window. I did not explain. I simply left his bag that he might carry it henceforth.

I might still be a servant but I did not serve him anymore.

Chapter Four

𝕴awoke to snuffling outside the stall. Wiping grit from my eyes, I blinked away the leaden weight of a dreamless sleep, into which I had sunk like a stone after checking on Cinnabar, whom I had found stabled with plenty of feed and so delighted to see me he nipped me hard to prove it. Righting myself on my elbows, I peered between my steed's legs to the stall gate. I had slept curled in my cloak in the back of the stall, on clean hay; it struck me that I had reverted to my childhood habits, seeking refuge in the stables as I'd often done to escape the Dudley horde.

A wet black nose pressed at the opening under the gate. When it caught my scent, an explosion of excited barking ensued, loud enough to rouse the entire palace.

Wincing at my still-sore back (I vowed never to sail the Channel again, so long as I lived), I ran a hand over my close-cropped skull and grabbed my boots and cloak, shedding hay as I rounded my horse to unlatch the gate. No doubt one of the stable hands had returned from walking a nobleman's dog, and I preferred not to be caught snoozing like a thief in the queen's own—

A silver-gray beast flew at me, jumping on muscular hind-quarters to slam its front paws against my chest. I cried out, staggering backward as Urian, Elizabeth's favorite hound, slavered my face, mewling and carrying on as though we'd been parted an eternity. "Stop," I gasped, fumbling at his collar. "Urian, no!" But I was laughing, too, for I was quite fond of the dog, and it was the first warm welcome I'd received. It was not until I managed to grasp hold of his trailing lead and yank him away that I saw her staring at me, immobile as a statue.

My heart somersaulted. Though she stood steps away, the distance between us yawned like a chasm.

"Brendan . . . ?" Her voice was low, unsure. In that one utterance, I heard an abrupt hesitation that punched like a fist into my gut. Kate took a step toward me. "So, it's true," she said. "You're back."

My four-year absence suddenly felt like an eternity. The last time I had seen her, she was walking into the Tower at Elizabeth's side to share her captivity. As I marked the toll of my absence on her face, the hurt and confusion, memories swept through me, of her laughing in our tousled bed in Hatfield, still warm from the waning heat of our lovemaking, her eyes shining as she traced the birthmark on my hip and spoke of the day when we could marry. It made me want to crumple to my knees.

I had left her without a word. I had never explained why.

I rested a hand on Urian as he sat beside me, gazing up in adoration. "Yes," I said softly.

"When—when did you arrive?" she asked.

I motioned to my hay-strewn person. "Last night. I found the ambience at court stifling, so I opted for bedding here instead. I can't be broken of my habits, it seems." In my nervousness, I heard myself start to chuckle. My mirth withered in my throat as she took another step forward.

"Don't." She pushed her hood to her shoulders, her deep brown eyes huge in a visage that I found too thin, too pale as she said, "You cannot make light of it. Not this time."

I swallowed. I had dreaded this moment, gone through my head a thousand times what I would say. How I would explain that I'd kept watch over her through Cecil's informants, menials he'd bribed in the manors where she and Elizabeth were confined; how I had wanted so many times to write but feared that my letters might be intercepted, that somehow my own whereabouts would be discovered, endangering her. Now, I realized my explanations would sound self-effacing, the protests of a man more interested in protecting himself. I had never found it easy even in the best of circumstances to reveal myself; now, it felt as if any excuse I offered would be a lie.

"You . . . you're so lean," she said. "I hardly recognized you. You've cut off all your hair, too, and your beard, it is so thick. . . ." Her voice trailed off, as if she were talking to a stranger who wore a familiar but suspicious visage.

I didn't know what to say. I hadn't paused to consider how much I, too, had changed.

She remained silent, studying me as if she couldn't quite accept that I stood before her in a rumpled tunic and sagging hose, my boots and cloak heaped at my feet. Then she whistled and she said, "Urian, come!" She turned to walk away.

The dog whined, lifting plaintive eyes to me. Taking up his lead, I hastened after her. "Kate! Kate, wait. Do not—"

She whirled around, bringing me to a halt. Something flamed in her eyes, like jagged lightning. "Do not?" she said. "Do not ask where you went after you left us in the Tower or where you've been these past years? Or do not ask why you never sent word to let me know you were alive? Do not ask anything: Is that what you want?"

"Kate, I—"

Her hand flew out, striking me hard across the cheek. My teeth cut into my lower lip. Tasting my blood, I said, "I know I deserve that. You have every right to hate me."

She was trembling, her hand pressed to her chest as though it had struck me of its own accord. "I don't . . ." Tears filled her eyes. "That's the trouble. I cannot hate you, but I want to. I *need* to." Turning about again, she staggered against her hem. I reached out, taking her by the arm to steady her. The moment she felt my hand, she froze.

"You must let me go," she whispered. "Please."

"Not until you listen to me." All of a sudden, my words tumbled from me in a frantic rush. "I did not leave voluntarily. The Imperial ambassador, Renard; he sent men after me. My life was in danger. Cecil and his household were in danger because of me. I had to go abroad. There was no other way."

She had to understand my predicament. She was Cecil's ward. After her mother's death, he and his wife had taken Kate into their home, raised her as their own. She loved them as she would her own parents, and they loved her. She would not have wanted them in harm's way, not even for my sake. She did not react as I spoke, her face averted, her body so tense that I finally let go of her arm. "I went to Basel," I added, "to stay with Walsingham. He agreed to take me in and train me. I was not allowed to write from there, either."

After a long moment, she raised her gaze. "I know. Cecil told me. He came to Hatfield after Mary died. He told me everything. I had just hoped to hear it from you instead."

"I wanted to tell you! Kate, I swear it. But I could not. It was too—"

"Dangerous. Yes, I've heard that before." She gave me a bitter smile. "It's always been too dangerous wherever Elizabeth is concerned. From the day you swore to serve her, we have dwelled on the edge of her plight. Now, she has won. She is queen." Kate paused. "But I don't imagine it'll be any less dangerous. And you will be at her side to see her through it, no matter the cost."

My throat knotted. "You know why I must serve her."

Her sigh had no rage left, no accusation, only heartbreaking resignation. "Sometimes, I wish I did not know it. Sometimes, I wish you had never told me. This bond you share with her, it consumes everything. It leaves no place for anyone else."

Desolation cracked open inside me. Sensing my distress, Urian barked in agitation. From the stalls behind us the horses whickered, Cinnabar's distinctive neigh among them. I longed to enfold Kate in my arms and reassure her that we could still forge a life together, forget the past and start anew. But I could not lie to her anymore; I couldn't maintain the illusion. Kate knew the truth: There would be no safety for us, and not only because of my duty to Elizabeth.

"I had no choice," I whispered. "I left because it meant that you would be kept safe. After what happened to Peregrine, I . . . I couldn't bear it if I lost you, too."

She raised her hand. This time, she set it upon my cheek, over the ebbing sting of her blow. "Instead, I have lost you."

"That is not true," I started to protest, and then I fell silent, remembering with a wrenching pain another pair of eyes, other hands. I had done more than forsake her. I had betrayed her with a woman whose cunning had blinded me, whose presence had led me into a darkness I had never fully escaped. Even now, she haunted my dreams. Never had I desired anyone as I much as I had Sybilla Darrier and never had my own desire proved so lethal to those around me.

Kate said, "I do not want any more promises. You must be true to the path you have chosen. I will no longer stand in your way. Good-bye, Brendan."

I stood as if paralyzed as she took Urian's lead and moved to the stable entrance, the dog padding behind her, looking over his shoulder as if entreating me to follow.

My cry burned in my throat, a vow to leave it all behind for her, to take her away this hour and find somewhere, anywhere, to build our love anew. But I remained silent, watching her vanish without a word into the cold light of day outside. When I finally moved, it was with a moan, as I buried my face in my hands.

I had done what I must to ensure her safety but she had not lied.

We were indeed lost to each other.

Walsingham glanced up as I walked through the door. He sat on a narrow stool, pulling on his boots. It had not taken long to locate him. I had gone to the oldest part of White-hall, in the lower wing, and now made cursory appraisal of our accommodations—a meager room, with two board beds stuffed with straw (I could tell by how lumpy they were) occupying most of the limited space, a chipped wooden chest for clothing, side table, and ubiquitous closestool. It smelled of damp and rank tallow. There was no window. I could feel winter seeping up through the plank floor laid directly over the stone foundation.

"Luxurious," I remarked, tossing my saddlebag onto the nearest bed. I could not tell which one was his. Both looked untouched. Had he even slept?

"It's only for a short while," he said, returning to his boot. "Cecil is renting a house nearby. I'll need a proper place for when my books and papers arrive, and I'd rather not spend too much time in such close quarters."

Though I agreed, I refrained from comment and rummaged in my bag for my poniard and cup. Stepping past him to the table, upon which were a decanter, a hunk of bread, and some hard cheese, I cut a slice of the latter and poured the watered ale into my cup. My stomach rumbled. I hadn't eaten anything since our fare at the inn, and despite the morning's upset, I was famished.

Walsingham cleared his throat. Looking around, I found him upright, fully attired in his habitual black. I had missed an opportunity by not joining him the previous night; having never seen him undressed, it seemed impossible that actual human flesh might lurk under that colorless armor of his, which he wore like a carapace.

"Dressed for court?" I asked.

He gave me a sliver of a smile. "I do not care to impress. You, on the other hand, must do everything you can to gain the queen's attention. I suggest you wash yourself and air out your clothes. She expects you this very afternoon in her apartments. Cecil was here this morning and left a pouch of coin in the coffer, along with the address of a tailor. If you're going to play the courtier, you will need to dress the part."

I deliberately sliced more bread and cheese, not revealing the jolt his words sent through me. I had not expected Elizabeth would ask to see me so soon. "I thought she was busy," I said.

"Apparently not." His brow arched. "Or were you planning on sleeping away the day? By the looks of it, you've had a rough night."

I set my cup down with an audible clang. "My plans are not your concern. I no longer answer to you." I recognized the absurdity of lashing out at him, for he was not to blame, but I couldn't control it. I suddenly loathed him. I loathed the court and wished I had never returned. At least in exile, I could pretend to aspire to another fate, believe there was some way to heal what I'd shattered. Not even the thought of serving Elizabeth assuaged me; all I could envision at this moment was a life of endless subterfuge, subject to Cecil's ploys and to Dudley's hatred of me—if I survived that long.

"You are right," he said. "You do not serve me. Thus, you are free to do as you wish. However, if you would permit me one last bit of advice . . . ?"

I glared. "When did my leave or lack thereof ever stop you before?"

He sniffed. "I realize the task at hand may seem unworthy of you, being bait to trap Dudley. Nevertheless, an intelligencer does as ordered, regardless of personal preference. I hope you have not wasted my time. You have the potential to be our most accomplished asset. Certainly our best-positioned," he added, "given your intimacy with the queen. But there is no room for error. If you have any doubts, you are unfit and should resign your charge at once. Disappointment is preferable to weakness."

His blunt rebuke made my jaw clench. Yet as he turned to

the door, I heard myself say, "I do not doubt." He paused, not looking at me. "And I'll be in her apartments," I said. "Wearing my best doublet and smelling of lavender, I promise."

"I don't care about promises" was his reply, in unsettling echo of Kate's words to me in the stables. "All I want is compliance. Remember what you are, not who you were." He pulled open the door. "You are expected at the stroke of one. Don't be late. She dislikes tardiness."

He left me standing there, my resentment curdling inside me.

Chapter Five

After consuming all the bread and cheese, and most of the ale, I felt better in my stomach, if not my spirits. Moving to the chest, I found my sword enveloped carefully in its scabbard and oiled cloth to weather the voyage. I hesitated, my hand hovering over it. It had come to me unexpectedly, thrown at me for my defense in a dying king's secret chamber. Would I have need of it today?

I did not think so. Moving it aside, I located the pouch of coin and clothing Cecil had brought: an elegant doublet made of maroon velvet, with matching hose, breeches, codpiece, and sleeves of crimson damask. I eyed the quality as I spread them on the bed. Cecil had thought of everything; he probably even had my measurements right. Taking a fresh chemise and underlinens from my bag, I draped them across the stool to air out the wrinkles and stink of travel before I went out in search of water. Whitehall had common bathing quarters, but I was in no mood for the company of gossiping, naked courtiers. A trough in a nearby courtyard yielded what I sought; splashing my face and hands, I used a cube of soap wrapped in linen to scrub myself, shivering in the cold as I toweled my body. I left a scum of grime on the surface of the water. Returning to my room, I ignored the curious glances of passing ushers and pages in the corridors.

The clamor of bells announcing the hour greeted me when I emerged, dressed in my stiff new finery. Walsingham had failed to provide directions but I assumed Elizabeth resided in the same royal apartments her sister had once occupied. After taking several passages, I found the sumptuous privy gallery fronted by mullioned bays overlooking the Thames.

The green river glittered in the sunlight, as if raw diamonds floated across its murky waters. It was a beautiful day, despite winter's approach. The storm clouds of yesterday had disappeared, blown away by a brisk wind that ruffled the hedges and pruned trees in the gardens; the palace itself was like a mausoleum, but it had never been warm, its gargantuan expanse ill-suited to comfort, regardless of how many braziers and hearths were kindled.

Around me, people began to appear—courtiers in finery, the rustle of weighted hems and embroidered sleeves, the clinking of pomanders and ropes of pearls and gold imbuing the air with chiming music. Sentries guarded an archway that allowed access into the royal abode; as I paused, feeling my dagger hilt press into my calf (I had stashed it in my boot, though weapons were forbidden in the sovereign's presence), I took a wary look about. I did not recognize any of those around me. For an unsettling moment, they all looked the same to me—polished peacocks with the sharp, hooded eyes of birds of prey, gauging my arrival as they might a fresh victim. All gathered in groups according to rank; all engaged in idle chatter. But none, I suspected, was actually interested in what the others had to say. They were intent only on the closed double doors behind which lay the beating heart of their existence: the queen herself.

Recalling how Mary had sometimes granted public audience at this hour, following her noon meal, I wondered if Elizabeth had summoned me to take my place among those eager to curry her favor. I had served her faithfully, yes, we had gone through trials together, but in the end, who was I to her? Certainly, I could not compete with the history she shared with Dudley. I had experienced firsthand the changes that being queen could wreak; Mary Tudor, whom I helped to win her throne, became a monster before my very eyes. Cecil had said Elizabeth's newfound power was going to her head. Had she, too, embarked on a transformation? If so, how would she welcome me?

As unexpected doubt assailed me, taking on a looming menace, as I recognized once more how precarious my position truly was, I nearly turned to depart. The sudden emergence of Cecil from behind the doors stopped me. He wore a dark robe, his chain of office heavy on his shoulders. He appeared flustered, pushing through the courtiers who surged at the sight of him. When he espied me at the edge of the crowd, he motioned.

I felt every pair of eyes cleave to me as I passed, heard someone whisper, "*Who* is he?" and then I stepped past the doors into the antechamber beyond. Cecil motioned to the guards. An outcry from the courtiers issued before the closure of the oak doors muffled it.

Cecil grimaced. Pulling off his cap, he dabbed at sweat beading his receding hairline. "It's a nightmare," he said. "They're at her night and day like Pharisees. They think that if they crowd her passage, she will have to notice them. I am considering drafting restrictions regarding the distance they must maintain from the sovereign's person. As it stands, she cannot set foot outside her doors without encountering that mob."

"You did want this," I reminded him. "You worked tirelessly to its end."

He sighed. "Yes, I did." Repositioning his cap, he glanced around us, though the splendid antechamber was empty. Behind the spangled curtain covering a nearby archway, I discerned voices. "Now, you must heed me. Lord Robert is with her," he began. He set a hand on my sleeve, detaining me. "I couldn't persuade her to see you alone. She says it is high time you and Dudley cease sparring. Indeed, she commands it. She told him as much, when he learned of your summons."

"I can only imagine his excitement," I said, wishing I had brought more than my dagger, though it was unlikely he would dare attack me in front of her.

Cecil sniffed. "Regardless of his sentiments, like all of us he must abide by her rule. She has taken this opportunity to begin opening the congratulatory gifts sent by foreign princes. She wishes to greet you informally." His voice lowered to a conspiratorial hush. "She has also expressed interest in bestowing you with a title and estate, in recompense for your efforts on her behalf. If she offers it, I want you to thank her but refuse, saying it is too great an honor. Humility is your weapon of choice."

"An estate?" I repeated. Without warning, hope flared in me, vanquishing the uncertainty of my future. A grant of land would solve everything; Dudley would rejoice to see the back of me and I would prefer to oblige him. If I accepted Elizabeth's offer, I could woo Kate back, marry, and raise a family. I could be free of the mayhem, the intrigue, the claustrophobia of life at court. Yet even as I welcomed the thought, my hope must have shown on my face, for Cecil's grip tightened like a vise.

"Would you deny everything we have fought for, to go off and play country squire?" he asked. "Is that what you want, to see her in thrall to Dudley and the rest of us on the scaffold?"

I knew. I knew it as if he had spat the betrayal in my face. Kate's appearance in the stables had not been coincidence. *He* had sent her to me, to rupture whatever frayed thread still bound us. "Up to your old tricks, I see." I yanked my arm away. "What did you tell her? That there is no place for me in her life because I devote myself body and soul to your service?"

"You did tell me you had forsaken her," he replied. "Only yesterday, in fact."

"God's teeth," I whispered, "just when I think you could not be more heartless. You had no right to interfere!"

He did not flinch. "Kate understands more than you suppose. She realizes we all must sacrifice," he said, as if he were talking of a piece of merchandise and not the very girl he had raised. "She knows how much is at stake now that Elizabeth is queen."

"Does she?" I riposted. "Because the way she spoke to me, it felt like—"

"Are you ready?" asked a woman from behind us. "Her Majesty is waiting."

With a furious glance over my shoulder, I saw one of Elizabeth's damsels peering from the curtain. I drew a taut breath as Cecil tugged at his robe and moved to the chamber where the queen and her company awaited.

A vivid recollection of the last time I had been in this airy room assaulted me. Here, during Queen's Mary reign, I had first met Sybilla. I shut my mind to the memory of her gliding toward me and focused on the chamber with its wide window bays offering a view of the windswept parkland outside.

Wrapped boxes, enameled caskets, and other containers sprouting ribbons and gewgaws were heaped on the central table, where Elizabeth's ladies had assembled to sort through the trove. I scanned their ranks; saw with a clench in my chest that Kate was among them, clad in blue velvet, her face drawn. She avoided my gaze, her somberness in marked contrast to the eager faces of her companions, all of whom were unfamiliar to me. Though the number of Elizabeth's attendants had of course increased, I found it unsettling to find no sign of the other two women who had served Elizabeth throughout her life. Times past, she would rarely have been seen without her protective chief gentlewoman, Lady Blanche Parry, or her former governess, the redoubtable Mistress Ashley.

Two contented spaniels dozed by the hearth. The atmosphere was warm, redolent with the bittersweet scent of crushed herbs underfoot. The carpets, I noted, were threadbare, as if our late queen had worn them out with her anxious pacing. . . .

Elizabeth's husky laughter rang out. Turning to my right, I found her seated near an alcove, clad in a high-necked gown of silver brocade. Tight-sleeved, with cuffs of black lace at her wrists, her garb showed off her perfect skin and slim hands to perfection—beautiful hands, which she liked to display, and which at this moment beckoned Dudley. He bent to her. Her head cocked to one side as he murmured in her ear. Her next burst of laughter was a purr in her throat. "You're too bold, my lord," she declared and she slapped him lightly on the cheek, even as a flush crept over her face, indicating that bold or not, she rather liked his suggestive whisper.

I tasted bile. Cecil's warnings returned to me, about her open indiscretion with Dudley, even as his wife lay secluded, perhaps already dying, in a manor far away. I had to resist the urge to stride to him and haul him from her side. As if she sensed my anger, she shifted her gaze in my direction. I immediately bowed, fumbling at my head. As I realized with a cold start that in my haste I had forgotten to don a cap, Dudley guffawed. "Lost your headgear again, Prescott? I seem to recall you mislaid it often when you were our foundling. I suggest you nail it to your head, seeing as you are so apt to roll around in the muck."

Elizabeth clucked her tongue. "Come now." She extended her hand with its signet ring to me. Her smile was inviting as I approached. Besides Cecil, Dudley and I were the only men in the room. She said softly, "Lest I am mistaken, it seems absence has not been kind to you, Master Prescott. You look tired."

I absorbed the tenor of her voice, seeking the underlying meaning in her words. With Elizabeth, there was always more than one meaning and I was not mistaken in detecting faint reprimand in her manner. It took a few moments to ascertain the cause; when I did, I replied, "Exile is never easy, Majesty. But my absence helped me return to serve you."

Her lips twitched. She held up a hand, prompting Dudley to reach for a nearby decanter and pour. He did not take his eyes from me. I ignored him, for in the daylight I could now discern the invisible burden she carried, though she disguised it with her usual skill. Triumphant as her accession was—indeed, some might say, miraculous—the violet smudges under her eyes and taut pull to her mouth, the slightly hollowed cheeks and pallor betrayed more sleepless nights than anyone supposed. Elizabeth had fought to attain this zenith; after a time, it had become her sole purpose in her otherwise imperiled existence. Betrayal, deception, even death had become her allies, and compassion welled in me as I watched her raise the goblet to her lips. Under her regal aura, a lonely woman sat before me—one who doubted my allegiance because I had left her, as she must doubt everything and everyone around her.

It was her curse—a curse which Cecil, for all his insight, and Dudley, in his arrogance, failed to understand. From the hour she had discovered how thin the line was between life and death, Elizabeth had learned never to fully trust.

Cecil said, "Master Prescott is entirely at Your Majesty's disposal."

"Is he?" She preempted Dudley, who started to scoff. She went quiet again, contemplating me. "Then we must give his disposition some thought."

Though it sounded like a dismissal, I knew it was not. I finally gleaned her purpose. This so-called informal gathering was as much a part of her ploy as her avoidance of overt acknowledgment of me in the hall the night before. She needed time to assimilate my return, to gauge where I could best be employed and set me on a course. She did not plan on setting me to dance attendance on her or relegating me to a country estate. Elizabeth had something specific in mind. All I needed to do was wait for her to reveal it.

Dudley, however, did not realize this. Focused only on his need to see me disgraced, he gloated as if I were about to be consigned to cleaning out the privies, preening at her side in his jeweled doublet, a hand at his hip. He looked exactly what he was—a handsome predator, whose only interest was the destruction of all rivals. Cecil's concerns were unfounded; though Dudley might have snapped his fingers and had any girl in this room on her back, for now he did not yet have the one he most desired.

All of a sudden, my trepidation about him vanished. I had dueled with him before. I was prepared to do so again to protect her.

"Majesty," I murmured. Bowing again, I stepped back. When I reached Cecil, he said under his breath, "You will stay." I had no choice but to watch as Dudley sought to dominate Elizabeth's attention once more by swaggering forth to the gift-laden table, swatting the women on their backsides and eliciting mock cries of protest and not a few surreptitious looks of admiration at his thighs in their fitted silk hose.

"Now, then," he said, "whom of these royal applicants most honors our queen with his largesse? Who among them is worthy to earn her consideration?"

With an indulgent smile, Elizabeth reclined in her chair, twirling her goblet as she watched her Master of Horse paw through her fellow sovereigns' offerings as though they were trinkets.

"Is it His Benevolent Highness the prince of Sweden?" Dudley flipped open a satin-lined box; within it nestled a necklace of pink rubies shaped in the form of the Tudor rose. He held it up to the light, examining it for flaws. He frowned. "Unimaginative," he announced. He dropped the jewel back into its box and swept both aside, prompting a genuine outcry from the ladies as they hastened to gather it off the floor.

Elizabeth chuckled.

The excitement at the table stirred the dozing spaniels, both of whom leapt up to round the table, barking as Dudley dug again through the pile and extracted a bigger case this time, bunted in scarlet. "Or is it His Imperial Majesty of Russia?" Throwing off the lid, he unloosed a length of white fur. "Another stole?" he groaned. Elizabeth could not contain her laughter. "Her Majesty has dozens," Dudley declared, and he flung the fur aside. The women squealed, losing all sense of dignity as they scrambled for it.

At my side, Cecil stiffened. It was evident that Dudley intended to distribute all the gifts among Elizabeth's women, thus consigning these first suitors for her hand to ridicule.

"Or is it—" Dudley paused with theatrical timing, dramatically extending the moment as he retrieved a narrow black-satin box. "His Majesty Philip of Spain?"

Silence fell in the wake of his words. Philip had been the late queen's husband; during my previous mission at court, I had contended with his ambassador Renard's fervent quest to see Elizabeth executed for treason. Renard had gone far beyond his master's orders; in truth, the young Spanish king had wanted only to hold her in captivity until the time came when he became a widower. His union with Mary had kindled the pyre of persecution, his Catholic stringencies inciting our late queen to burn hundreds of English martyrs and send hundreds of others into exile. His name was no laughing matter, and Elizabeth responded accordingly, her voice turning sharp as she said, "That is sufficient. I'll not hear anointed princes mocked."

"Who is mocking?" exclaimed Dudley, and I heard Cecil gasp at his confident rebuttal of her. "I merely wish to discover which of these exalted princes is best qualified to pay suit to Your Majesty's person. We all know how eager Philip of Spain is to impress. The question is, how much is he willing to spend?"

Elizabeth's gaze narrowed, but I could tell she was enjoying this. She could not help but relish hearing disparagement of the very king whose machinations had cornered her during her sister's reign, though Philip had intervened on her behalf and persuaded Mary to release her from the Tower. I had not been in England when she and the Spanish King met face-to-face, having already gone abroad, but I could imagine the merry jig she had led him on, the insinuations she must have dangled before him as she determined to safeguard her person. Indeed, I had no doubt that Philip must now regret that he had both released her and failed to convince Mary to kill Dudley, as rumor must have already reached him of Dudley's intent to supplant him.

"I said, that will suffice." Gaining control of her better judgment, Elizabeth thrust out her hand. "I will open his gift and judge for myself whether Philip of Spain can impress."

Dudley froze. It was only a fraction of a second, but I saw the rage flicker across his expression as he proceeded to her, bowing with flourish before presenting her with the box.

"Have some wine," Elizabeth suggested, and as he stomped to the board in the alcove and the decanter, my breathing inexplicably turned shallow.

Elizabeth plucked at the embossed wax seal, which bound a ribbon around the box and held the lid in place. Leaving the other women, Kate hastened to take a jeweled letter-opener from the table and went to assist the queen, the spaniels scampering at her heels. Elizabeth smiled—"How thoughtful of you, Mistress Stafford"—and Kate said softly, "Allow me, Your Majesty," swiveling the box in the queen's lap toward her, kneeling down to slide the blade under the seal.

I did not know that I had moved toward her until Cecil said, "What are you doing?" His rebuke brought me to a precipitous halt. In rapid succession, the seal on the box cracked apart and Kate rocked back with a little cry of surprise. The lid fell off. Elizabeth tried to hold on to the box as it slipped from her lap, tumbling its contents to the floor—a mess of gilded tissue, wrapped about something leathery.

Kate scrambled up, making a grab for the bundled article. But one of the spaniels dove at the same time and clamped the gift between its jaws, shredding the tissue, worrying it as if it were a rat.

Elizabeth gazed at the dog as it tore apart the king of Spain's gift. "Are those . . . gloves?" she asked, bemused. Her tone indicated that Philip had indeed failed to impress.

I didn't hear Kate's response, however, deafened by a warning roar I did not realize was in my head, as I remembered another broken seal on an unexpected letter, the curiosity on Peregrine's face as he held it, then his gasp as he lifted fingertips already singed from—

The women shrieked as I leapt forth, pushing them aside. Elizabeth recoiled in her chair. From the alcove, where he had been drowning his humiliation in wine, Dudley flung aside his goblet and barreled at me. I scarcely felt the bone-jarring impact of his body nor the fist he slammed into my gut, quenching my breath as he cried, "Now, I've got you, mongrel!" Twisting sideways to evade his yanking me to the floor—a maneuver learned through Walsingham's tests of endurance—I rammed my own fist under his jaw as hard as I could.

Blood dripped from his cut lip. He hunched his powerful shoulders; as I prepared for his full onslaught, Cecil cried, "Stop it! Stop this instant!" and Dudley snarled, showing me blood-stained teeth. He might have charged again had Elizabeth's frightened voice not shattered our confrontation: "God save us, what—what is wrong with it?"

I whirled about. Horror flooded me.

Kate stood as if paralyzed. At her feet, black foam bubbling from its snout, the spaniel thrashed, one gnawed glove still clenched between its teeth.

The other glove dangled from her hand.

Chapter Six

o not touch anything," I said and I had to force back a surge of panic, drawing a steadying breath as I stepped to her.

The chamber's stunned hush was broken only by the spaniel's death throes, as if it were being disemboweled from within. Arching its spine, the dog released a vile stream of spew, choked, and went still. The other spaniel whimpered but did not try to approach.

Her color drained to an ashen hue, Kate dropped the glove and started to turn to Elizabeth. I heard Dudley shout, "No! Do not approach the queen!" and a stiff rustle of petticoats as he pulled Elizabeth bodily off her chair.

Kate lifted wide eyes to me. "Am I . . . ?" she whispered. She knew this was how Peregrine must have died, intoxicated by poison smeared on a letter's seal.

I made myself look at her hands, hanging limp at her sides; to my overwhelming relief, I did not detect the blisters that had been the beginning of Peregrine's doom. Still, I could not be certain. If the poison had seeped inside her, nothing I did could save her. The spaniel had died within seconds. It would not take much longer to kill a woman—

Something snagged at my attention, dragging my gaze downward. Gilded shreds, stuck in the dog's now-rigid mouth . . .

"The wrapping inside," I breathed. "It was poisoned." To no one in particular, I added, "I need something to cover my hands with, so I can gather it. And keep the other dog away."

There was no movement until Elizabeth said, "Do as he says. *Now!*"

One of the women took the surviving spaniel by the collar and hauled it from the room. Within moments, Cecil had handed me a pair of hawking gauntlets and as I pulled them on, the fit loose but close enough, Kate said, "What should I do?" She remained immobile, a tremor in her voice, but there were no other changes. I took her hands in mine and turned them over, examining her palms, closely this time.

"Am I going to die?" I heard her ask. I shook my head. "No. It wasn't on the gloves." I glanced at the tumbled box, the up-ended lid. "The box . . . it looks as though it was altered—"

Dudley said angrily, "What do you mean? How could it be altered? *Who* would dare?"

Elizabeth hushed him. Cecil shifted to Kate, leading her to the other women, who were holding each other and crying. I started to bend to the shredded papers when I felt someone hand me a shawl. "Cover it," Elizabeth said. "Lord Robert," she added, lifting her voice. "Fetch gloves and help Master Prescott." Not awaiting Dudley's answer, she directed her next orders at Cecil: "Take my women to my rooms; they look ready to faint. And make sure the outer doors are secure and no one is admitted.

Disperse the parasites outside. Tell them I will make no public appearance today. No one says a word of this to anyone, on pain of my worst reprove. Is that understood?"

The women nodded in unison, sniffling, and allowed Cecil to herd them out. After I shrouded the dead dog, I began picking up the torn paper and half-chewed glove. Dudley delayed for as long as he possibly could, joining me as I finished making a heap by the hearth, his own hands sheathed in gauntlets and his expression grim.

"What is your intent?" he asked, and while I'd expected derision in his tone, perhaps even a hint of accusation, he seemed begrudgingly willing to listen.

"Burn it, of course," I said. "What other remedy is there?"

He bristled. "Poisons can be traced. My own Dr. Dee knows a great deal of these matters and could tell us where the poison originated, help us find whoever did—"

"It will not tell us anything," I interrupted. "I've seen this type of poison before. It is fast acting and untraceable." Even as I spoke, I had a terrifying notion of who was responsible, and Dudley must have gleaned it, for he snarled, "Whatever you know, you had best spill it now. It is treason to do otherwise."

"I will decide what is or what is not treason," cut in Elizabeth. "If Master Prescott says we can't discover anything from this—this abomination, then I would prefer it were burned and out of my sight, lest some other hapless creature suffers. And the same for that poor dog." She motioned to Dudley. "If you would not mind, my lord . . . ?"

Tight-lipped, he went to assume charge of the corpse. Footsteps entered the room. Cecil had returned with Walsingham.

"Did I not just say I wanted absolute secrecy?" exclaimed Elizabeth.

"Your Majesty," said Cecil, "Master Walsingham is familiar with poisons. He has traveled extensively in Italy, made a study of the art—"

"Art?" Elizabeth was outraged. "Christ's wounds, this so-called art was meant for me!"

"Yes, it was," Walsingham said. "Which is why we must examine it first. I have asked Lord Robert to have the dog's body brought to the cellars. With Your Majesty's leave, I can perform a necropsy that might help determine the type of poison and its origin."

Elizabeth hesitated and Cecil drew her to the alcove. As they engaged in urgent conversation, Walsingham stepped to the hearth. "Excellent," he murmured, so that only I could hear, "already you've made yourself indispensable, the hero who saved the queen's life. But, you're about to make an error, albeit an understandable one, given your experience. Don't you think it wise to sift through the evidence first?"

"My squire perished like that dog," I said. "I've seen this poison before. It is odorless, tasteless; it strikes within seconds and leaves no trace. You can cut that dog up in pieces and it will tell you nothing."

"Indulge me. Have you searched the box?"

I started. In the uproar, I had not considered it. Abandoning the hearth, I gingerly righted the box by Elizabeth's chair. It was, as I had supposed, empty, save for a crumpled lining. I reached for the lid. The same fine cloth upholstered both; as I took up the lid, something crinkled under my fingers. I paused, probing. "Walsingham," I said.

He rose from his crouch over the tissue, striding past Elizabeth and Cecil, who broke off their argument to stare at us. "I think there's more paper under this." I patted the lid. "Not tissue. By the feel of it, it could be a letter parchment." Even as I relayed the information, I was pulling my poniard from my boot to slash at the covering.

"Careful," warned Walsingham. "Some poisons release their toxin when exposed to air. It could be a trap, in case the first attempt failed."

"Or it could be a message," I said, "because the assassin anticipated that the attempt would, in fact, fail." Still, I did as he instructed, meticulously slicing the fabric and rocking back on my heels, to avoid being directly over it as I gripped the shorn edges and ripped them apart.

A folded parchment slid out—unsealed.

Walsingham's mouth curved into an icy smile. "He plays with us. Allow me." He removed gloves from within his doublet. My breath stalled in my lungs as I braced for the worst, but he unfolded the parchment without incident. Passing his gaze over it slowly, he went still as if contemplating its significance. Then he removed his gloves and passed his fingertips deliberately over and around the paper.

"Well?" Elizabeth demanded warily after enough time had passed and Walsingham had not started foaming at the mouth. "Will you tell us what it says, sir?"

He turned to her, dazed, as if he had forgotten she was there. "I cannot, Your Majesty. Though it does appear to be a letter, its code is unfamiliar to me."

"Then it must be deciphered," said Cecil. "And while that is being done, Her Majesty must leave for Windsor at once, the coronation postponed until we can ascertain—"

Elizabeth held up her hand. "No."

Cecil gaped at her. "But Your Majesty, I must insist. An attempt has been made on your life. This monster could try again and Whitehall is too large to protect you. We have too many people coming and going; if we restrict access to your person or post extra sentries, it will rouse suspicion that something is amiss—which is not the impression we wish to convey."

She regarded him as though she were counting seconds under her breath. I knew that look; I had seen it before. Elizabeth was not going anywhere.

"I am afraid," she said. "Terrified, in fact. But I'll not be chased from my own city before I have even been crowned, with every sovereign in Christendom expecting me to fail. A queen who flees at the first sign of trouble is not long on her throne."

"This isn't mere trouble," I said, bringing her attention to me. "If it's what I suspect, Your Majesty's life could indeed be in grave danger. We both know Philip of Spain employed a secret agent to see you imprisoned by your sister." I did not add that the agent had been Sybilla, unable even now to voice her name aloud, even as I stood in midst of a chaos that had her mark.

"Yet seeing as no evidence could be found against me," she said, "I was freed."

"Precisely my point: Philip may have interceded on your behalf with Mary but only because he hoped to eventually win your hand and retain England as his vassal state. He wanted to be your king-consort, and now he has failed." Her eyes flared at my assumption that she had already discarded the Spanish king as a suitor but I ignored it. "You will not wed a Catholic," I added. "Philip knows this; he fears that in time you could become his enemy. Therefore, he must eliminate the threat. Though we do not know whom he has hired this time to do his deed, I think it is safe to assume the assassin had his consent. As it did not succeed, then my lord Cecil is correct in assuming that he will probably try again."

Elizabeth arched a brow. "Then we're fortunate that my knowledge of Philip surpasses yours. He may fear my enmity but he has one important reason to keep me alive, though I may reject his suit. Should I die without an heir of my body, the succession dictates my Catholic cousin Mary of Scots stands next in line to the throne. Under any other circumstance, I am sure Philip would rather she rule here than me; but Mary is wed to France. Philip would crown me with his own hands to keep the French from overtaking this isle." She let her words sink in. "This cannot be his doing; but someone clearly wishes it to *appear* as if it were. You said earlier you thought the box had been altered in some manner; I would hear your reasoning first, before we call his ambassador to task and further risk our already tenuous relationship with Spain."

I nodded, gathering my thoughts. As I turned back to the box, aware that Cecil and Walsingham observed me, I said, "There is a problem with the seal."

"What of it?" said Elizabeth.

"If it had arrived from Spain, after such a long voyage, it wouldn't have cracked so easily. It might have been brittle, fallen into pieces. But look: It broke apart in distinct sections."

"Ah, yes," said Walsingham. He sounded pleased. "Which could indicate it was recently applied. How clever of you to notice."

"And see here." I pointed to a faded area where the seal had been affixed. "There are still flecks of wax, but of a different color. That may indicate the original seal was taken off and replaced." I returned my gaze to Elizabeth, who regarded me intently. "Whoever did this could have removed the first seal, added poison to the tissue, and then resealed the box. Therefore, the gloves, one of which Kate touched, are not poisoned. The dog died because it grabbed the glove *inside* the tissue. Biting into the paper killed it, not the glove itself." I held back my suspicion that the poisoning of the tissue was not intended to be lethal but merely to sicken and frighten. If the assassin had wanted Elizabeth dead the gloves would also have been tainted, to ensure her demise. Whatever ultimate motive lay behind this attempt, fear was its primary goal.

Elizabeth turned to Cecil. "Can we find out who brought this gift? We must have some record of its delivery, an inventory, perhaps?"

The lines on Cecil's face deepened, making him look older than his years. "I believe envoys brought the majority of these gifts," he said haltingly. "My staff accepted them, of course, and recorded the date of arrival, but . . ." His voice faded. Elizabeth tapped her foot. He swallowed. "I cannot guarantee we annotated every one. There were so many messengers in those first days, so much confusion. The former secretary to your late sister had files we had to look through and store; we had papers everywhere to sort through. . . ." His voice turned brisk, to compensate for his deficiency. "I believe that at the very least, we have no other alternative than to question the Spanish ambassador."

"Then do so," said Elizabeth. "Only be discreet. Remember, His Excellency the Duke of Feria is a confidant of Philip's.

Moreover, if this gift came directly from Philip and was not a mere token of his esteem chosen by some menial, why did His Excellency not deliver it to me in person? The other royal envoys presented most of these gifts, as is the established custom. Yet seeing as Feria did not, indeed that he has shunned all but the most obligatory contact with me, is it possible these gloves did not come from Spain at all?"

Walsingham gave a grunt of consideration; Cecil looked even more troubled. To me, her question was valid. If the new reign's bureaucracy was as unsettled as Cecil described, anyone with knowledge of the inner workings of the palace could have hired someone to deliver the box. Her mention of Feria unsettled me, however. I recalled him well, a rigid Spanish nobleman I had met during my time in Mary's court. He had stood by and watched Peregrine die in my arms. I also knew he bore Elizabeth no love. Could he have orchestrated the assassination attempt at Philip II's behest? I had to doubt, if only because it was so obvious an attempt. Feria would surely have anticipated suspicion falling upon him and covered his tracks. Given what we knew thus far, taking into account the lack of poison on the gloves, it increasingly felt to me as if this would-be assassin was taunting us. Which left—

"The message," I said to Walsingham. "We must decipher it. If the culprit wants us to know his intent, it is there. He will not make it easy for us."

"So it would seem." Walsingham cleared his throat. "I'll work on it at once, Majesty—"

Elizabeth did not let him finish. "I will see to it." She extended her hand. "Lord Robert spoke the truth about Dr. Dee; while the man is an eccentric, I'll grant you, he is also a marvel with ciphers. Robert can bring the message to him. In the meantime, you will perform the necropsy and assist Cecil with searching the delivery records and questioning Feria."

Walsingham inclined his head, giving her the parchment. Though he must have been taken aback to have his own expertise supplanted by the seer dubbed a "madman" by Cecil, he did not comment on it, and neither did I. It was evident Elizabeth sought to entrust Dudley with a weighty task that would satisfy his ever-urgent need to feel important.

"And your women?" asked Walsingham. "Are they all familiar to Your Majesty or is it possible that one of them could have slipped this box among the other gifts? It would not be difficult, with so many to keep track of and your time in the palace so recent. And if you have strangers in your employ . . ."

"Do you imply that I cannot trust my own household?" Elizabeth sounded brusque, but she was not questioning his judgment. He simply confirmed a fear she already harbored, that anyone in her life could be suspect.

"I merely suggest the women should be questioned as well," replied Walsingham. "We cannot be too cautious. May I request leave to arrange it with your chief gentlewoman?"

For a moment, I thought I saw Elizabeth falter. Then she said, "Yes, of course. Though I fear Lady Parry, who oversees my women, has gone to visit relatives, while my other matron Mistress Ashley is still at my manor of Hatfield. However, you may apply to Mistress Stafford, who was nearly poisoned here today. She has served me many years and I trust her implicitly."

"Majesty." Walsingham made his retreat to the door. Cecil lingered. Realizing he desired to talk with her in private, I decided to join Walsingham. I might be of help to him, though the thought of cutting up the dog made my stomach turn. As I made my leave, sidestepping the jumble of caskets, coffers, and other items littering the floor, the white pelt of Sweden flung in a corner like a melting snow, Elizabeth called out: "Brendan."

I halted in my tracks. Walsingham had already left but her uttering of my first name startled me anyway. It conveyed an intimacy that until now she had evaded. Standing like a pilaster sketched in silver against the windows, her red-gold mane escaping the net at her nape to curl about her face, she said softly, "Do not stray far. I may have need of you."

"As my lord Cecil mentioned, I am entirely at your disposal," I said, and with another bow, I slipped from the chamber.

I wanted to dismiss it as more of my overwrought imagination, kindled by the turmoil, but the raw entreaty I had glimpsed in her eyes assured me otherwise.

Elizabeth was not only afraid.

She was hiding something.

Chapter Seven

The antechamber was quiet, Walsingham nowhere in sight. He had not tarried, and I moved past the sentries at the doors into the privy gallery.

Most of the courtiers had dispersed, save for a few desultory figures feigning games of cards or walking leashed dogs in the stubborn hope that the queen might yet make an appearance. Cecil had demonstrated his usual efficiency and tact; word had obviously not spread or the gallery would have been swarming with officials and gimlet-eyed ambassadors, eager to garner news of the near catastrophe for their masters.

Wondering where the cellars might be and how I might access them (for while I could get around Whitehall well enough, I had not explored its entirety), I started down the gallery, turning into a corridor leading to the great hall. I thought of finding my way to the kitchens; the cold storerooms would surely be near any cellars and—

A shift in the shadows caught my eye. Spinning about, I gleaned movement before I had the chance to whip my blade from my boot. A fist crashed into my face. As I gasped, darkness exploding behind my eyes, the fist hit me again. The brine of blood flooded my mouth. Hands grasped me by the shoulders, dragging me into a recessed alcove.

"Finally!" Dudley flung me so hard against the wall that my teeth rattled. "I have you."

Blinking back whirling stars, my head pounding, I met his ferocious stare. He was palming a dagger. "To what do I owe this honor?" I managed to utter, even as I debated whether it would be worth trying to go for my knife before he slashed me open.

"You know what." He thrust the blade at my throat, hard enough for me to feel it nick my skin, preempting any idea of reaching for my own weapon. "Move an inch and it'll be the last thing you ever do. You will be singing chants in hell while I set your balls in a bag at her feet. No matter how highly she may regard you, she cares for me more."

I took a moment to gather my composure as he jutted his chin at me. "What? Have you nothing to say?" He paused, eyeing me. The dark timbre of his voice stirred the hairs on my neck. "I'm of mind to gut you here and now, like your friend Walsingham is about to gut the queen's dog. That would teach them a lesson they'll not soon forget."

"Oh?" I remained still. "And what lesson might that be, my lord?"

"That I am not to be trifled with," he bellowed, and then he went quiet, trembling. He might think to prove his prowess to the world, but I had the disquieting impression the lesson he sought to impart was for me alone. I had humiliated him too many times. Now, he wanted to rouse fear in me again, the same fear I had felt when he had terrorized me in my youth.

I waited for his next move, my breathing gone shallow. If all else failed, I could resort to Walsingham's training; all Dudley need do was ease back on his dagger and I could bring my knees up and hit him in the groin, double him over long enough to—

"You should never have come back," he said suddenly. "But you always were more cur than hound; and like the cur, you always return to your own vomit. The question is: What to do with your body?" He pressed on the blade. I was becoming quite alarmed. I could feel a trickle running down the side of my neck, seeping into my collar. He had cut me. I had to do something.

"If you harm me," I said, freezing the murderous contempt on his face, "you could come to regret it. You have forgotten how much I know about you."

He chuckled. "As I said, more cur than hound. Once you are dead, who cares what you know? And besides, what proof have you?"

I had nothing to lose, save my life. Forcing out a smile, I said, "Proof enough."

His mouth contorted. "What are you saying?" he hissed. "Tell me now before I slice your throat and leave you here to bleed."

I made myself smile. "Just know that if I should disappear, I've left word for a certain packet of information to be delivered to Cecil, detailing everything I learned about your plot to depose our late Queen Mary. I daresay, Cecil will be most interested. Indeed, your past misdeeds could give him the very means he seeks to undo you. Treason runs in your family, my lord. Her Majesty will be obliged to act. So, either you kill me now or we reach an understanding that can benefit both of us."

His eyes glittered. Not for the first time, I wished Elizabeth could see him as I did—the feral ambition, usually tethered under his polished countenance, rising to the surface, so that he resembled nothing more than a ravenous wolf.

"What exactly do you propose?" he asked in a tone that implied he did not care. But he had swallowed the bait. He did not trust me anymore than I did him and safeguarding incriminating information was something he himself would have done in my shoes. He also knew Cecil plotted against him and that evidence of his past treasonous activities was not a credential to earn him the crown of king-consort. In fact, if his actions during Mary's reign were made public, Elizabeth would have no choice but to distance herself from him—permanently.

"Our queen is in danger," I went on. "Perhaps for once, we can put our differences aside and find a way to work together."

The suggestion tasted vile in my own mouth, as if I'd spewed my own brand of poison. It was the only solution I had, seeing as I couldn't kill him. Much as I believed this world would be a better place without Robert Dudley in it, I would never survive it. He was a nobleman, the queen's favorite; even if Elizabeth could forgive me and others breathed a sigh of relief at his demise, there were always the righteous highborn who would bay for my head, if only because an example must be made. Dudley, on the other hand, could slay me with impunity; and as he tightened his hold on the dagger, for a horrid moment I thought he would. God knew he was capable of it. Though I might gain respite by instilling caution and appealing to his self-interest, in the end he would have his revenge.

He knew it and so did I.

"Work together?" he echoed. "You think we should *collaborate*?"

I nodded. "Elizabeth has ordered us to find accord, and while you took the dog away I found a message hidden in the lid of the box. It is in cipher; she wants you to convey it to your astrologer. That message could reveal who is behind this attempt. Once Dee deciphers it, you will of course be the first to know. We can solve this mystery together and—"

"Reap the rewards!" He guffawed, with his familiar mocking gusto. "Ah, Prescott, you have not changed. You always did seek advantage in the mire." His good humor faded. "Chaffing at Cecil's shackle already, are we? It was all fine and good when she was a princess and you could sneak around, conniving behind my back, but now that she's on the throne, you want a heftier reward."

I gave him another smile. If that was how he saw it—indeed, with Dudley, it was the only way he *could* see it—why should I dissuade him? Let him believe I was as rapacious as he, as avid to betray my morals for sable on my cloak and gold in my pockets, providing it gave me the opportunity to find some way to bring him to his knees.

"A reward ample enough to earn my gratitude," I said, and though every part of me recoiled, I made myself incline to him, with masculine camaraderie. "Ample enough to make me destroy the evidence I have and leave court, if you so desire it."

"Oh, I desire it," he said, his eyes narrowing to slits. "I do and you will, either of your own volition or wrapped in a winding sheet—it matters not."

I watched his emotions flicker across his face, doubt leading into frigid consideration of what I presented, wrestling with base instinct to be done with it and sever my throat. Then, with a decisiveness that made me sag, he smiled. "Very well. I'll bring the message to Dee so he can decipher it, and once we catch this varmint you can accept her reward and retire." His smile turned cruel. "But if you try to double-cross me in any way, if you seek to betray or gain favor over me, I'll see that you end up in the river." He came so close I gleaned a chip on his front tooth. "But first, I will strip the skin from your bones. No one will recognize a faceless corpse. You will end up as you started: a foundling, fit for the pauper's pit." He slid his blade down my cheek. "I shall be watching you, Prescott. Every moment."

He stepped back, his gaze fixed on me as he sheathed his dagger. I did not move until he turned heel and stalked back to Elizabeth's apartments.

Only then did I let out my breath, touch the smarting wound he had made on my throat. It had stopped bleeding; my fingers came away sticky. Dabbing at it, I exited the alcove and made for my room, to gather my cap and cloak.

To hell with Walsingham and his necropsy. To hell with Dudley.

I had to get as far from this snake pit as I could.

I rode Cinnabar through the park of St. James. At first, I reasoned I needed some fresh air, to clear my head and exercise my horse, as he had been in the stable for too long and I could feel his extra girth under my thighs. Cinnabar reacted with enthusiasm, cantering with head held high and muscles flexing, but soon enough, I found myself guiding him toward the Thames and dockyards, to that inn where Archie Shelton lived.

I had not seen Shelton in years, not since he accompanied me to Cecil's manor after Elizabeth was imprisoned in the Tower. I now knew he had had a forbidden liaison with my mother, Mary Tudor, duchess of Suffolk; it was entirely possible that he was, in fact, my father. I had no other explanation for why my mother had hidden her pregnancy or entrusted me to her intimate servant, Mistress Alice, who took me in secret to the Dudley estate. By strange coincidence, my birth had coincided within days of Elizabeth's own. Only days later, my mother died of childbed fever, disguised as the fatal result of a long illness.

Thus, I had grown up unaware of my royal blood. Shelton spent years searching for me; when he did find me, he instigated himself in the Dudley employ. I had believed him my foe. Only later did I learn he had been protecting me all along.

We had reached an understanding. His own terrible experience during my first assignation at court had left him maimed. He now eschewed the life of a nobleman's menial, opting instead to work as a publican with his love, Nan, a former doxy who had inherited her uncle's tavern. This was the Griffin, where I headed now, drawn to the only family I had.

Riding down Tower Street near the old city wall, I had an impressive view of the forbidding fortress brooding on its bloodsoaked hill, the crenellations of its keep stabbing into the early dusk. The district seemed seedier than the last time I had been here, ramshackle tenements, brothels, taverns, and warehouses leaning into each other, a corkscrew tangle of alleyways threading between them, the haunt of footpads and whores who plied their illicit trade across the river from Southwark, against city regulations. Packs of skeletal dogs skulked as I passed. Vagrants sat in pools of their own filth or wandered about shouting at devils in their heads, while night-soil collectors hauled their stinking carts beyond the walls. Those who lived or worked here moved quickly, heads down and eyes on the path before them; only slatterns lounging in doorways met my eyes, bony hips cocked and fingers snaking up their tattered skirts to offer a glimpse of cunny. I could see the effects of Mary's persecution everywhere, from the desolation on the residents' faces to rotten bodies swinging in scraps from gibbets, evidence of a fervor that had no compunction. I remembered what Cecil had said about the destitution of the realm. Elizabeth had a monumental task before her if she was to rebuild everything her sister had laid to waste.

I was heartened to reach the swinging sign over the Griffin's threshold. Perhaps Dudley knew me better than I thought. Perhaps he was right and it was indeed only here, in common mire, that I truly belonged. It was what I knew, after all. I had grown up among people whose only experience with the court was watching the occasional royal procession.

Sliding off Cinnabar, I was looking around for a reliable place to tether him when a skinny jumble of knees and elbows with a thatch of unkempt hair raced out from a nearby side street—an urchin, no older than twelve by the looks of it. With an inept bow, he said, "Will my lord need a stall for his horse?"

I repressed a smile. Boys like him were ubiquitous in London, orphans or foundlings who made a meager living doing anything they could to keep body and soul together, from running errands to driving livestock to engaging in thievery and less savory deeds. This one looked honest enough, scrappy and none too clean, but with an earnest gaze that did not sidle away to assess the richness of my trappings.

"What is your name?" I asked.

"Thomas. Or Tom to my friends, if it please my lord." He

bobbed another clumsy obeisance, bringing a lump to my throat. He reminded me of Peregrine.

"Well, Tom-to-your-friends," I said, "I do need someone to watch my horse. However, I'd not look kindly on him disappearing." I reached into my cloak, extracting several coins from my pouch. Tom's eyes went wide. It was probably more money than he had seen in his entire life. "Can I rely upon you to take good care of him?"

Tom gaped. "Yes, my lord, on my life."

"Let us hope not." I flipped him two coins; he caught them in midair. "Two more when I come out," I said. "I trust you'll be close by, in case I have need of you?"

"Oh, yes. I work here in the mornings sometimes, helping the master and mistress."

I remembered him now, the grubby boy whom Nan let sleep by the hearth. He had not recognized me, however. "Good." I handed him Cinnabar's reins, taking a moment to make sure he would not balk, as my horse could be skittish with strangers. The boy seemed to know what he was doing, though, murmuring to my steed and putting him at ease. I moved with confidence into the tavern, ducking under the low lintel.

Smoke from tallow lights thickened the air, making my eyes prickle. There were several patrons seated at tables, tankards of ale and platters before them. The rattle of dice and conversation hummed around me; I paused to adjust to the surroundings, wishing I had had the forethought to change my attire. I must be as noticeable here as a swan on the Fleet.

Nearing the hearth, I espied the battered armchair where Shelton often dozed, his old dog at his feet. The chair was empty, but the scarred mutt was there, opening one lazy eye to stare at me. Women in swishing skirts, loose-laced bodices that offered plenty of cleavage, and sweat-soaked caps weaved through the room, bearing trays and swatting away pinches to their buttocks. Approaching the serving hutch, I heard a voice call: "Get those pies out now before they burn!" and saw Nan herself at the counter, rubbing a meaty forearm across her forehead as she glared at someone unseen. Her serving girls, I noted, were all hips and saucy manner, adept at fending off inebriated advances. Former doxies, I surmised, who had abandoned their thankless trade for an honest living under Nan's tyrannical employ.

I paused before her, smiling. A quizzical look crossed her flushed features as she took in my appearance. Then, as recognition dawned on her, she cried, "Scarcliff!" and a large, heavy figure limped out from behind the hutch, wiping dirty hands on his apron.

She had called Shelton by his assumed name. I still marveled at the change in him, struck for a few moments by the mutilated patchwork of his face, so that he appeared like a monstrous pirate from a child's nightmare, his beard scarcely concealing the contorted shape of his jagged-toothed maw, his left eye a puckered welt. The damage inflicted on him had visceral impact, but his garbled chuckle at the sight of me was warm. Before I could utter a word, Shelton enveloped me in his arms, his yeasty beer breath in my ear as he said in his broken voice, "Of all the knaves to walk through the door, you are the last one I expected to see."

I grinned, drawing back. "Still handsome as ever, I see."

He slapped me on the back. "She likes me that way, don't you, Nan?" He cast a roguish wink at his love with his good eye.

Nan harrumphed, "Get away with your tomfooleries, old man," and took my face between her palms. "Look at you," she said softly. "Such a sight in your fancy sleeves. I almost didn't recognize you."

Her maternal solicitude overwhelmed me. With a gentle pat on my cheek, she said, "You look tired. Go on: Take a seat. I'll have one of the lasses bring you a nice quail pie and bottle of our best wine."

"No wine," I said. "Ale will do. My fancy sleeves don't have fancy tastes."

At my side, Shelton's laughter rattled like nails on cobblestone as he guided me to his battered chair, yanking up a stool next to the rickety table. "Move, Crum." He shoved his pet with his foot. The dog growled, grudgingly making room for us. As soon as Shelton sat, the dog settled down again, close to his side.

"Crum?" I asked. "As in, Cromwell?"

"Aye." He reached down to ruffle the dog's clipped ears. "I figured he needed a name. It was the first one that came to mind. He's a good watchdog, my Crum. We leave him downstairs at night and no one dares break in. Much as I imagine Cromwell must have kept the friars from breaking back into their monasteries after he stripped them bare."

I found myself laughing. It felt good. Normal. A few moments later, a blond girl with sparkling blue eyes appeared, placing a steaming pie and tankard before me with exaggerated flourish, her lascivious regard moving up and down me.

Shelton grunted, eyeing the lass as she sauntered away. "If you're in the mood for a bed warmer, none's saucier than Margie. But," he added, lowering his voice, "don't let Nan hear of it.

She's forbidden the girls from selling their wares during working hours, though after we close for the night, well . . . what they do then is no business of ours, eh?"

He had a bawdy humor, I thought. Who would have known the former Dudley steward would end up making jokes about the whores employed in his tavern?

He motioned at the pie. "Nan will want every bite accounted for. It's her special recipe."

I ate with relish. The pie was greasy, so fresh from the oven it burned my mouth, but it tasted like manna from heaven after days of stale bread and cheese. The ale was exactly as I remembered it: thick and foamy as it slid down my throat. I drank it down in two gulps. Shelton gestured to Margie for a pitcher. He served me himself this time, leaning over the table, his sleeve rucking up to display the latticed scars on his forearm.

He caught me staring and remarked, "I look like Christ's passion. I vow those guards at the Tower whacked me so many times, it's a miracle I am still alive to tell the tale."

"Indeed," I said. I remembered all too well that night of chaos when London declared for Queen Mary. The Tower shut its gates, trapping hundreds inside. I had escaped by throwing myself into the river—a memory that still made me shudder—but Shelton was not so fortunate. Assaulted by the guards cutting a swath with their pikes through those amassed at the gates, he was cudgeled unconscious. He might have died if Nan had not found him.

"But that," he went on, "is no matter now." He reclined in his chair, his hand straying again to his snoring dog. "Tell me about you, lad."

I had been gone for years but in his usual way, he did not ask for specifics. For a moment, I wondered how much I should re-veal. Taking another long draft from my cup—the more I drank, the more the ale's quality improved—I began to tell him of the events that had transpired since we'd last seen each other, of my refuge with Cecil and how word eventually reached us that the Imperial ambassador had sent men after me, prompting Cecil to dispatch me abroad. Then I faltered, recalling Elizabeth had for-bidden any of us to speak of the incident in her chambers.

Sensing my reluctance, he made a cursory examination of those seated around us before he said, "No one is interested. This lot works the shipyards all day. All they care about is their drink, filling their bellies, and wasting their hard-earned wages on dice and cunny. Griffin's safer than any hall at court, I can assure you."

All of a sudden, I yearned to unburden myself of the pain of my encounter with Kate, if nothing else. When I finally began to speak, my words were awkward, uncertain, as if I sought to make light of it. Once I was done, he gave me a pensive nod.

"But you still want her. Do not bother to deny it. I may not be much to look at, if I ever was, but I was young once. I know a fool in love when I see him."

"My love cannot protect her," I said. "It didn't protect Pere-grine."

He sighed. "You're like a flagellant. The lad died by accident. You are not to blame."

"I should have known!" Hearing the flare in my voice, I had to make myself lower it. "I will not put Kate in any more danger. Ever since I entered Elizabeth's service, foes have hunted me. Kate's only hope is for me to put as much distance between us as I can."

"Yet she too serves the queen. It seems to me that is danger enough."

I started to protest, but he was right, and so I looked away. Shelton leaned toward me, setting his gnarled paw on my knee. "You cannot be responsible for her safety, lad. You can only do the best you can." He paused. "I may not have been much of a father to you these past years, but I would like to make amends if you let me. And I can see something more is troubling you."

My throat knotted. He removed his hand. "I will not force you. You are back and that is enough. We each have our burdens to bear. You've managed well enough with yours; another might not have been so willing to sacrifice everything you have."

In a low, almost emotionless voice, I told him about the events in the queen's chamber. "Now, do you understand?" I asked, as he sat silent. "I have barely been back two days and already she came close to death. Yes, I still love her. I think I always will. But I would rather forsake her now than lose her that way."

"Aye, I can understand that," he said. "Though it seems to me that again, this weight you carry is not of your doing. That box was tainted and sent to the queen. You could not have prevented it. Do you have any idea who might be responsible?"

"I do," I said, and as he met my gaze, he went still. "No, lad. It is impossible."

"Impossible things happen every day. And it has her mark— the quick-acting poison and cryptic message. It's just like that letter she left in my chamber, the one that killed Peregrine."

Shelton reclined in his chair. "What exactly are you saying?"

"That if I did not know better, I would think Sybilla Darrier has returned from the dead."

He whistled through his teeth. "That would indeed be a feat. We both saw her leap willingly from the bridge. It was a hard fall."

"Precisely. She did it *willingly*. What if she planned to jump from the bridge in order to escape because I had discovered her true purpose?" Sybilla was a secret Catholic working for Spain, bent on revenge because Elizabeth's father, King Henry, executed her father and brothers during the revolt against the closure of the monasteries, the Pilgrimage of Grace. "I have never met a woman so skilled at deceit," I added, as his frown deepened. "I believed she took her own life to evade capture. But, what if that is only what she *wanted* me to believe?"

"Even if it were true, and I'm not saying it is, where has she been hiding all this time?"

"She . . . she could have hidden anywhere." Uncertainty crept into my voice. I realized how ludicrous I must sound, how devoid of reason. Still, I could not dissuade myself. "Her body was never found. If she did plan to survive that fall, she would have had her hiding place arranged in advance."

He rubbed his chin, with a troubled sigh. "No, her body was never found—or if it was, I never heard of it and I kept an ear out for any word. Most of those who ply the waters for corpses come here to drink; they would have mentioned finding a woman like her. Countless others have been dragged from the Thames since then, but none I heard about matched her description." He went quiet for a moment, considering. "Perhaps she was never found because she was dragged under by the current and swept out to sea?"

"The river was nearly frozen," I reminded him.

"Then she was trapped under the ice and when the river thawed, her remains were swept out to sea." His voice softened.

"You cannot chase a shade, lad, not when you have more pressing troubles at hand. Whatever happened to her, whatever evil she caused—it's over now."

I wanted to believe him. I had every reason to. I had seen her plunge from the bridge with my own eyes, her last enigmatic smile on her lips before she leapt. She had looked at me in that final moment as if she had won a victory. Perhaps because she had escaped me, because I would now never know what that smile had meant, I had let her haunt me. It was possible that deep inside me, in that dark place where lust twisted into monstrous shapes, I wanted her to be alive because it meant I would see her again. If so, it only proved my weakness, how much harm I might yet bring upon those around me.

I said quietly, "I took her to my bed."

Shelton started in his chair.

"I disregarded my promise to Kate," I went on, "everything I held sacred, because I desired her. I wanted her from the hour I first saw her, among Queen Mary's women. She was so beautiful—" I paused. "Christ, she was unlike any woman I'd ever seen. Even now, the mere thought of her . . . She used me. She saw my desire and she honed it as a weapon against me."

He went quiet for a moment. Then he said, "You are but a man. How were you to know?"

"Because it was my duty to know!" To my horror, tears scalded my eyes. I forced them back, summoning the fury I had nourished like an invisible scourge. "I should have known. There were plenty of signs she was untrustworthy, if only I had heeded them. Peregrine's death alone should have been enough, but it was not. I let my grief for him become so vast, I stepped right into her snare."

"You are too hard on yourself. No"—Shelton shook his head, silencing me—"you always were. You always felt you had to prove yourself since you were a foundling in the Dudley household. No matter what those ruffians flung at you—the taunts and dunking in stable troughs, the beatings and black eyes—you fought back. You never let yourself be defeated."

"How could I?" I said, stung by this unwelcome reminder of my childhood. "If I'd shown a single instance of weakness, they would have killed me."

"Indeed. Yet defeat can take many forms. You succumbed to a woman. God knows, there is not a man alive or dead, I wager, who has not made the same mistake. Nevertheless, you protected Elizabeth, and Kate, too; you helped save the kingdom. Unfortunately, it is most often our mistakes, not our triumphs, that define us. Do not let that happen to you."

I did not want to hear it. I evaded his advice, because it made me recognize my morbid attachment to my self-inflicted culpability, a dismal refuge I had built around my heart, so atonement would always be out of reach. Sybilla was dead, but part of her lived in me. I had kept her memory alive to torment myself. I had to forget her if I hoped to ever find peace.

"You are wise," I said at length. "I should not let the past cloud my future. I must focus only on finding out who now seeks harm on the queen."

"And you must do it before Dudley finds out you misled him," added Shelton. "He may have struck a pact with you out of fear you'd reveal his treason, but when he discovers your ploy, he will try again to destroy you. He hankers for revenge."

"I know." I found myself finally smiling. "I do seem to have a talent for riling him up."

Shelton chuckled. "I have never known anyone more prone to stepping on his tail." His mirth faded. "I still have Sybilla's sword, the one she dropped on the bridge. I had it repaired. It is the finest Toledo steel money can buy. Beyond price. It's yours, if you want it."

I shook my head, reaching for the pitcher. "Keep it. I do not want anything of hers."

Two hours and two more pitchers later, I could barely stand. The smoky room swam about me. Looking around through bleary eyes, I realized it was empty, girls sweeping up gristle and ashes from the floor while others clanked dishes in the washing tub behind the hutch. I was too drunk to ride, Nan emphatically informed me.

"You will sleep here," she said, in a tone that brooked no argument. "The streets are no place for a law-abiding person at night, what with the riffraff and the curfew in effect." Turning to Shelton, she said, "He can bed on the settle. Take him now before he falls flat on his face."

As Shelton wrapped an arm like a beam of lumber around my waist, guiding me to the narrow staircase, I slurred, "My horse . . . Cinnabar. I left him with a boy outside . . ."

"I've already seen to it," said Nan. "The horse and Tom are stalled out back, with plenty of feed and a brazier to keep them warm. I will check on them again before I close for the night, don't you fret. Now, go on upstairs. You have no head for ale."

"Or much of anything else these days, it seems," I muttered, but I allowed Shelton to take me up to their small living quarters above the tavern, where I collapsed in a heap on the settle as he pulled off my boots, unlaced my doublet, and divested me of my breeches like a child.

Slumber overcame me within seconds of him setting a blanket over me. I feared I would dream again of Sybilla, straddling me with a knife in her fist.

Instead, I saw Elizabeth, a spaniel dying at her feet as she whispered, *Do not stray far. I may have need of you.* . . .

Chapter Eight

I left the Griffin before dawn with a sour taste in my mouth, an aching head, and repeated assurances to Nan that I would return as soon as I was able. Shelton gave me a hearty embrace and fetched Cinnabar himself. My horse seemed content, and I tossed Tom his extra coins as promised, bringing a cheerful grin to the boy's grime-stained face.

The ride to Whitehall was quiet, the city only starting to stir to its usual ear-numbing cacophony. Flurries of snow pirouetted in the icy air; I could see my own breath coming in puffs from my mouth and sensed this winter would be as frigid as the last time I had been in London, when the Thames froze over and children took to it with skates made of bone strapped to their feet.

Above me, the morning's brisk exhalation washed the sky clean of its pall of smoke, revealing a patina of crimson and gold flushing the horizon. After presenting my credentials to the yeomen at the gates (ever-efficient Cecil had enclosed a note in my doublet pocket bearing his signature and seal, stating I was in his employ), I stabled Cinnabar and paid the sleepy-eyed groom to brush him down and feed him. I then made my way through the palace to my room, holding my nose and resisting gagging as I passed the reeking jakes. The overcrowding would require a move soon, if only because Elizabeth had a sensitive nose.

I expected to find Walsingham waiting. Instead, the chamber was empty, his few belongings gone. He must have moved to the house he had said Cecil was renting for him, I thought, wincing at the persistent throb in my temples as I unclasped my cloak. I really should not ever drink ale again. Nan was right: I had no tolerance for it.

A knock came at the door just as I was splashing water on my face from the ewer on the table, having shed my court garb for my comfortable, worn clothes.

Cecil stood on the threshold.

Dark circles under his eyes betrayed an anxious night. The gravity of his expression, too, doused the aftereffects of my indulgence with remarkable efficacy. Looking at him, I felt stone-cold sober. I also found myself bracing for the worst, thinking something terrible had happened while I had been gone.

"She wants to see you," he said. "Make haste."

We went together into the privy gallery without saying a word. At first, I thought he was angry that I had wandered off after such a calamity, when he might have found need of my assistance, but the terse line of his jaw was not indicative of any particular anger toward me. He would have had no problem venting his spleen if it were. Nevertheless, I could not abide his silence any longer and ventured, "Is something amiss?"

"I take your meaning to be, is anything else amiss besides the fact that someone tried to poison our queen?"

"Yes," I said, resisting a roll of my eyes.

"Indeed. Well, fortunately for you, it was an uneventful night. She stayed in her rooms, despite ceaseless badgering from the court, which seems to think she must now make appearance every night in the hall, dressed to the teeth with roast at her table, eager to strew her favor."

"Have you any indication of who might be the culprit?"

"We do not. We did question His Excellency de Feria at length and had his rooms searched, rousing his outrage, but we found nothing to indicate he is party to any plot, instigated by his master or otherwise. Of course, these Spaniards always have a few knives up their sleeves, but Walsingham is of mind that in de Feria's case, his outrage is genuine. The duke swore to lodge a complaint with King Philip himself and take ship for Spain on the next tide, of course, but we reminded him that he requires royal leave. As you can imagine, he is not pleased."

"No, I should think not. And the delivery records . . . ?"

He scowled. "That infernal gift seems to have materialized out of nowhere. I've had my assistants devise a new system for tracing everything that arrives for her henceforth, and to detain anyone suspicious, but in the meantime we have no clue as to who brought such an abomination into the palace." He paused before the doors to the royal apartments, clearing his throat. "I've been up all night, poring over every possible route in and out of Whitehall, both official and unofficial. All doors and passages not currently guarded are now closed. I also spoke to the queen's women at length. All swear on their honor that they know nothing; no one approached them or entrusted them with the box. It's inconceivable that poison could have made its way into the queen's very own hands without anyone being the wiser, but there you have it."

Now I understood the reason behind his rigidity. Cecil was horrified. Not a month on her throne and already Elizabeth had come within inches of her death. It was an ominous start to what had been an often dangerous rise to power; she was not yet crowned and we faced an unknown opponent who would most likely strike again. Should she succumb, the crown would devolve on her cousin Mary of Scots, to the papist depredations of France abetted by our own scheming Catholics. On Elizabeth's narrow shoulders now rested England's entire future. Without her, this realm would be torn apart.

"Do you know why she asked to see me?" I said, tugging at the edge of my old dark wool doublet. I should not have changed, though it was so early there was no one about to witness an ordinary man in plain fustian, entering the queen's rooms.

"I do not." He motioned the granite-faced guards at her doors aside. "I assume she has a purpose. She also insisted on speaking to you alone." He stared at me. He did not need to add that as soon as I learned this purpose, he expected me to report it to him.

The watching chamber was deserted. I paused, discomfited by the absence of servants. I knew Elizabeth valued her solitude; during our short time together at Hatfield, she had often taken to the gallery to read or walk on her own. All of us who lived with her had sensed how much she needed her time, that a mind such as hers, so nimble yet elusive, so keen, required privacy. Nevertheless, whenever she had asked to see me alone it had been for a reason, and I suspected that I was now about to discover why she had summoned me from Basel to attend her.

A dog's whine turned me about. "I am here," she said, her voice issuing as if out of thin air. Looking toward the far window, I saw her draped in shadow, Urian resting at her feet, silhouetted against the wine-dark folds of her robe. As I started to bow, she held up a hand. "There is no need for ceremony, as you can see. We are alone."

As she stepped forth, I noted her marked pallor, her skin stretched so taut over the angular bones of her face it seemed almost translucent, a blue vein traceable in her brow. Her hair hung loose, her slim waist cinched by the jeweled clasp of her garment. Her sleeves, unstiffened and full, hung like velvet wings to her exquisite hands; other than her royal ring, she wore no jewels. She murmured to the dog and Urian bounded to me, shoving his sleek head into my hand. I ruffled his ears.

"Are you well?" she asked.

"Yes, my lady, as well as can be expected under the circumstances. And you . . . ?"

She blew out a frustrated breath. "I am not ill with worry, if that's what they think."

"I do not think it," I replied.

"No? Cecil thinks I should be, as does that brooding Moor of his, Walsingham, who cut up my spaniel. Had they their way, I'd be rushing about in a panic, ordering departure for Windsor or, better yet, the Tower, where I can lock myself behind stout walls like a prisoner and refuse to see anyone until that madman, whoever he is, is drawn and quartered."

"Then they did not know you as I do." I allowed myself a smile, using my hand to settle Urian at my feet. "They do not understand that you never run from a fight."

She went still, regarding me with that intensity that could make me feel like her most intimate companion or an enemy poised on the jagged edge of her worst reprove. "No," she said at length. "I have never run. What would be the point? In the end, they always find you. It is not a matter of when but rather how, and who shall disarm whom first."

I remained silent, watching her walk to a small cabinet, where a decanter, goblet, and stack of papers rested. Urian whimpered again. Unease went through me, reminding me of the impression I had yesterday that she was hiding something.

At the cabinet, she placed her hand on the papers. "You said you were entirely at my disposal. Is that true?" She glanced at me. "Be very sure of your answer. If someone says they are at my disposal, I take them at their word."

I nodded, even as my heart quickened. She selected one of the papers. "I wish for you to undertake a special assignment for me."

"Of course, anything your Grace requires."

"Be careful with what you promise; times past, your labors on my behalf have often led you into danger."

"Is this one of those times?" I asked warily.

"I sincerely hope not. But of all those who serve me, you are the only one I can trust with it." She returned to me with the paper—a torn section of a letter, I thought—in her hand. "I need you to travel to Withernsea in Yorkshire as soon as possible."

For a moment, I did not know how to react. "But that is—"

"About four days from London," she said, "if you ride a fast horse."

"Is there any indication the man we seek is there?"

She gave an impatient shake of her head. "This is a private matter."

"Your Grace," I said carefully, "I fear I do not understand.

Yorkshire is far away and Cecil expects me to investigate the recent attempt against your person, as I witnessed the event and have in the past protected you from those who would do you harm."

"He may expect it of you, but this is more important—to me." Her voice trembled. She always kept close hold of herself but whatever was written in that fragment in her hand had perturbed her. "Are you aware that my Lady Parry went to visit her cousin at his manor?"

"Yes, I heard you mention it. I trust it's not too serious?"

"It wasn't at the time." She paused. "I did not care to explain to Cecil and all those others who watch me like hawks that Blanche had received word that her nephew's wife, Lady Vaughan, had taken with fever. Blanche requested leave to travel to Vaughan Hall near the village of Withernsea; the family has two young children, one of whom had also taken ill. Blanche was worried, so I told her of course she must go. At the time, my sister Mary's health was failing, but we had no confirmation that her illness would be fatal. I did not want to refuse Blanche leave, given the circumstances."

It sounded reasonable, if unorthodox, for one of Elizabeth's favored attendants to have left her side because of a family ailment, but if so, then why the secrecy?

"Blanche must have arrived safely," Elizabeth went on. "But then . . ." She went silent again, struggling to contain her emotion, the mysterious paper still clutched in her fingers. After a long moment, she said, "I did not hear from her after she left. I should have inquired; I know that now. But Mary's health took a turn for the worse and at Hatfield, we were on tenterhooks waiting for her demise. It seemed as if the entire court had abandoned

Whitehall to set up camp on my doorstep. When the news finally came of her death—you can imagine the furor: Cecil and his minions at me day and night, with mounds of papers to sign; Mary's funeral to attend to; the new Council to oversee—it overwhelmed me. It was only after I'd contended with all of it that I belatedly sent word to Blanche that I needed her back at court as soon as possible."

"Did she respond?" I asked.

"No. I sent my missive with an escort, so she could travel here by litter. I reasoned she must be weary after tending to a sick family and would prefer to be without the burden of riding on horseback. When my escort arrived, Lord Vaughan told them she had left four days prior, accompanied by the children's tutor, who had some business in London. As soon as Lord Vaughan realized something must have happened, they went in search of her. They eventually discovered her horse, still saddled and wandering the road, but Lady Parry was nowhere to be found. No body; no sign of any struggle. She had vanished."

Dread crept through me. "What about the tutor?"

"He had disappeared, as well; not even his horse was found. Lord Vaughan assured my escort that he had engaged the man from London to educate their children. He must have been trustworthy, if Blanche went with him. Then, this note was found under her saddle."

With a visible quiver of her hand, she finally extended the paper to me. It was rain-streaked, its ink smeared, but the boldly written words were clear:

You must pay for the sin.

I looked up. "Do you know what it means?"

"No, but it must be a threat." She could not hide her fear anymore—a faltering of her self-control that I had rarely seen her display, not even when her dying spaniel thrashed at her feet. She reached abruptly for my hand, another rarity for her. Her fingers were icy. "You must find her. Blanche is my most cherished companion. She has been far more than my chief gentlewoman these past years, for she attended my birth and cared for me when I was but a child, the daughter of a queen everyone wanted to forget. If she had not been there to fight for me, to defend me even against the will of my father, I might not have lived to see this day. She is like the mother I never knew. I cannot abandon her to whatever fate has befallen her."

I went quiet, restraining my rush of questions.

"Will you help?" she asked.

Even if I had wanted to, I could not refuse. I had sworn to serve her, though I had the disquieting impression there was more here, a tangled skein buried under the surface. Here was another message, albeit not in cipher, coupled with the unexplained disappearance of a woman Elizabeth valued above all others. I had to broach the obvious, and she knew it.

"Do you think the poison attempt is related to Lady Parry?"

"I don't know. I do not care to contemplate it, but yes, I suppose it is entirely possible."

I considered. "Cecil will not like it," I said at length. "You do not wish this matter made public but how can I explain my leaving to him in a way that will not rouse his suspicions?"

"You can leave the explanations to me." She withdrew her hand, her features hardening into that inscrutable royal guise. "I will tell Cecil I decided to send you elsewhere and he must abide by it, for I shall not be questioned. Besides"—she managed a tremulous smile—"I assume he can manage without you. He has Walsingham now, who seems to me quite determined."

"Oh, yes," I said. "Like a hound after the fox, I can assure you of that."

"Then we must place our trust in him. Robert took that message yesterday to Dr. Dee's home in Mortlake; if anyone can decipher it, Dee will. You must leave at once. You will need a map, my letter of introduction, and funds." She turned back to her cabinet and yanked open a drawer to pull out a small leather folder, rolled into a cylinder and fastened with a cord, as well as a pouch. She was prepared; she had been biding her time, but this was indeed the reason she had called for me. "Here is the map. The funds in the pouch should be sufficient. However, should you need more, you must send to Thomas Parry, who manages my personal accounts. Write by courier to Hatfield; Ashcat is there, tending to the manor. Whatever you do, do not write to me at court. As matters have shown, anything here can be tampered with, so whatever I wish kept private must go through other means."

"Is that why Mistress Ashley is still at Hatfield? I had wondered at her absence."

"She knows where I am best served" was Elizabeth's reply. "Like Blanche Parry, like you and Kate, she obeys my command." She thrust the purse into my hand. "Go now, before my women arrive. I don't want them to know you were here."

Tucking the pouch and folder into my doublet, where it made a noticeable bulk, I met her gaze. Implicit understanding passed between us. I had no idea what perils awaited me on this new errand, but her trust in me cemented my resolve. We had been through worse, and I had found a way through it. I would find a way now. Urian came to his feet. Elizabeth patted her thigh, bringing him back to her side.

"You must take care while I am gone," I told her. "Promise me. If anything else should occur, if there is even the hint of another threat, you must heed Cecil and depart London at once. The kingdom cannot survive if you are not here to rule it."

She nodded, impatient. "Yes, yes. I promise. Now, *go*."

As I stepped to the door, she suddenly said, "Brendan," and I stopped. "I never thought I would come to rely on you as much as I have, but I need you now more than ever. You must find Blanche before it is too late. Bring her home to me and I shall grant anything you ask. No recompense will be too great for her safe return."

I inclined my head. "I will do all I can."

As I turned away, it did not escape me that she had failed to mention what my punishment might be if I failed.

I hurried back to my room, avoiding the courtiers already gathering in the gallery for their daily vigil outside Elizabeth's doors. Cecil's grim words came back to me; Elizabeth had become the focus of incessant scrutiny. I wondered how she would contend with it, after having spent most of her life in country manors, left to her own devices save for the occasional foray to court. Already I had sampled a taste of what her new life entailed, the lengths she must go to preserve her privacy. It would not be easy, that much I knew. Much as Elizabeth reveled in attention—she was a Tudor, above all else—she always relished her freedom to seek refuge. She had escaped countless dangers simply because she knew when to retreat.

Now, she had no retreat. There were only sets of doors between her and the exigencies of the world—doors and the service of those trusted few on whom she could rely, which included Blanche Parry. I had witnessed how much Elizabeth depended on Lady Parry during our ill-fated sojourn at Queen Mary's court and knew Lady Parry for a sensible, middle-aged woman whose devotion to her mistress was unquestioned. She would not have willingly abandoned her duty. Whatever had befallen her had happened against her will, and Elizabeth was no doubt correct in assuming it was she, not Lady Parry, who was the ultimate target. Indeed, the more I dwelled on it, the more it seemed the poisoning incident and Lady Parry's disappearance must be linked.

The question was: How?

Turning these ruminations over in my mind like a puzzle without a key, I failed to notice the door to my room stood ajar. When I did, I slid to a precipitous halt, unsheathing my poniard. Had I failed to latch it in my haste to follow Cecil? Reaching out, I eased the door open, braced for an attack. It had happened before. I peered inside to find a well-dressed woman with her back to me, waiting.

My heart leapt in my throat, my grip on my dagger tightening convulsively. She wore a coif with a long veil, her shoulders rigid. Shelton's voice tumbled in my head—*You cannot chase a shade*—and I found myself whispering under my breath like an incantation, "It cannot be, it cannot be," even as I took a step forward, ready to plunge my blade into her heart.

The echo of my words or clack of my heel on the threshold caused her to turn around. I heaved relief as her hand came up, lifting her veil. It was Kate, only she wore an unfamiliar elaborate gown, its heavy fur-lined sleeves and pearled hem marking her as one of the royal attendants. Like everyone else who shared Elizabeth's inner sanctum, she looked in dire need of rest, her gaze embedded in pockets of shadow as she said, "Brendan! You startled me."

"As you did me." I sheathed my blade, tasting bile. "I could have knifed you."

"Yes, I . . . I did not think to warn you. I heard you were with the queen and did not want to intrude. It seemed . . . important."

"It was." I tried to keep my anger from my voice as I shut the door. I wanted to berate her for lurking in my lodgings like this, risking a blade in her back before I realized my mistake, and yet simultaneously welcomed the very sight of her. She was here. It must mean she had not intended what she said in the stables, or, if she intended it, she had found cause to regret it, which only told me she had indeed done it solely at Cecil's behest.

Her next words were not about us, however. "She is sending you away, isn't she, to find out what happened to Lady Parry?"

I went still. "How . . . how do you know? Were her ladies eavesdropping?"

She flinched. "Only me. She had me bring Urian from the kennels and wait for her in her chamber. I have served her long enough to know when she is worried about something, and Lady Parry had been absent longer than expected. It did not require much to deduce that something may have happened to her. Then, you returned to court."

"I see." I swallowed, softening my tone. "I cannot tell you anything, Kate. I gave her my word. Besides, I don't know anything yet."

"But you know enough to assume it could be dangerous." She remained rooted to her spot. "And if so, then you mustn't go about it alone."

I said quietly, "I can fend for myself," and she stepped so close that the very scent of her—of clean soap, for Elizabeth deplored cloying perfumes—overwhelmed me. I could not speak, could barely breathe, as she said, "For all your skill, you are still a fool. Like most men, you think when a woman is angry she loses her reason. This isn't about my doubting you. *She* is the one I doubt."

I lifted my gaze. She must have read my intent, for she drew back abruptly, as if in belated cognizance of our proximity, her skirts brushing against my legs, her breath quickening visibly, swelling her breast against her tight-laced bodice.

I said quietly, "You should not say such things about her," and I too stepped away, the erratic beat of my heart loud in my ears. The moment between us was extinguished, like a candle guttering in its own wax.

"I do not ask you to confide in me," she said. "Only, that you confide in someone."

"Such as . . . ?" I already knew what she would reply.

"Cecil. You cannot depart court without advising him. He has placed his entire trust in you. He thinks of you as his own—"

"Slave," I cut in. "He thinks of me as his vassal, beholden to him in all things. Is that why you are here? Did he send you after me to do his bidding, like he sent you yesterday to the stables?"

To her credit, she did not try to deny it. "He did ask me to listen in on your talk with her. I have not told him anything. I came to you first because you are blind where she is concerned, though her business is always more complicated than it seems. She never tells the entire truth if she can avoid it, and what she does not tell often ends up costing someone their life. First it was her brother, Edward; then poor Peregrine—"

"Don't." I thrust up my hand. "Elizabeth . . . she had nothing to do with his death."

"Yes, she did." Kate's voice was unflinching. "She may not have known what would befall him but she never told you or Cecil everything you needed to know about her dealings. He sent you to court to safeguard her, not knowing she was neck-deep in intrigue." She searched my eyes. "How long will you continue to do whatever she asks, without paying the consequences? How long before you give your own life to save hers?"

Her stark honesty took me aback, though it should not have. Kate knew Elizabeth's ways; when we had first met, *she* had been the spy, ferreting out secrets for the embattled princess. She only spoke the truth as she saw it. Elizabeth indeed thrived on evasion, but never without some risk to her own person. And while I would not admit it to Kate, something ominous did hover over Lady Parry's disappearance, though I was confident that no matter what she may have withheld, Elizabeth's distress in this case was genuine.

"I appreciate the concern." I turned deliberately to fling open the lid of the clothes chest. "And if I need Cecil's help, I'll ask for it." I did not look up as I spoke, yanking out my belongings and strewing them on the cot, the knot in my throat threatening to choke me. It seemed impossible we could have reached this impasse: locked in confrontation after all the passionate hopes we had shared. "You must not tell him what you know, either," I added, though it was unjust, insulting, to suggest she might. "You too swore an oath of loyalty to your queen."

"My God. Do you think so little of me?" she said, and I heard her step to the door. "I will tell him nothing. But you are still mistaken to think he is your enemy."

I clenched a fistful of folded hose. "How can you say that to me, after everything he has done?"

"Because no matter what he may have done, he did not do this to us."

I went still. Paralyzing fear swept through me. Did she *know*? I made myself focus on her expression. She had gone imperturbable, as if a stony mask had slipped over her features. I could not tell if she had somehow sensed the betrayal lurking behind our estrangement, though I had not told anyone of the terrible night when, crushed by my grief, I surrendered to Sybilla's seduction. I had buried it under a morass of guilt, distanced myself from it with the adage that it would serve nothing to confess now, that what I had done must go with me to my grave. The pain of it now made me want to roar like a caged beast that Cecil was indeed my enemy. He had put me in the position of having to forfeit any right I had to Kate's heart, to lay claim to her and dream of an ordinary life; and he had profited by it. It suited him to see me unencumbered, to sever any ties I had outside his interests so he could tighten the tether, as he might on a falcon he had trained to kill. I had become another weapon for him to exploit.

"If you believe that," I told her, "it is you who makes the mistake. He has only one goal: to see Elizabeth on her throne, regardless of the cost."

"Then you've more in common with him than you think." She reached for the latch. "I hope you heed my advice, if only for her sake. Yorkshire is still loyal to the old faith; many there are not happy she is queen and will not welcome a man of hers in their midst. You will be far from court and her protection, too far to send warning or request for help. Should something happen to you, who can she trust to send after you, a spy sworn to secrecy, whose mission is known only to her? You will disappear without a trace."

She did not await my response. Opening the door, she departed, her footsteps fading away, leaving me more alone than I had ever felt.

Chapter Nine

After shoving my clothes into my saddlebag and strapping on my sword, I made my way to the stables, where I saddled Cinnabar and paid the groom more than enough to ensure at least his temporary silence. We cantered furiously out of White-hall under a darkening sky.

Flurries of icy sleet stung my face like needles. The weather had turned foul, the morning's clarity subsumed by an incoming storm, and as I rode, I welcomed the chill seeping into my marrow. I did not want to dwell on the implicit accusation in Kate's words, the charge that I had once again chosen to risk my personal safety for Elizabeth.

I hated to admit that to some extent, Kate was right: To venture alone to the north on a secret assignation was reckless. If whoever had taken Lady Parry was the same person who sent the poisoned box, I could not fail in my task, as more than just Lady Parry's safety hung in the balance. Should something befall me, whom could Elizabeth turn to?

Still, I had not fully acknowledged what I was about until I found myself riding down Tower Street to the Griffin, reining outside the door. Tethering Cinnabar to the hitching post, I stalked into the tavern. The clammy smell of spilt ale and dissipated smoke greeted me; in the dismal gloaming of the storm brewing outside, the tavern resembled what it was—a seedy establishment with warped plank flooring, daub walls stained with grease, stools stacked on the scarred tables like pitted mushrooms, as though rats had been gnawing at them with tiny teeth.

I came to a halt. The Griffin might be tawdry, a watering hole for dockhands, whores, and laborers, yet at least here was a place someone called home, while I, with my king's sword and expensive clothes, my royal favor and enviable repute, had nowhere of my own.

Shaking aside my contemptible self-pity, I called out. From behind the hutch, young Tom stumbled into view, his mop of hair askew, grimy hands rubbing at his sleep-swollen eyes. He gasped. "Your . . . your lordship—"

"No lordship today, lad. Just me. Where is your master?"

"Upstairs, still abed." Tom looked anxiously to the door. "Was it unlocked?"

"Well, I am no ghost," I replied dryly, and he let out a moan. "I forgot! Mistress Nan told me last night to bolt it but I forgot. Please, my lord"—he clasped hands before him in supplication—"don't tell her. She'll kick me out and I have nowhere else to go."

His plea cracked the hardening shell inside me. Looking at his thin, disheveled person, oversized breeches hitched about his skinny waist with a bit of twine, revealing dirty ankles above ill-fitting shoes he must have stolen from some corpse, I saw my lost squire again. Peregrine had also been obliged to fend for himself until I hired him, an anonymous piece of gristle for the court to devour. Bowing my head, I said with a catch in my voice,

"Do not worry, boy, I won't tell." I looked toward Shelton's empty chair. "Where's his ugly dog?"

"Crum?" Tom shrugged. "Upstairs, too; he follows the master everywhere."

"So much for guarding the establishment," I muttered. I could not look into his eyes for too long. Memories of Peregrine threatened to engulf me as I rummaged in my purse, tossing out a coin. "See that my horse isn't stolen," I told him.

He eagerly scurried out, heaving the tavern door shut. Its closure echoed in the empty room; as I stood there, uncertain, thinking I had made an error in coming here and should just make for the North Road before the storm struck, I heard the dull thud of footsteps. Moments later, a heavy clamber down the staircase preceded Shelton in a rumpled shirt, his thick, veined legs bare and limping under the hem, one visibly deformed and shorter than the other. He brandished a cudgel as he peered suspiciously at me with his one good eye. At his side, Crum growled, baring discolored stumps of teeth.

I yanked off my cap.

"Lad." Shelton lowered the cudgel. "Rather soon for another visit. Missed us that much, did you?"

Nan sidled around him, clutching a shawl to her throat. Silver-threaded hair escaped her flattened hood. Despite her evident anxiety that an intruder had broken into the tavern, the telltale blush in her cheeks made me grin.

"Do I disturb you?" I said.

"Not at all," she declared, more loudly than required, betraying that I had. "We were just waking. The hour . . . it got away with us." She scowled. "Good thing you returned when you did. That slattern Alice was supposed to be here by now, to scrub the hearths. And where is good-for-nothing Tom? I told him to—"

"I sent him outside to mind my horse. He opened the door for me." I met Shelton's eye as I spoke; his expression shifted, indicating he had read my unvoiced purpose.

"Hungry?" he asked. I nodded, sending Nan straight to the kitchen. Shelton set the cudgel aside. "I'll be a moment. You wait here and break your fast." He trudged back up the stairs, leaving Crum to stare balefully at me. "Don't mind him," Shelton called out. "He won't attack unless I tell him to."

I was hardly reassured. Though the dog's teeth looked fit only for gnawing boiled meat, fending him off would still be an unpleasant experience. Easing a stool down from the nearest table, I sat cautiously. With a snort, Crum lowered himself onto the staircase landing and broke wind.

Nan returned with a tray. She winced. "God save us, he feeds that cur too much." She set the tray before me: a tankard of small-beer, carter's bread, and a bowl of porridge. "I haven't been to the market yet, and they ate us out of everything last night. The winds: No one could do much work on the docks, so every lazybones ended up here. Not that there's much to choose from at the market these days," she added, "what with the whole country in the poorhouse: The harvests have been terrible and we're lucky to find decent turnips, let alone much else. But, I have my sources."

"This is fine, thank you." As I reached for the food, she planted her hands on her hips and glared. "I assume this isn't a friendly waking call? Not that we're not delighted to see you, but you were just here." She paused, waiting. When I did not answer, she harrumphed. "Just as I thought. You've come to drag him off into more mischief."

"Nan, I—"

"No, no." She wagged her finger at me. "It's none of my business, as that old goat upstairs would be quick to remind me. I'm not to say a word." She thrust her chin at me. "Except that I will. I do not like it. I do not like it and I never will. He has had enough of the highborn and their intrigues. Almost killed him the last time, that Wyatt revolt; after it was quelled, we spent weeks keeping our noses down so the authorities would not come knocking on our door to ask if we knew something. Lucky for him, he wasn't seen running around with you, because you'd already gone into hiding and it wasn't as if grand Master Cecil was about to vouchsafe our contribution to helping save the kingdom."

"I know," I said quietly. "He risked his life. I won't ask him, if it will upset you."

"Bit late for that now," she retorted. She went silent again, considering. "I can't say he didn't warn me. When you showed up, he told me he was going to do whatever you asked. He says he owes you, as he was not the man he should have been when you were growing up. But whatever mistakes he's made in the past, he's different now," she said, her voice quavering. "He's a decent soul and God knows there are too few of them these days. Swear to me you will not let anything happen to him. It would be the end of me. I'm not worth a farthing without him."

"I swear it. I will lay down my life for his, if need be."

She hesitated, as if she was going to say more, then she

turned away as Shelton trudged back down the stairs. He wore outdoor garb: a hooded cloak and sword sheathed at his hip, his battered wedge-heeled boots that balanced his stance. Crum sighed in dejection.

"Not done yet?" Shelton eyed the platter before me. "Best hurry and fill your belly, lad. The day's not getting longer, or any warmer, by the looks of it."

Dutifully breaking bread, I averted my eyes as Shelton cradled Nan in his arms and she rested her head on his shoulder.

Chapter Ten

Storm clouds piled in the sky, the sleet and wind tearing through our layers of wool as we made our way through the city to crowded Cheapside, Shelton riding on his large prized destrier, Cerberus, whose very appearance scattered people in our wake. I explained to Shelton the bare facts of my mission, that I was going to investigate a disappearance of one of the queen's women, but refrained from adding that I suspected there might be more at stake, because for the moment it was only my suspicion.

As usual, however, he sensed what I would not say. "York-shire is a long way off, especially this time of year, what with the state of the roads and kingdom at large. Plenty of wolves on the hunt, both of the four- and two-legged kind." He eyed me over the black cloth tied across the lower half of his face to stop the chill, his ruined visage shadowed by his large cap and his empty eye-socket covered by a patch. "Is this lady so important to her?"

"She is; one of her most trusted. Fever beset the household Lady Parry went to visit, too. Nan made me promise to see you safe, so I think you should know, in case—"

"In case of what?" he growled. "By the cross, I'm not a lily-livered youth. At my age, I've had more fevers than most; and worse to boot, as anyone with two eyes can see."

I had to smile. "I'm only doing as I promised. Nan would have my head otherwise."

"Aye, she frets too much. She thinks I can't go to the privy without a hat and scarf."

"She also thinks you feed that dog of yours too much. I must say, I have to agree."

Shelton threw back his head in guttural laughter—"Smelled one of his farts, did you?"—and led us through Bishopsgate onto Ermine Street, the old north road that would eventually bring us to Yorkshire.

I had not seen much of my native land. Though I had once rode as far as Framlingham Castle in Suffolk during the struggle between Northumberland and Mary Tudor, like the majority of my fellow Englishmen great parts of the realm remained a mystery to me, a collection of anonymous names. As we distanced ourselves from the serpentine huddle of the city walls and variegated spill of orchard, pasture, and wealthy manors that had sprung up outside them, expanding London's boundaries, the wind abruptly mellowed, the biting sleet fading into a desultory rain that dampened half-shaped drifts of snow smudging the landscape.

I had already accepted this trip would not be easy. Though the old road had been in existence since Roman times, a carefully patrolled stretch that had conveyed their troops from London to the edge of Hadrian's Wall bordering Scotland, the passing of the years had eroded it, turning a once well-maintained route into an unpredictable patchwork of mud, baked dirt, and occasional cobblestone. Few people traveled it these days, save for enterprising merchants with packhorses drawing their loaded carts and escorts of strongmen hired to keep thieves at bay. Even so, sometimes they too fell victim to the predations that had resulted from King Henry's dissolution, which had evicted thousands of friars, monks, and nuns from their ancestral homes to wander the land, begging or stealing, hunters or hunted in a world turned upside down.

Now, the road stretched before us like a frayed ribbon, dense woodlands clustered right to its edges, so that at times it was as though we traveled under a sunless tunnel of leaf and twined branch, the darkness of thickets enclosing us in a feral embrace.

Shelton had been on the road before, he told me, during his time in his former master Charles of Suffolk's employ. The duke had been an intimate of the king's, a fellow jouster and ribald companion, whom Henry dispatched to put an end to the rebels of the Pilgrimage of Grace, that massacre that had shocked the country into total submission to the king's will.

"You were still a boy, barely four," said Shelton, slouched on his mount's ample back as though he had no worries, though he kept one gloved fist close to his sword. "But that day will go down in infamy, for Henry had given his solemn word he'd treat with the rebels, who wanted only a return of the old ways and an end to Cromwell's rapine. Instead, the king betrayed his promise and had over three hundred souls drawn and quartered as traitors."

He did not betray discernible emotion, as if he recounted something in which he had had no stake, but I glimpsed the edging of his jawline under his scarf and wondered if he had been with Suffolk to witness the executions.

Hours passed without incident. Eventually we outpaced the storm, leaving it to brood behind us in a rumble of angry cloud, but the cold seeped into our bones, icing our feet in our boots and turning our hands numb in our gantlets. We finally stopped at the crossroads of an impoverished hamlet to rest our mounts and sup in a smoke-choked tavern. I had hoped to reach Huntingdon in Cambridgeshire, where the road crossed the Great Ouse, but it was twice the distance most men could ride in a day, Shelton warned. He doubted we could get there before nightfall, not to mention that we would overexert our horses and risk our lives to bands of highwaymen who swarmed the road after dusk.

"It's either that or camp in a field," I said. I made a subtle motion with my chin, directing his gaze across our table to the corner alcove, where three mean-looking men with the shrunken expressions of those who have nothing left to lose eyed us with that peculiar blend of suspicion and interest that isolation inevitably breeds toward strangers. "I'm not about to let those blackguards slit our throats for whatever we have in our purse."

Shelton immediately squared his shoulders and glared, causing the men to shift their gazes away. One of the ruffians, however, looked back at me. He was no seedier than his companions yet he had a certain air about him, his ferret-like features and beady eyes alight with a greed that made my nape prickle. As soon as we finished our repulsive meal of unidentifiable meat pie and rancid beer, Shelton pushed back his stool and rose to full height, towering over all in the low-raftered room. Together, we walked into the yard, blades unsheathed. We mounted quickly and cantered onto the road, looking behind us the entire time. I did not settle down until forested countryside wreathed in mist surrounded us.

Shelton turned to me. "Have you truly told me everything I should know?"

I winced, hoping I sounded more nonchalant than I felt. "Why do you ask?"

"Because I think you think those men were expecting us."

"That's impossible," I said at once, even as a shudder went through me. "No one knows where I am." Except Kate, I thought, and perhaps Cecil by now, given his penchant for uncovering secrets. Much as I hated even to consider it, Kate might have told him anyway.

"You are certain?" Shelton eyed me. "Because if this affair turns dangerous, I'd rather not be caught with my breeches about my ankles."

I had no choice. "No, I have not told you everything. But I have not only because I don't know anything else yet."

"I see. But whatever it is you don't know anything about yet, I wager it has to do with more than some favored lady's disappearance."

"I think it might, yes." While I disliked going back on my vow to Elizabeth, he did not deserve to be blindsided should our situation take an ugly turn. "I swore not to tell anyone," I added. "So, no one knows you are with me except Nan."

He chuckled. "Then I'll be invisible. Would not be the first time, eh? Scarcliff is not someone most people care to remember."

I nodded uneasily. People might not want to remember him, but in my experience, he was not someone you could easily forget. It struck me in that instant that I had been more than reckless. I had not thought any of this through. Goaded by Kate and the hurt I felt, I'd tossed caution aside and put Shelton in jeopardy. I did suspect hirelings of Cecil's had just spotted us. I could not think he would have left my departure unexplored, no matter what Elizabeth told him, and though we had made excellent progress, I had tarried long enough at the Griffin for his informants to gain a head start. For all I knew, he had outliers at every crossroads between here and York by now, primed to report on me—or to do more than report. That, too, was not something I could ignore. If Cecil had decided to interpret my absence as a threat, he would have no compunction in acting upon it.

My life was secondary to his ambition. It always had been.

"Is there another way to Yorkshire?" I asked abruptly.

Shelton's brow furrowed. "I'm sure there is, through the fens, but it's not wise. It'll take us off the main road and those wolves I mentioned earlier—the forests seethe with them."

I withdrew my dagger, palming it. "Better wolves than Cecil. I think those men in the tavern will come after us. They are waiting until we get far enough from the hamlet that we cannot turn back. Come." I kicked Cinnabar off the road into the woodland, Shelton riding behind me, grumbling he would have done better to stay in London with his feet propped before the hearth rather than be murdered in some godforsaken field in the middle of nowhere.

I had to agree.

Dusk fell swiftly, dragging a black hem across the horizon and snuffing out the light. We stopped to let the horses graze, while we chomped on dried venison, cheese, and bread Nan had packed for us in Shelton's saddlebag. After watering the horses in a brook, we located a meadow nestled among a copse of trees, sheltered from the elements, though still icy as a witch's cunny, Shelton remarked, hauling his saddle blanket to his chin as he bedded on the ground, using his bag for a pillow.

We did not make a fire, in case it betrayed our location. I assumed first watch; within seconds, Shelton was snoring loud enough to make me think we hardly needed anything else to alert our would-be trackers. I had to smile as I remembered the time he had first brought me to London and I dozed off on my horse, losing my cap. Apparently, I was not the only one who could sleep anywhere.

Not tonight. Crouched under a large oak with my sword unsheathed at my side and dagger in hand, the horses tethered nearby in the shadows, I was alert to every sound. In the brush, unseen animals rustled and branches snapped; the eerie ululation of a fox echoed, and the rising wind flushed the sky clear, revealing a black firmament strewn with a thousand stars and a sullen sliver of moon. I might have admired this display of grandeur, which I had not seen in years, living as I had been in crowded cities where thickets of eaves and spires blotted out the sight. Instead, I cursed the way the wind agitated the air and swirled among the trees, scattering leaves and making boughs creak. I could not tell if the sounds I heard signaled a stealthy approach.

Then I did hear it: the unmistakable pad of footsteps. Ducking farther into the shadow cast by the oak, I edged around its wide trunk to see three figures in cloaks creeping toward us, glinting steel in their hands.

In the distance behind them, seated immobile on a horse, was another cloaked figure.

My pulse quickened. I had thought Cecil would have me

watched, but now it did not appear quite so simple. Perhaps he had ordered me captured and brought back to court, or perhaps my suspicion that I had outlived my usefulness was on the mark. Whichever the case, I had to assume that mounted figure was not here to ensure my health, and I took up the handful of pebbles I had collected by my sword and tossed them at Shelton, aiming above his head. The rattle as they struck the earth woke him instantly; like the former soldier he was, he did not cry out but was on his haunches within seconds, sword out and ready as he crawled away to hide.

If these fools thought to catch us unawares, they were in for a surprise.

I discerned urgent whispering among them as they neared; some type of argument. They were making more noise than professionals would, I realized in relief; they must be the locals they seemed to be, hired on the spot. As I braced for their arrival, I took another glance at the mounted figure silhouetted against the night sky. He had not moved. He seemed to be studying the impending situation with detachment, restraining his horse with an expert hand.

I could only hope he did not have a crossbow or firearm aimed at us.

The approaching men's voices became clear: "He says not to harm the younger one. The older one we can rob and kill."

"Good," replied another with glee. "I didn't like the look of that old bastard."

They were so close I could have reached out and grabbed one of them by his knotted rat's nest, slicing my dagger across his throat. I made myself stay still until they slipped past me to enter the clearing, making for the crumpled blanket and saddle-bag. In the dim moonlight, it appeared as if someone was still asleep there, and on reaching them, they came to a halt.

Shelton exploded from his hiding place in the woods, his sword raised, roaring like a dragon. In his other hand, he brandished a broken branch, thick as an arm, which he swiped at the group, causing them to leap back and stagger into each other. Blades razed the air; they were so intent on evading him they did not think to look behind them until one turned about and impaled himself on my sword.

Blood spewed from his mouth. He crumpled and fell to the ground. The stench of his loosening bowels clogged my nostrils as I ripped my blade out and whirled on the second one, slashing down to block the thrust of his dagger, my sword's edge biting hard into his wrist. He yelped, dropping his weapon. As he spun about to grapple for it, the third one rushed toward me, knifing his wounded companion and pushing him aside to thrust his dagger at me. With a heave of the branch he carried, Shelton delivered a solid blow to the back of my attacker's head that sent him sprawling. The wounded one, I realized, was the ferrety man I had seen staring at me in the tavern; he clutched at his wrist, gazing open-mouthed at his friend who had turned on him. Then he lifted his gaze to me. As panic flared in his eyes, I warned, "Do not move. Do not shout. If you so much as breathe, I will kill you." I looked at Shelton, who stood over the one he had clubbed. "Watch them," I said, and I dashed back to the oak tree, prepared to find that mysterious mounted figure galloping upon us. Our own horses were tethered close by, their hooves and bridles muffled with cloth, but we had only seconds to get to them and mount before whoever the leader was came galloping into the clearing to finish what his parcel of knaves had bungled.

When I looked, the horizon was empty. The figure had vanished.

I heard my own panting in my ears as I waited, thinking he must have gone around, using the trees as cover. After minutes passed and no one appeared, I turned back to find Shelton hauling the wounded one by the scruff of his jerkin. He threw him at my feet, eliciting a howl of pain.

"Who hired you?" I asked.

Shelton snorted. "The town idiot, apparently, seeing as none of this motley lot could hunt down a rooster, much less a man. I hope whoever he was didn't pay you by the head, fool."

The same thought had occurred to me. No one of experience would ever hire men like these. To inform from a distance, perhaps, if they could stay out of the tavern long enough, which, judging by the reek of ale wafting off the one at my feet, had not been the case. Cecil would not have given them a second look, not for something as important as apprehending his own intelligencer.

"Is that other one . . . ?" I said. Shelton shook his head. "I must have hit him too hard."

The man at my feet gave a plaintive moan. I returned my regard to him. He was a pathetic sight, soaked in his own blood, the bone of his wrist gleaming within the deep gash where my well-honed blade had cut through his flesh, severing tendons and arteries, no doubt. His side, too, was bleeding profusely from the dagger stuck in it.

"You are going to die," I said, "lest we tend to you. Which we will—if you talk."

"Please don't let me die," he whispered. "I'll . . . I'll do anything."

I leaned to him. "I'll ask you one last time: *Who* hired you?"

His choked reply iced my veins: "I don't know who he was. But he said you are a spy for the new queen."

Chapter Eleven

We bound the man's wrist with a strip of cloth ripped from the hem of my shirt and used the saddle blanket to staunch the wound in his side, but both articles soon turned sopping red, and within a few hours fever arose and glazed his eyes.

Shelton wanted us to leave him and give chase to the leader. But I knew he was long gone and refused to abandon this man who'd been injured by my hand. Propping him against the oak, I sat beside him and plied him with questions.

What I managed to glean only increased my apprehension. A stranger in a hooded cloak had approached him and his companions hours before our arrival, instructing them to watch for two men who would pass by and detailing our descriptions.

"He said you would fight," he told me, between gasps of pain. "But he wanted you alive. The other one . . . he said we could kill him."

"Did he say why he wanted me?" I said, deeply alarmed that this stranger not only knew that I served Elizabeth but had ordered my capture. Could it have been Cecil's work, after all?

No one else but him would have done this; it had to be, and yet every instinct in me rebelled against the idea. Cecil was capable of many things, and was ruthless when it came to protecting his interests, but he detested clumsiness. If this was indeed his doing, then he had to be desperate.

"Coldhearted villain," growled Shelton from where he bent over the dead man, rummaging in his jerkin. "I ought to crush your skull in like I did your friend here." Extracting a purse of coin, he let a low whistle. "This is quite a sum. Whoever hired them had means."

"What happened then?" I asked the dying man.

"He gave us that money and left. He said there would be more if we caught you alive. So, we sat in the tavern to wait." He coughed bloodied foam. He did not have much time left. "After we spotted you and followed, he appeared on the road. He . . . he must have been watching us, to see if we would do as he bid. He showed us the spot where you turned into the woods."

"Bastard." Shelton loomed over him, his fists clenched.

"Go," I said. "See to the horses." With a begrudging grunt, Shelton went to Cinnabar and Cerberus, who were neighing, yanking at their tethers, distressed by the smell of blood, while I remained intent on discovering everything I could before the man lapsed into delirium.

His fever crested. He began to babble, of a sister who would starve without him and he never meant harm, but his parents had died of flux and left him nothing, so what could he do, when his sister wasted away with only him to depend on?

Then he shifted suddenly lucid eyes to me, his fever ebbing for a moment. He whispered, "That man . . . he said something else. About you. He said . . . you must pay for a sin."

I swallowed, watching him until his chin drooped against his chest, his mouth parting to release a final seepage of breath. Blood pooled about him.

By the time Shelton returned, he was dead.

And I knew that the shadow of my past had found me.

We left the man under the tree; we had no means with which to bury him, and as we took to the road once more in the opalescent light of dawn, leaving his corpse and those of his two companions behind for the forest beasts, I did not speak.

Shelton allowed me my silence until we were well into our travel, before he said, "You're white as a ghost. What did that coxcomb tell you?"

I did not look at him. "He and the other two were pawns. This stranger who hired them, he wanted them to die. He knew from the start they would be no match for us. He did it to scare us, to prove he has the upper hand. He must be the same man who seized Lady Parry."

"But how did he know you'd even be here?" said Shelton in disbelief. "I thought only you and the queen were aware of the situation surrounding Lady Parry."

"Somehow, he knew. He planned it." I gripped my reins. "You were right: We should have gone after him. He is taunting us. God, he must have reveled in it, watching those fools sacrifice themselves for his sake—and all so he could deliver his message."

"Oh? What message would that be?"

"That I must pay for a sin." I turned to him. "Those are the same words that were written on a note found on Blanche Parry's saddle after she went missing. Elizabeth showed me the note. Whoever he is, this stranger has a purpose."

Shelton regarded me for a long moment. He did not press me for more, though I sensed he wanted to. "What now?"

"We proceed as planned. He did not come after us, so I assume he accomplished what he intended with those men. He must have gone back into hiding but when the time is right, he will find me. I only pray it isn't too late for us to find Lady Parry."

We reached Kingston-upon-Hull three days later, exhausted, saddle-sore, and so soiled from the mud and sleet of the road, not to mention the blood crusted like rust on our clothes, it was a marvel the sentries granted us entry through the gates. The city, situated on the northern bank of the Humber estuary, was prosperous, unlike much of the rest of the realm. As we rode through the streets, we noticed evidence of this wealth in the many shops and the open marketplace displaying a variety of goods, in baskets of wool carded by women and children on house stoops, and from the clatter of looms that produced the coveted wool stockings exported to London.

Locating a well-appointed bathhouse, we stabled our horses and I divested myself of my filth-stiffened garb to soak in a hot tub for an hour. Changing into a fresh shirt, jerkin, and hose, having done my best to brush the clotted soil from my cloak, I felt almost normal again.

I was also ravenous.

Shelton awaited me outside. He brought me to a tavern near the bathhouse, where we ordered food and ale. He, too, was much improved, having bathed, changed his shirt, and buffed his boots, though nothing could be done about his face, which prompted the servers to eye him as if he were about to upend the table like a disfigured giant and initiate a rampage.

I devoured fried haddock in beer sauce. It was not court fare, by any means; it was better. Still hot from the kitchens and devoid of the heavy creams and spices that court cooks used to disguise the food's lack of freshness, I finished every bite, down to the flaky bits on the bones.

"I see you haven't lost your appetite," remarked Shelton.

With my mouth full, I muttered, "A man has to keep his strength up."

"Aye, he does." Shelton drained his tankard, lifting his hand to signal for another round. As the server warily set a pitcher before us, the bells of a nearby minster tolled the hour.

"We'll have to hurry if we want to reach Withernsea by nightfall," I said.

Shelton grunted. "We'll make it. I think I have earned the right to your trust, don't you?"

I nodded.

"Good. Because fond of you as I am, I do not like secrets when my neck is on the block. I know you believe this stranger has a purpose. What I want to know is what you think his purpose is."

I reached for the pitcher and filled my tankard. "I told you already. He knew the queen would send someone to find Lady Parry. He left me a message that—"

Shelton made an impatient gesture. "Forget all that. Do you think he has something to do with that woman Sybilla?" He set his big hands on the table. "I'm no dimwit, lad. You came to me only four days past convinced she was still alive, and you barely said three words until we were well on our way here. So, do you think this man who has taken Lady Parry could be an accomplice of hers, that you're being stalked to avenge her death?"

I did not answer at once. Around us, customers and servers harangued. Shouts from the hutch and raucous laughter collided in the dense atmosphere. Outside on the busy streets, the people went about their business, tending to shops or errands, dragging children by the hand and stopping to exchange news with friends and neighbors—all the ordinary activities of those who live without the double-dealing and soul-crushing deceptions of serving a queen.

I heard Elizabeth in my head: *I have never run . . . In the end, they always find you. It's not a matter of when but rather how, and who shall disarm whom first.*

"Yes," I said. "I do not know how or why, but I think this man knows about her and has set in motion a dangerous gambit. He set his trap by abducting Lady Parry, leaving a note on her saddle with the same words as the message he gave those men. And he must have sent the box to the queen, for it was tainted with the same type of poison that killed Peregrine. I also found a note hidden in the lid, composed in cipher. We have yet to decipher it, but would you not say that is too many coincidences?"

"Aye, but not proof that he holds you responsible for Sybilla's death," said Shelton. "I thought you agreed to not let the past cloud your reason. This would be the time, lad. Whatever gambit this stranger plays—and I have no doubt, gambit it is—if you are wrong about his motive, it could be your undoing. *Our* undoing."

"Perhaps. But I must trust my instincts, until I find evidence to the contrary."

"Just as long as you accept it if you do not," Shelton replied. He said nothing more as we paid our bill and went to fetch our horses.

Icy wind flecked with snow gusted as we left Kingston-upon-Hull. Several hours later, we reached the sullen hamlet of Withernsea and asked directions from a peasant on an emaciated mule weighted down with kindling, a black dog skulking at his heels. He pointed us to a narrow road alongside a chalk-gnawed ridge overlooking the North Sea.

I had never seen a body of water like this, roiling onto a beach scattered with jagged spines of rocks, its shallow color burnished by the white light, like a tarnished mirror.

"There's a roke coming." Shelton shielded his brow to the blackened horizon.

"Roke?" I frowned.

"A fog local to these parts: fast-moving and treacherous. Within the hour, we will not be able to see our hands in front of our faces and risk our horses losing their footing. Where is that blasted manor?" He grimaced, tugging his scarf up over his nose. "Must be quite a house for them to live all the way out here—and well defended, too. Not a hundred years past, this whole shire was prey to Scots who came over the Marches to steal cattle and pillage."

Reaching into my doublet, I pulled out the leather tube containing the map Elizabeth had given me and tried to establish our bearings within the scoured landscape around us. I too was prepared for an impressive estate like those I'd known in Hert-fordshire; instead, we came upon it quite suddenly—a stark sentinel rearing from a bluff facing the sea, enclosed by a half circle of walls, seeming about to tumble into the crashing waters below, not at all the elaborate edifice I had been expecting.

"This . . . cannot be it," I said, as the wind tore at our cloaks and flung salt spray, to the horses' snorting discontent. But the map confirmed it could be no other.

We had reached Vaughan Hall.

Chapter Twelve

We struggled up a road no wider than a goat path, hugging the precipice and buffeted by the wind as the roke rolled in and blanketed us in a shroud. It was unnerving, how swift the fog's transformative power was. Within minutes the daylight disappeared, the rumble of waves shattering against the rocks the sole distorted sound in a world gone blank as canvas.

A lichen-stained turreted gatehouse, adorned with heraldic beasts worn smooth by the elements, materialized before us, the only entrance through walls that were higher than they had seemed from the distance. I reined in Cinnabar. Square iron gates served as a portcullis, barring our passage. The manor loomed behind it, fronted by bedraggled hedgerows around an outer courtyard, a cluster of smaller, timber-framed outbuildings huddled at the house's edge.

"A welcoming sight," said Shelton wryly. He caressed Cerberus's muscular neck, easing the destrier's labored breathing. We had ridden our horses past endurance. Welcoming or not, we had to rest here for the night. We could not risk them going lame.

I dismounted, barely reaching the ground before I espied a figure running toward us from one of the outbuildings. At first, I thought it was a short man, but then he reached the gates, and as he peered at us through the bars, I saw he was in fact a youth, fumbling for a key tangled on a chain about his throat.

From the tube containing the map, I removed the queen's letter. I did not have time to show it before Shelton barked: "Open those gates, lad. We are here by royal command!"

I scowled. So much for being invisible. Shelton shrugged in response, his shout having startled the gatekeeper, who promptly bent over and jammed his key into the gate's lock, without removing it from the chain about his neck.

The gates creaked open. The boy stood staring, his mouth ajar.

"I come by order of Her Majesty Queen Elizabeth—" I started to declare, until Shelton muttered, "It's no use. Look at him: The lad's boil-brained."

The youth cocked his head as if he understood Shelton's disparagement. He had wide-set small hazel eyes, an upturned nose, and small mouth. Lank ginger-hued hair was plastered to his brow from the damp and his jerkin and breeches were rumpled, with bits of straw clinging to his hose as if we had woken him from an illicit nap. He was very thin, but not ill formed; I thought he must be eleven or twelve years old.

"Are you here to pay your respects?" he said, shifting his regard to Cerberus as he spoke, his eyes growing wider as he took in the impressive size of Shelton's steed.

"No, we . . ." I faltered. "Respects? Who has died?" As I spoke, my stomach sank to my feet. God save us, we had come too late. Lady Parry was dead.

"The little master," said the youth sadly. "He took the fever. My lady said, why poor Master Henry? Why is that stupid Raff alive when Master Henry is dead? My lady hates me because I never get ill."

Shelton muttered, "Boil-brained, just as I said."

I ignored him, taking a cautious step toward the youth—only I still held Cinnabar's reins and as my horse also clopped forward, shaking his mane, the boy edged backward, his gaze riveted to Cerberus as if he feared the destrier might tramp forth next, right over him.

"Are you Raff?" I asked, and he said, "Yes. That is my name."

Shelton snorted.

"Can you show us to the stables, Raff?" I said.

His brow creased for a moment before he exclaimed, "Your horses must be hungry. I feed the horses, too!" as though it were a revelation that he might be of use.

Shelton rolled his eyes when I looked at him. "I know. I'm to go with him so he doesn't overfeed the horses and give them bloat."

"He won't," I said quietly. I returned my gaze to Raff. "This is my manservant, Scarcliff. He will help you with our horses."

Raff wagged his head. "No, no. No one can help me in my work. My lady says I must work on my own. You take your manservant with you."

I leaned to him. "It will be our secret, eh? No one should help Master Scarcliff, either. He is supposed to be invisible. Do you know what that means?"

Raff paused, jutting out his lower lip, making me think perhaps Shelton was right, and the boy was a little slow. "It means he's not supposed to be seen," I said. "If he goes to help you in the stables, it can be our secret, too. Would you like that? Can you keep a secret?"

His eyes gleamed. "Yes, I know secrets. I know how to keep—"

"Good, very good," cut in Shelton, his exhaustion rousing a bout of ill humor. "Raff knows how to keep a secret. Bully for him." He jumped off his horse, taking the reins. "Lay on, then. Show me the way."

Raff whirled around. "Come with me!"

Shelton shot me a scathing look. "Isn't this grand? I'm to bed in the hay with an idiot when I could be up against my Nan's warm backside right now, a meat pie in my belly."

"Remember, you are my servant now," I said. Unhooking my saddlebag, I handed him Cinnabar's reins and watched him trudge after Raff, disappearing into the fog.

Shouldering my bag, I walked alone to the manor.

Up close, Vaughan Hall displayed the relentless assault by wind and sea, its solid sandstone façade mottled with discoloration, creeping ivy-like tendrils of vine clinging to the mortar like collapsed veins, winding about oblong windows inset with panes of discolored horn. Devoid of ornamentation, the entire structure appeared impermeable, thick enough to deflect the extremity of the weather, if not the pervasive damp. A square watchtower squatted on the west end; gazing up, I noted the tips of chimneys poking through the fog like incongruous fingers.

Passing under a vaulted stone porch, I came before a stout oak door braced with enough ironwork to impede a battering ram. A sprig of rosemary tied with a white ribbon was affixed to the postern, signaling a child's death. I was reaching up to seize the brass handle when it abruptly swung open to reveal a thin, sallow man dressed in black frieze.

In a supercilious tone, he said, "Yes? What is your purpose here?"

"My name is Master Brendan Prescott and I come by command of Her Majesty Queen Elizabeth to inquire into the disappearance of Lady Blanche Parry. If you would be so kind, I wish to speak with the master or mistress of the house." As I spoke, I handed him the letter of introduction, which he peered at with feigned indifference even though he must have espied Elizabeth's elaborate signature at the bottom, the paper imprinted with her royal signet. She had not been queen long enough to have a privy seal crafted for her.

The man's face twitched. It was nearly imperceptible, the slight stiffening of his expression, but sufficient to convey that despite my credentials, he did not view me as anyone of significant rank. Given his attitude, I guessed he must be the household head steward. Only stewards behaved as though they owned the place.

"*Lady* Vaughan is abed, resting," he said, placing marked emphasis on her title. Suddenly, I realized how little I knew about the people I had come here to question; what their backgrounds were, if they were gentry or noble, impoverished or wealthy. My instinct told me the former in both regards. The house itself might be imposing, but its location, so far from London and the court, indicated that high noble blood did not run in their veins; or that if it did, they had fallen on hard times. Likewise, the dual duties Raff performed as gatekeeper and stable groom betrayed a scarcity of coin. Nevertheless, this man's manner indicated how my arrival might be perceived, and I inclined my head in an appropriate gesture of deference.

"I beg your forgiveness. I have only just learned the family has suffered a recent loss."

The man sniffed, opening the door wider. "I am Master Gomfrey and I manage the household. You will address your concerns to me in all matters pertaining to your stay." He paused. "Your boots are soiled," he remarked. As I surreptitiously wiped each of my boots in turn on the back of my hose, he added, "Have you no servants?"

"Yes, one: my manservant, Scarcliff. I sent him to assist with our horses. He is a rough sort, ill accustomed to fine accommodations. I thought it best if he bed with your groom. I trust that is amenable?"

Master Gomfrey sniffed again. "It is. Pray, come inside."

The manor's interior was stark as its exterior. The steward led me into a large hall with a high timber-framed ceiling and narrow arched windows whose dirty panes barely permitted any light, let alone a view of the surrounding area. The furnishings were sparse—a long central table arranged before a smoke-blackened hearth, with upholstered chairs of a purely functional nature. A wrought-iron chandelier hung from the ceiling, affixed by a rope to a pulley for lifting and lowering, its iron circle festooned with gutted wax stubs, as was the one standing candelabrum. The plank floors were clean but lacked carpets or the usual herb-strewn rushes; I detected a draft coming from somewhere, billowing spider-webs clinging to the eaves and the lengths of white mourning cloth pinned to the walls.

The damp, I suspected, must be a constant presence. A few

months here and even the hardiest man would begin to complain of ague in his bones.

"My lord attends the gravesite at present," Gomfrey told me in an emotionless tone. "Master Henry's funeral took place only this morning and the family is naturally quite bereft. If you care to wait here, I shall have our maidservant stoke the fire." He paused, as if to measure the echo of his explanation and decide if he had relayed it as well as he should. "Are you intending on bedding here in the hall or would a private chamber be required?"

"A chamber, if it does not inconvenience," I replied, thinking that surely Gomfrey could not expect the queen's appointed representative to sleep on a pallet in the hall.

"I will inform our housekeeper, Mistress Harper." Stiffly, the steward turned heel.

"Master Gomfrey."

He stopped, not moving for a moment before he turned back to me. "Yes?"

"The gravesite: Is it nearby? Could I go there to pay my respects?"

He regarded me in silence. Then he pointed past the hall. "Through that archway, to your left, past the private chapel. The cemetery is situated outside behind the house, near the bluff."

"Thank you." I made my way past the hall and an empty watching chamber into a passageway narrow as a tunnel. Here, I felt the damp keenly, making me pull my cloak closer about my shoulders. As I neared a set of tarnished filigree gates, I smelled the unmistakable must of incense. Beyond the gates lay a chapel carved of stone, upheld by pilasters that showed prior evidence of gilded paint. The altar was nearly lost in shadow, its frayed cloth adorned with a dull-stoned crucifix set in its center. In a niche to my right stood a chipped wooden statue of the Virgin, a peeling oversized Christ child in her arms. At her feet rested a bouquet of dusty silk lilies.

It took me a moment to understand what I was seeing. When I did, I stepped back quickly. I heard Kate in my head: *Yorkshire is still loyal to the old faith; many there are not happy she is queen and will not welcome a man of hers in their midst.*

The household was Catholic. This would explain my sensation of feeling unwelcome. I'd come at the behest of the new queen; while Elizabeth had yet to declare her stance on religion, it was no secret she'd been reared in the Reformed faith like her late brother, Edward. Such were the vagaries of faith since King Henry's death that in less than twelve years, we had gone from stringent Protestantism under his son to vicious Catholic reprisal upon Mary's accession, and now, back once more, to an unknown future embodied by an untried queen.

Turning about, I made my way back down the passage to a narrow door, pulling it open to reveal a mist-shrouded garden—or what I assumed had once been a garden. Now, it was more of a haphazard collection of ragged herb beds and overgrown paths, lichen-stained birdbaths and lumpen statuary giving it an air of forlorn neglect.

The wind had ceased, and the roke blanketed everything as far as I could see. With tentative steps, I moved toward where I could glean a huddled pile of gravestones, several of which were blackened, inscriptions erased by time, teetering against each other like decayed teeth. The soil here must be chalky, brittle to excavate; I wondered how many of the dead had actually ended up seeping out of their graves to dissipate, ash-like, into the air.

I did not see anyone until abruptly, near a copse of wind-twisted pine, where the crash of the sea below thundered, I saw a small mausoleum guarded by forlorn stone angels. Above its closed gates was chiseled the name of Vaughan.

Two figures stood before it, clasping hands—one tall but stooped, with a cloak hanging limply from its shoulders, the other diminutive, in a short cape and gown.

I cleared my throat, not wanting to startle them. Without warning, I heard a low menacing growl and turned to see a large black mastiff stalking up to me, a studded leather collar about its bullish neck.

I went still, aware that any sudden move or sign of panic would indicate I was prey. The little figure turned to look over her shoulder, her pinched wan face overpowered by aqua-blue eyes, a cascade of fair ringlets escaping her askew hood—a girl no older than six, clinging to the veined hand of a man whom I assumed must be her father, Lord Thomas Vaughan.

She whispered to him. The man turned to me, without surprise. He had a long, furrowed face, with jowls sagging against his high collar, as if he had recently shed a great deal of weight. His thick beard could not conceal the stricken expression on his features, his hollowed eyes deep in their sockets, his downturned mouth bracketed by etched lines.

He whistled sharply, bringing the mastiff to a halt. "Bardolf, hold!"

The enormous dog immediately dropped to its haunches.

"Do not fear him," the man said, beckoning me forth. "He only attacks at my command. Otherwise, he is gentle as a lamb."

I doubted it, but guilt overcame me as I sidestepped the watchful dog and took a wary step forward. Vaughan had the mien of a man lost to grief and here I was, a stranger, from court no less, about to make his time of mourning even more difficult.

I bowed. "Forgive my intrusion, my lord, but my name is Prescott and I am here by Her Majesty Queen Elizabeth's command."

Lord Vaughan's expression remained blank, as if he was having trouble deciphering my words. It was the little girl instead who piped, "Elizabeth? She is not our queen. Queen Mary is."

"Hush, Abigail." Lord Vaughan tightened his hand about hers. In a low voice I scarcely heard above the din of the sea, he said, "Yes, Master Prescott, we have been expecting you."

I must have looked taken aback, as I had encountered nothing thus far to indicate it. He let out a weary sigh. "We assumed Her Majesty would send someone to investigate. I am glad to see you, though I regret it comes under such circumstances."

"Indeed," I murmured. "Please accept my condolences on the loss of your son, my lord. Had I been apprised, I would have—"

"Henry isn't lost," Abigail interrupted. "Isn't that right, Papa? My brother has gone to heaven with the angels and the saints because he was shriven in the one true faith." She spoke with the earnestness of an innocent seeking reassurance and I saw Master Vaughan's mouth quiver, though I could not tell if he reacted to her guileless reminder of his son's death or the fact that his daughter had just confirmed that the household was indeed Catholic.

Then he said, "Yes, my child. Henry is with the angels." His tender attempt to muster a smile brought a knot to my chest. I had never known such tenderness in my childhood from anyone save the humble woman who raised me, my beloved Mistress Alice. Such care for innocence, particularly among the privileged, was a rarity.

Lord Vaughan said to me, "We cannot conduct our business here before the tomb. We only saw my son into the vault yesterday."

"No, naturally we cannot," I said, aware I had broken into a private moment. "I only wished to tell you I was here and pay my respects. Master Gomfrey is seeing to my accommodation."

I was about to return to the manor, bypassing the dog by a wide margin, when Lord Vaughan said, "We shall speak later. I will have supper served in the hall, as you must be hungry after such a long journey. You must ask Mistress Harper or Master Gomfrey to provide you with anything you may require, such as hot water for a bath or extra comforters for your bed. I assume a chamber has been prepared for you? It has?" he said, as I nodded. "Good."

He was doing his utmost to convey the solicitous attitude of a nobleman for his guest, even as I sensed his composure fraying. "We have always been loyal subjects to our sovereign, so rest assured we welcome any inquiry you care to present and will do our utmost to assist you in your investigation. Lady Parry is my aunt; I wish to find her whereabouts as much as you do."

"Thank you, my lord." Bowing again, I paused to smile at Abigail. Giving Bardolf wide berth, I walked back into the swirling mist.

As Lord Vaughan returned to his vigil with his daughter, I pondered how, in all this, his wife was nowhere to be seen.

* * *

Cutting across the garden around the side of the house, I passed the cluster of outbuildings—a henhouse and live-stock enclosure devoid of anything save for a thin lowing cow and a few ducks—and moved to the larger structure that must be the stable block. As soon as I entered the building, with its smell of hay and musk of horses, hearing stamping in the stalls, the burden of my task lifted from me. I allowed myself a moment of reflection on the fact that while I had long since escaped my days of toil and fear as a Dudley minion, all it took was return-ing to a simple place where beasts dwelled for me to feel safe.

Dudley had been right: I was indeed more cur than hound.

"Getting settled in silk and feathers?" Shelton's greeting pulled me from my reverie. He stood by one of the stalls, sleeves rolled to his elbows, a long-handled brush in his hand.

"Hardly. Where is Raff?"

"Who knows?" Shelton grimaced. He had removed his eye patch. "That lad may be daft as a hare, but he gets about quick as one, too. He had the horses unsaddled and in their stalls faster than any ostler I've seen, then went out for water from the trough, brought in feed, and dashed out once more." He glanced up to the hayloft. "Could be up there for all I know. He's clearly lived here all his life; he knows the place like a man knows his prick."

I smiled, approaching the stall where Shelton had been brushing down Cerberus. Next to him in the adjacent stall was Cinnabar, who whinnied at me.

"How's the manor?" Shelton lowered his voice as if Raff might indeed be perched on one of the rafters above us like a hidden owl.

"Strange." I went into Cinnabar's stall to give him some

attention. He had been brushed down, his russet-colored coat gleaming as he munched on oats. I told Shelton what had happened, and that Lady Vaughan had yet to make an appearance.

"Well, she's lost her son," he said. "She must be distraught. The steward told you she was abed. It is what women do when they grieve. I see no reason for suspicion."

"No," I agreed, "neither do I. But I still have this feeling something is not right." I crouched down to inspect Cinnabar's hooves, even as Shelton said, "No need for that. Raff already checked and removed two pebbles lodged in the back shoe. I tell you, that dimwit's got a knack for horses I haven't seen since you were a boy." He paused, grimacing again as I turned to him. "Sorry. I know I need to be more circumspect."

"You do. We both do. It's imperative we appear to be only master and servant."

"How Fortune likes a joke, eh?" He guffawed. "Once you quaked at the sight of me and now look at us: I am answering to you." He paused in his steady stroking of his brush over Cerberus. "You were saying you had a feeling something isn't right?"

"Yes, but I can't explain it." I rose to my feet, caressing my horse. "Though Lord Vaughan went to pains to explain he will be as cooperative as I can expect, I feel as though more than a child's death and Lady Parry's disappearance affect this house." I went quiet, trying to unravel the vague unease I harbored. "I found a chapel," I added. "They revere the old faith."

Shelton grunted. "Perhaps that can explain your unease. They must be worried. No papist will be sleeping well, now that Anne Boleyn's daughter is on the throne."

"Yes, perhaps that's it." Now that we had broached the subject, I wondered how he stood on this perilous matter. "Are you still . . . ?"

He resumed his brushing of his horse. "Venerating saints and creeping to the cross? Nay, I was never one for priests either way. Nan would have my hide to hear me say it, but to me one religion is much like the other. Take away the gewgaws and Bibles, and both preach the same dire end to anyone who does not live by their rules."

My surprise must have shown, for he went on. "Don't go thinking I am a heretic. I believe in Christ. I just don't have use for those who tell me how I should go about it."

"I think that makes you a Protestant," I said.

He grinned. "Well, if it does, you must keep it between us. Nan is still papist to her marrow, no matter that she abides by whatever order happens to be the rule of the day." He went quiet for a moment before he said, "And you? I know Alice raised you in the old ways. She hid it well enough from the rest of us, but I know she kept a rosary in her box of herbs. It is nothing to be ashamed of; we were all papist once. Even old Henry, for all his bellyaching that no pope should tell him how to conduct his affairs, kept to the old ways to his end, despite making himself Head of the Church and making us the foe of every Catholic in Europe."

"Honestly?" I said. "I cannot say. Alice did raise me in the old way, but she also made sure I learned the reformed one, as well. There was a time after Peregrine . . . I attended a requiem mass in his honor. I remember thinking how beautiful it was, how worthy of grief. But Protestants also hold services for the dead."

"Aye. Death is death, while the living are left behind. Still, you'll want to reassure them you're not here to inform against their faith," he suggested.

I nodded. "I will, if need be. They are not trying to hide it, at least not in their chapel. And if they intended to, their daughter Abigail disproved it in front of me." I turned back to Cinnabar, busying myself with running my hands over his legs, dispelling the awkwardness that had fallen in the wake of our conversation.

At length, I said, "You might ask Raff if he can tell you anything."

"Such as what? No, he never gets sick? No, no one can help him with his chores? No friends for Raff now that poor Masters Henry and Hugh are gone? The lad is mad as a hare. He's no use to anyone save to open and close those gates and feed the beasts."

"Shelton."

He frowned. "Oh, fine. I'll entertain myself tonight by asking the idiot if he knows any secrets about the family who feeds him and—"

"No. You just said, Masters Henry *and* Hugh."

"Did I?"

"You did." I leaned over the short divide between the stalls. "Did Raff actually mention both those names to you?"

He considered, raising a hand to scratch at his beard. Suddenly, he growled, catching a stray louse and squeezing it between his fingers. "Bloody hell. Forget my lack of faith; Nan will have my hide anyway, and in boiling water, too, for bringing such filth into our bed."

"Shelton, can you please answer me?"

"Yes, yes. Wait a moment. I am thinking." He gingerly searched through the gray grizzle on his chin. "Yes," he said at length. "He said it: Henry *and* Hugh. I am certain of it."

"You did not mishear him? He said those exact names and called them 'masters'?"

"I am. What of it?"

"Well, I have not heard of a Master Hugh who lives here, to start."

"And? The name is common enough. Half the men who toil in the London dockyards hail by it. Perhaps they have a spit boy or kitchen lad. Have you asked?"

"Somehow, I doubt it. The household is most definitely in arrears," I said. "The son who died was Master Henry. So, who is Master Hugh?"

"I have no idea. If not a servant, maybe another son who died before? What about the tutor? Did not the children's tutor accompany Lady Parry when she disappeared? They have not found him yet, either. Maybe he's called Master Hugh and he was friendly to Raff."

"Maybe." The unease I had felt earlier returned. "Whatever the case, we should find out. You can ask Raff tonight. I will have food brought to you. Fill his belly and then ask him who Hugh is." With a pat on Cinnabar's rump, I exited the stall and strode to the stable entrance.

"Better send ale, too," Shelton called after me. "And plenty of it."

Chapter Thirteen

Dusk had fallen, quenching the last of the feeble light intermingled with the fog and creating an eerie penumbra that had me staggering around like a drunkard. Finally, after stubbing my boots on various obstacles, I found my way back to the garden and door through which I had come, but when I tugged on the latch, the door held fast.

I cursed under my breath. I was not looking forward to venturing back around the manor to the front door and contending with Master Gomfrey's disapproving face. By now, I was in desperate need of a bath and change of clothes; my skin crawled with a perceived infestation triggered by Shelton's discovery in his beard, and if I was to dine with Lord Vaughan in the hall, then no doubt I was already late. Not to mention, ruffians had ambushed me once already and the stranger stalking me could be hiding anywhere. This infernal soup of fog and dark would provide the perfect cover; even if he was not lurking nearby, I had no idea if that household mastiff was.

I yanked on the latch again. Just as I was about to admit defeat and brave the blackness enveloping the garden, I heard a voice whisper, "You can come through here instead," and I spun about, not seeing anyone. Childhood memories of ghost stories told by Alice to keep me firmly in bed made the hair on my nape to prickle. If ever there was a place for malign spirits, this was it, though I had always prided myself on being the least superstitious man I knew.

"Here," said the voice again, and something tapped my boot. I gasped, jumping back as a seemingly disembodied hand reached up from the fog at my very feet. Gut instinct took over; as I began to cross myself, finger to my forehead, left shoulder, then right, the hand became an arm and a pair of shoulders in a plain dress, below the pimply face of a young woman. "Here," she said again, and I saw she stood on the worn steps of a root cellar, its trapdoor flung open. "That postern door is always locked by nightfall," she said, as if I were a fool not to have known it. "Come this way and I'll take you through the kitchens to the hall."

I paused, looking down at her. "Who . . . are you?"

She pursed her already needle-thin lips. "I am Agnes, the maidservant who made up your room. Are you coming with me or not? Hurry, before the sprites get in." As she spoke, her watery eyes scanned our vicinity with trepidation. She, too, it seemed, had a fear of the unnatural, though in her case it was an invasion by night fairies.

As I eased past her down the steps into a moldy space situated beneath the manor's foundation, which piles of wicker baskets and rickety tables heaped with jars denoted as a place for storage of perishables, I heard her slam the trapdoor behind me. For an instant, I saw nothing. Then the faint glow of a hand-held lantern materialized.

"This way." Agnes lifted the lantern higher, casting a feeble interplay of light over her uncomely features. She was like the manor itself, I thought, as fetching as stone. She moved around me; I lurched after her, practically treading on her patten-shod heels. She cast a look over her shoulder. "You might have a care, my lord. We have only just met."

I might have laughed at her presumption had I not been desperate to get out of that cellar. I loathed enclosed spaces almost as much as I did deep water. To me, they were one and the same: bottomless caverns waiting to swallow the hapless.

"You'll be late for the feast," she said, echoing my previous thought, though the manner in which she pronounced *feast* held distinct sarcasm, as if plentiful food was the last thing I should expect. "You have yet to bathe and reek of horse. My lady will not be pleased; she values punctuality and cleanliness above all else."

Again, she spoke with marked scorn. Servants must be hard to come by here in Withernsea, I thought, for Lady Vaughan to put up with such insolence. However, having been raised myself among servants, I knew they often carried hidden resentments.

We traversed a dank passageway and climbed another short flight of steps to a door that Agnes took her time opening, using a key she produced from her apron pocket as if it were a talisman. The lantern was guttering by now, producing more smoke than light. Between its oily stink and the darkness around us, I was starting to feel sick. When she pulled open the door to reveal the kitchen, with its fire pit and basting heat, I rushed past her as she gave a nasty giggle, such as a wicked child might emit after drowning a pet.

A robust woman with rubicund cheeks and floppy bonnet

fastened under her numerous chins barreled from behind the kitchen's block table, which was strewn with guts. I smelled the disemboweled fowl cooking on spits arrayed above the fire—and took quick note there was no kitchen boy present—as the woman declared, "Agnes, by the rood, I told you to fetch herbs, not dawdle your heels. His lord and ladyship are already in their chambers preparing to receive our guest—" She came to a standstill. "Who might this be?"

Agnes said, "Our guest. I found him outside the garden postern. He did not realize that we always lock that door by nightfall."

"Yes, I am Master Prescott," I said haltingly to the woman, brushing my horse-soiled hands across my breeches and attempting to bow before I remembered she was also a servant.

The woman was aghast. "But, you—you are supposed to be in your chamber. We serve supper in less than an hour! Agnes, you were to fetch him and bring hot water for his bath." She directed her wrathful stare at the maidservant, who seemed not the least concerned as she proceeded to the table and deposited a handful of crumpled leaves from her apron pocket.

"I did," Agnes said. She turned to hang the key on a hook by the door. "The water must be cold by now. He was not to be found. What was I to do? Search the roke and be taken by sprites? You told me to fetch herbs for pies." She pointed at the pile. "There they are."

"Well, I—I never . . ." Mistress Harper—for she must be the housekeeper—bulged with outrage until I said quickly, "It is entirely my fault. After greeting my lord Vaughan in the cemetery, I went to the stables to check on my horse and manservant. The time got away with me. My abject apologies; if you could direct me to my chamber, I promise to wash, change, and be in the hall promptly within the hour."

Mistress Harper clucked her tongue in disbelief. It reminded me of Alice, whenever I told a fib and she caught me in it, and made me warm to the housekeeper at once. I knew this sort of woman—efficient and solicitous, as Alice had been.

"I doubt that," she remarked but her gaze warmed in return. "But you must hurry along, regardless. My lady does not take to tardiness." She jabbed her hand at Agnes. "Show him upstairs and return here at once. We still have these pies to garnish."

Agnes gave me a slithering look as she led me across an inner quadrangle separating the kitchens from the manor, through another door, and back down a passageway toward the hall, turning from the chapel to a main staircase leading to the upper floors. I noticed a faded tapestry adorning the balustrade. It must have been fine once, with hints of glittering silver threads that proclaimed it an expensive import from the looms of Burgundy or Flanders, but now it was as faded and neglected as the rest of the house.

On the second floor, Agnes opened a door to reveal a simple chamber with an arrow-slit window set in the far wall, the room furnished with an oversized bed hung with a tester, a stool, a chair, and a chest for clothes. My saddlebags sat unopened on the chest. A smaller room off the bedchamber served as garde-robe and privy; upon its chilly floor was a linen-lined tub filled with—as Agnes had supposed and a dip of my finger confirmed—cold water.

I turned back to her. She lounged in the doorway, rolling the door key about her spindly finger. Her knuckles were red but not chaffed; for being the only maidservant I had seen in the house, she appeared remarkably unharried.

"Shall I assist my lord in disrobing?" she asked with a sly affectation that set my teeth on edge. Insouciant *and* a slattern: I decided I did not care for Agnes at all.

"No, thank you."

"As my lord wishes." She dipped a shallow curtsey that offered me a good glimpse of small breasts tucked within her gaping bodice. She was about to turn away when my hand shot out and caught her thin wrist. She whirled on me.

"The key," I said, before she could issue another uninvited solicitation.

Agnes cocked her head. "Lady Vaughan does not care for locked doors."

"Except for that garden postern," I reminded her, and a flush crept into her concave cheeks. "The key, if you please. There are items in my saddlebag I must protect."

Her gaze darted toward my bag, even as she pretended to consider for a moment before she handed me the key. "As you wish, my lord. Lady Vaughan will not be pleased."

"I am sorry to have displeased her so much before I have even made her acquaintance," I replied, "but as I said, I carry important items and my door must be locked when I am not in my room. And," I went on, as her eyes narrowed, "I am not a lord. Master Prescott will suffice."

Before I shut the door, I gleaned covetous greed on her face.

Oh, no, I did not care for Agnes at all. But resentful servants had eager tongues, and hers, I suspected, could be unloosed, if I had the need for it.

I was late. As soon as I descended the stairs in my somber court doublet of muted green velvet, matching breeches, and dark hose, I heard voices in the hall and among them was the high tone of a noblewoman. Whatever distress Lady Vaughan had undergone at the death of her son had been set aside in lieu of her visitor, as I discerned the moment Gomfrey pompously and unnecessarily preceded me with the announcement of my arrival. I stepped into the hall to find Lady Vaughan with her husband before the fire-lit hearth.

The candelabrum flickered with fresh tapers, as did the overhead chandelier, but this excess of light scarcely banished the brooding shadows at the walls, as though the hall had only reluctantly released its habitual gloom.

As I bowed, I heard rustling skirts approach and looked up to find myself appraised by a haughty figure dressed in a high-necked black gown of antiquated design, its sleeves voluminous and lined with squirrel pelt. She wore a crescent hood that revealed a seam of fair hair tucked underneath its rim, the seed pearls adorning the hood's edge muted, of inferior quality.

Lady Vaughan appeared at least ten years younger than her husband. She had been fine once, much like the tapestry on her stairs. Yet like that tapestry, her beauty had dissipated, her flesh pared so that her green eyes under plucked brows were like watery emeralds in an assiduously pale face that had rarely seen the sun. Her nose was arched, her bone structure angular. A slight slackness under her chin betrayed premature bitterness and encroaching age—though, judging by her demeanor, she must have inspired covert desire once, even if she had probably disdained it. I detected rank in her face and manner: she held herself as though she came from noble blood. If so, life here must have been a purgatory. Women like her were bred for court, to serve royal mistresses and marry into their own pack; they were not meant for decaying manors, wed to husbands with little to commend them.

How had she ended up in Vaughan Hall?

She held out a slender hand. "Master Prescott?"

Taking her hand, I grazed it with my lips. "My lady, it is an honor."

Something dark flashed in her eyes. "Is it?" she said, and before I could reply, she pivoted like a damsel before a coterie of admirers to her husband. "He is most charming. But so young: You did not tell me he was so young, dearest Thomas."

Lord Vaughan muttered, "I did not think of it, Philippa. His age seemed irrelevant."

Their affectionate use of first names rang false but the smile she bestowed on me was definitely not. It was dazzling, seemingly welcoming yet tinged with malice.

Lady Philippa Vaughan had the smile of a practiced predator.

Again, this I had expected. I was the uninvited guest who had interrupted their mourning and personified the power of an unwanted queen. Nevertheless, it put me on guard. Why would she feel a need to disarm me, unless she was already prepared to deceive?

She let the silence between us settle. Then she said to Gomfrey, "Have the first course served." She led me to the table set with pewter fingerbowls, plates, goblets, and decanters, her hand light on my sleeve. Leaving me at my chair, she assumed her place with Lord Vaughan at the head of the table. I was surprised no one else was present. "Is Abigail not joining us?"

Lady Vaughan laughed. "She's a child. And children, however

delightful, do not share the board with adults." She paused, again with that air of someone gauging a potential enemy. "Do you have children, Master Prescott?"

"No. I am not married."

She lifted her chin, as though the concept were anathema. "How unfortunate. Marriage can be such a joy in the best of times, and a necessary solace in the worst."

I deliberated her words even as I leaned back to allow Gomfrey to pour perry wine from the decanter into my goblet. Was she trying to say she had married below her rank and now found she must endure, as her situation had turned sour? I did not see anything remotely approximating joy or solace in Lord Vaughan. He motioned to Gomfrey to serve him as well, and drank from his goblet at once, down to the dregs, despite the sharp disapproving glance his wife shot at him.

Nor, I thought, did I see any sign of the distraught mother who had recovered from a near-deadly fever only to return to her bed in anguish, so much so that she could not join her husband and daughter at her son's gravesite. She appeared both healthy and reveling in the novelty of having a guest on whom to test her claws.

The time had come to see how sharp those claws were.

"I was deeply sorry to hear of your son Henry's death," I began. "Had Her Majesty known of it beforehand, she might have delayed my visit until a more appropriate time—though, given the direness of Lady Parry's situation, I fear time is of the essence."

"My son died in God's grace," she said. "I grieve him as only a mother can, but, as you say, Her Majesty's interests take precedence. We can only assume that whatever mishap has befallen Lady Parry is most urgent, seeing as we have had no further word of her. We cannot suffer another tragedy. Better you are here now, when a remedy might yet be found."

Her sentiment sounded rehearsed, as did Lord Vaughan's solemn nod at her side. Was I obliged to deal with his wife alone in the matter of his own aunt's disappearance? Agnes and Mistress Harper entered with platters of food, preempting my next question. As Gomfrey remained by his master's chair, the sweating housekeeper and stone-faced maidservant served. It suddenly occurred to me that I had forgotten my promise to Shelton; turning to Mistress Harper, I said, "Can you please see that some hot fare and a jug or two of ale are taken to my manservant in the stables? He has a hearty appetite, and I'm afraid we ate little during our travels."

Mistress Harper shifted a nervous glance to Lady Vaughan, whose entire countenance turned glacial. She clearly was not amenable to sharing her largesse with menials, especially not a manservant who did not work for her. But she did not contest, nodding curtly to Mistress Harper to indicate approval. I thought of the name Raff had mentioned, considered letting it slip as I took up my knife to cut into the roast capon on my plate. If I asked who Hugh was, would Lady Vaughan tell the truth? I had the distinct impression she would not, if it did not suit her interests, and so I decided to trust in Shelton instead to pry the necessary information from Raff. Besides, I did not care to expose Raff to censure from his mistress, should his slip of the tongue provide a necessary key to the mystery I sensed brewing here.

"Upon my report, I am sure Her Majesty will be sensitive to your period of mourning, but, yes, I fear she does expect full cooperation," I announced. Let the weight of my authority subsume whatever double-dealings Lady Vaughan had up her sleeve.

"Lady Parry's disappearance has affected our queen most grievously. She demands a solution, preferably one which entails her lady's safe return." I knifed my capon. "I know a note was found on Lady Parry's saddle and tendered to Her Majesty by the escort she sent here. I have read the note. Tomorrow morning, I wish to see the spot where it was found. Upon my return, I will question every member in the household, including Abigail. I trust that suits, my lord Vaughan?"

The direction of my request was deliberate and Lady Vaughan's clenched jaw revealed she knew it. Without looking up, Lord Vaughan mumbled, "Yes. I'll take you there myself."

"Thomas, you cannot!" The clatter of Lady Vaughan's knife on her plate brought everything in the hall to a standstill. She paused, gave a self-deprecatory laugh. "I mean, you can, naturally, but surely we can direct Master Prescott to the location where we found the note without the need for accompaniment? It is nearly a half day's ride, after all, and I had hoped to have you here to help set the household in order. We require a return to some normalcy, if only for Abigail's sake. The poor child has lost her only brother and now she—"

"Is in need of a new tutor," I cut in, with an understanding incline of my head. Lady Vaughan froze. "He, too, disappeared with Lady Parry. What was his name again, pray tell?"

"Master Godwin," she said through her teeth. "Master Simon Godwin."

I kept my expression impassive, hiding my rush of satisfaction. Shelton had guessed wrong. Whoever Hugh was, he was not a servant or the tutor.

"Ah, yes," I said. "And he was accompanying her because he had urgent business in London, if I understand correctly?" I did not await her response, stating what I believed to be a fact. "It must have been challenging to find a tutor in these parts. The distance from York: I imagine finding a replacement will not be easy. Perhaps I could offer my assistance by sending word to court . . . ?"

"I see no need for you to inconvenience yourself," said Lady Vaughan in a clipped tone. "Strange as it may seem—given, as you cite, our relative distance from any place of note—I am of noble birth. My father was a peer of this realm, a baron of impeccable repute who once served at court. Though he is now deceased, God rest his soul, as is my lady-mother, both my sisters are married and living in London; they are acquainted with men of letters. Indeed, it was by my eldest sister's recommendation that we hired Master Godwin six months ago. I shall write to her on the morrow, which is why I hoped to have my husband present to help compose my letter."

I did not believe for a moment she needed help with a letter, any more than I believed she had neglected to mention her father's actual name in error. I wished in that moment that I could consult with Cecil; I had to discover everything I could about Lady Vaughan and her family. But Elizabeth's mandate had prohibited me from involving Cecil or anyone else at court.

"Well, then," I said, "my offer still stands, should you wish to avail yourself. Perhaps you could tell me something more about this Master Godwin? I would need as much information as possible, if I am to have any hope of finding both him and Lady Parry."

With a hint of impatience, Lady Vaughan said, "He was a servant. I did not discuss anything with him beyond matters pertaining to the children. As I have said, my sister Lady Browne referred him to me."

"So, you do not know in which households he had served previously?" I was not about to let her have her full rein nor condone her suggestion that I would do better to return to London to inquire with her sister, but she laughed again and replied, "Why, he tutored her own children, of course!" She turned to her husband, who had his nose buried in his goblet. "Thomas, did Master Godwin ever speak to you of his provenance or such?"

Lord Vaughan shook his head. "Not that I recall." He finally lifted his bleary eyes. I had noted that while he ate sparingly, he had already consumed the contents of an entire decanter, Gomfrey ever-present at his side to refill his goblet. By now, he must be quite drunk, yet his voice barely held a slur. "Master Godwin was a gentleman. He knew Latin, as well as several other languages, and was well versed in the humanist style of learning. He suffered an accident in his youth, it seems; one of his legs was crippled and he relied on a cane. He was always polite but he mostly kept to himself when not engaged in his duties. My son . . ." Lord Vaughan swallowed, visibly fighting back his emotion. "Henry liked him very much."

I felt like an insensitive rogue as I pressed on. "Did you know anything about the type of business he wished to conduct in London?"

"Books," said Lord Vaughan. "He had placed an order in the city a few weeks before and was going to collect them."

"He had been in London previously? Why did he not ask that his books be sent here?"

"They were imported works from the continent. It was too costly to have them transported so he went to fetch them himself from the bookseller. As it so happened that my aunt needed an escort to London, he offered to accompany her. He assured us he would be back within a week at most. As I said, he had gone before so I saw no reason to impede him."

"And yet he and Lady Parry vanished on the road," I said, as Lady Vaughan stared at me, "and have been unaccounted for . . . for nearly two weeks now. Is that correct?"

Lady Vaughan nodded, her mouth curled in distaste, as if the matter were both sordid and beneath her. Moments later, the servants returned with a course of herb-spiced pies. The rest of the meal proceeded uneasily, with Lady Vaughan making her own inquiries as to my origin, which compelled me to offer vague explanations that established me as a man of low birth taken in by a noble family who educated me and placed me at court. I did not mention the Dudleys or how I had come to serve the queen, but she did not probe further, as though she merely sought to establish her superiority by putting me in the position of having to justify myself.

By the end of the meal, I was tired of her ploys and wanted only to retreat to my chamber to mull over everything I had thus far learned. Yet I still had the matter of Lady Parry's stay at the manor to discuss, and was about to do just that when Lady Vaughan abruptly rose.

"I fear I have overextended myself," she said. "I'm still weak from my fever and the loss of my son. By your leave, I must retire." Her timing was perfect. Casting a stern look at Lord Vaughan that brought him clumsily to his feet, she let him take her by the arm and lead her from the hall. I stood and bowed; the instant they were gone, Mistress Harper and Agnes began to clear the table.

Gomfrey stepped to me. "Will Master Prescott be requiring

anything else?" His tone conveyed he would not be pleased if I did.

"No," I said. "Thank you. I am tired myself. I trust food and ale went to my manservant?"

"It did." He paused. "I humbly suggest you remain indoors tonight. In the past, there have been unfortunate accidents when curious guests took to wandering the grounds at night and ended up falling from the cliff. It's impossible to see in the dark, and if one is unfamiliar with the environs and the effects of the roke . . ." He let his unsettling implication linger. When I did not reply, he added, "In the winter, at high tide, bodies are rarely found. It would indeed be a calamity if another mishap befell us."

"Yes, I can see that it would. Do you think such an accident befell Lady Parry?"

His gaze turned, if possible, even more remote. "Lady Parry was in excellent health when she left us. Both she and Master Godwin took to the road after sunrise. I saw them off myself. Beyond that, I dare not speculate." He paused. "Though in such lawless times, I did warn them of the risks. They insisted they would find other travelers in York with whom to share their journey. I could hardly argue, seeing as his lordship granted them leave after Lady Parry expressed herself eager to return to court."

"Indeed." I turned to leave. Once again, inexplicable foreboding overcame me.

What secrets did Vaughan Hall hide?

Chapter Fourteen

ᚠatigue fell upon me as soon as I entered my chamber. Un-
lacing my sleeves, doublet, and breeches, I let my codpiece
drop to the floor and blew out the guttering tallow light in a
shallow dish by the bed. Someone, perhaps Agnes, had taken
advantage of my absence to leave the light in my room—no
doubt to warn me that while I might retain the key, there must
be others that unlocked my door. A quick search of my bags
revealed nothing out of place. With my mind in tumult, I fell
onto the bed in my hose and shirt.

It was evident that my arrival had disrupted something beyond a family's grief. Lady Vaughan had demonstrated as much
by her presumptive manner, and the steward struck me as someone I should watch. Agnes was also one to be wary of, a sullen
maidservant who sought advantage wherever it might be found,
while Mistress Harper appeared a sensible woman unlikely to
participate in anything illicit. Nevertheless, all three servants
depended on the Vaughans for their livelihood. I could not rely
on any of them to assist me.

Adding to my troubles was Master Gomfrey's statement that

Lady Parry had left the manor in good health with Master Godwin, whom both she and everyone else at the house had apparently trusted—though allowing an older woman to take to the
road with a crippled man unable to defend her seemed to me the
height of carelessness. Gomfrey had stated he tried to warn
them of the risks of traveling unescorted; now, she and the tutor
had vanished without a trace, that cryptic note under her saddle
the sole indication of something untoward, perhaps fatal.

I let out a breath. I had thought this stranger must hold a
connection to Sybilla, that he had initiated a gambit to lure me
away from court to exact revenge; but here in the darkness, surrounded by the unknown, I began to doubt my own conclusions.
My imagination could be blinding me, fueled by years of guilt.

What if the stranger I sought had another motive?

You must pay for the sin.

I thought then I would never sleep and decided to wait until
the hour when everyone else had retired. Exploration of the
manor might prove useful, particularly with no one to impede
me. But I could not keep weariness at bay. Without realizing it,
my eyelids drooped. Soon, I was lost to slumber, plunged once
more into the terrifying nightmare in which I lay paralyzed, as
Sybilla came toward me, clothed in skin and night, the glint of
steel in her hands. I felt her weight as she straddled me, the
warmth of her mouth; as I struggled to resist, she giggled and—

I jolted awake with a shout, flinging the figure upon me from
the bed. As it tumbled, gasping, onto the floor, I pulled my dagger from under my pillow and lunged upright, about to thrust
my blade downward when the figure cried, "No!"

I blinked, pushing away the furious haze of my dream to see
Agnes glaring at me, coming to her feet and yanking at her di-

sheveled skirts. "Would you skewer an innocent woman?" she spat, wiping her hand across her mouth. "I was just trying to—"

"I know what you were about." I tugged my rumpled shirt, to disguise my evident waning arousal under my hose. "And I'd hardly call a woman innocent when she creeps into my bed."

She simpered. "I thought my lord would welcome the company."

"You are wrong. Now, remove yourself at once before I report you to Mistress Harper."

"Do so." Her smile turned nasty. "She's drunk as a bishop on her stool in the kitchen. She likes a nip, does our Mistress Harper, after everyone takes to their rooms." Her contemptuous tone overcame my better judgment. With two strides, I had her pressed against the wall.

"What do you want?"

"I told you. I thought you'd like some company," she said. "But if you rather I remove myself, then I shan't tell you secrets they don't want you to find out—" She let out a painful gasp as I seized her by the arm.

"Speak plainly, girl. I tire of your insolence."

Up close, her breath was foul with the tang of onion as she said, "Unhand me or I'll not say a word."

Reluctantly, I released my grip. Rubbing at her arm and scowling, she said, "They're all lying to you: Lady Vaughan, Gomfrey, even his lordship—they don't want you to know the truth of what happens under their roof. If I were you, I'd be very careful, because if you get too close, they'll make you disappear just as they did Lady Parry."

I eyed her, hiding my interest. "And I suppose you want a reward for helping me?"

She showed in that instant she was not merely any slattern seeking advantage; in her dull eyes surfaced a cunning that made me want to thrash her. "I am no fool. The old queen is dead and the new one is not likely to look kindly on papists. I'm not going to be arrested and put in the Tower for protecting them."

I refrained from informing her that larcenous wenches like her did not go to the Tower; they were imprisoned instead in the Fleet, where putrid underground cells and hordes of hungry rats would make an end of her with far less mercy.

"You have coin." She thrust her hand at my saddlebag. "I saw it. You must know important people at court. You can take me there when you go."

"To court?" I smiled. "What do you think you'll do there: wash Her Majesty's linens and serve her at her table?" I watched the cunning on her face harden into defiance.

"Do not make sport of me," she hissed. "You need me more than I need you, Master High-and-Mighty Prescott. Others will pay good coin for what I know."

"And what is it you know?" I said through my teeth. "I'm not in the habit, nor, I wager, are those others you mention, of paying coin for information without verifying it first."

She shrugged. "As you wish." She started to the door, but she had to edge around me first and kept looking at me as if she anticipated a blow.

I was tempted to oblige her. With a clench of my jaw, I went to my saddlebag. She was a clever vixen: She had gone through my bag so expertly, I had not noticed. Taking out three shillings from my pouch, I tossed them at her. As she bent down to scrabble for them, I started to say there would be more if she talked now, when a querulous voice called from the corridor: "Agnes? Agnes, where are you? The fire needs stoking."

It was Mistress Harper and she indeed sounded to be in her cups. The scratching of nails on floorboard announced that the mastiff Bardolf had climbed the stairs and was prowling the passage. His snuffling under the door froze Agnes in mid-crouch.

"God help me, she'll have my head," Agnes whispered. Her eyes had gone wide in fright; the revelation of her fear gave me pause. Was she afraid of the tipsy housekeeper?

"Stay put," I said. "Do not move. Do not say a word."

Bardolf was pawing at the door, the tip of his nose snuffling under the door's seam. Pocketing the coins, Agnes stood frantically.

"Agnes," I hissed as she whirled to the door. "Tell me this: Who is Hugh?"

Her hand froze on the door latch. Then she dashed out, closing the door behind her before the dog could get in.

I heard her outside, explaining in a hasty, tremulous voice that should not have fooled anyone: "I . . . I was seeing to Master Prescott's water and candles. I . . . I had forgotten them."

Her falsehood was so blatant, I braced for Mistress Harper's retort. But the housekeeper only grumbled, "Is that so? Well, get back to the kitchens. You have no business up here with your betters. What need has he of water or wax at this hour? He should be abed."

Their footsteps moved away. Moments later, I heard the dog lumber off, too.

Bunching my fists, I cursed under my breath. I should have restrained her—by force if necessary; make her confess what she knew. For I was certain she knew something. Her fear had been so obvious, as was her reaction to the name Hugh. I would have wagered my very life on it.

Tomorrow, I vowed. Tomorrow, I would question every one of them. I would drag the truth out if I had to threaten them with the Tower, the rack, or the scaffold itself.

I would start with Agnes.

𝕴 slept poorly, in fits and starts. As soon as sullen sunlight leaked through the window, I rose, bathed hastily using freezing water—Agnes had indeed left a pitcher in the garderobe to substantiate her story, along with two candlesticks; she was not such a bad liar, after all—dressed, and went down to the hall to break my fast. I had no appetite, forcing myself to swallow the brown bread, goat cheese, and watery ale Mistress Harper served me in stolid silence, her movements deliberate, betraying she had indeed imbibed too much the night before. As she was clearing the table, I asked her if I might speak to Master Gomfrey.

"He went out with his lordship early," she replied, her eyes averted. "They said they would be back soon, to take you to that place where Lady Parry and the tutor disappeared."

They had risen before dawn. Why? To hide evidence, perhaps?

"Mistress Harper," I said. She lowered her face farther, until her chins sank into her collar. "May I ask you if you know anything about the circumstances in which Lady Parry left this house? Was there any disturbance I should know about?"

"Disturbance?" she repeated, as if she failed to understand.

"Yes. Was there a quarrel or disagreement? I had understood she came here to tend to her ladyship and Master Henry, who had both taken ill. Clearly, the boy, at least, was not yet recovered when Lady Parry left, seeing as he died soon after. Why would she have departed with only Master Godwin as her companion, leaving behind a very sick child?"

"She . . . she insisted on it." Mistress Harper glanced warily around us, as if unseen witnesses might lurk nearby. "She said that Her Majesty had urgent need of her and she had to go. There was no disagreement. Master Gomfrey did advise them both to wait until we could arrange a proper escort, but Lady Parry . . . she would not hear of it."

It was difficult to tell if she was lying. Her explanation sounded rehearsed, as if she recited words she had taken pains to memorize, but by now my suspicions were at such a pitch, everything I heard would seem like a falsehood.

"You do realize," I said, "that should I discover that anyone in this household seeks to obstruct my investigations or hide important information that could help locate Lady Parry, the queen herself could consider it an act of treason. And God forbid that Lady Parry should be found harmed: Her Majesty will impose severe punishment on all those involved, whether they were directly responsible or not."

My threat sufficiently dismayed Mistress Harper for her to lose her color. Grabbing up her tray with the remains of my breakfast, she muttered, "I have told you what I know. I am the housekeeper. I do as told and stay clear of their lordships' affairs. If there was any disturbance or disagreement, I am surely not aware of it."

She hastened away to the kitchen, leaving me more frustrated and angry than before. Throwing on my cloak, I stormed from the house through the thinning scrim of fog to the stables, hoping Shelton had had better luck questioning Raff. I intended to put a few questions to the boy myself, but when I entered the stables I found the first stalls that held the Vaughan steeds were empty. Cinnabar whinnied as he heard my approach. I did not find Shelton where I expected, up and tending to our horses.

Panic flared. Yelling his name, I began to search every stall, narrowly avoiding an ill-tempered bite from Cerberus, who, like Cinnabar, was hungry and restless. I was about to rush back to the manor to shout everyone into the hall with threats when I suddenly espied him, lying faceup in a hay pile in a far corner near a heap of detritus: a stack of old apple barrels, broken crates, and a tangle of rusted, hanging hooks.

At first, I could not move. He must be dead. He was so still, he could not have been anything else. A wave of despair choked me as I willed myself to step toward him.

He had one arm flung over his brow, his battered face slack, his skin tinged with an awful grayish hue. His mouth under his beard was open; as I bent over him, a howl of grief clawing at my throat, I realized with a start that his chest rose and fell, so slight it was almost imperceptible.

He was breathing.

"Shelton!" I shook him by the shoulder. "Shelton, wake up!" I could smell ale on his breath; saw now at his side a tray with the gristle and bone of a capon and a jug, tipped over in a pool of liquid. "Shelton, damn you, wake up!"

He did not stir. Seizing the pitcher, I ran to the outside trough and raced back inside, dumped its entire contents over his miserable head.

He spluttered, the water hitting him in the face. As he groaned and tried to open his eyes, I said furiously, "You old fool!

You drank yourself into a stupor. I'm supposed to rely on you to watch my back, and here you are, passed out with drink, when I need you to—"

I leapt back as, rolling to one side, he spewed a bellyfull of vomit.

He gasped, wiping the filth from his mouth and chin. With excruciating caution, he sat up, his head hanging between his knees as he coughed and dribbled spittle.

My outrage faded. He was sick. He must have somehow caught the fever that had sickened Lady Vaughan and her son—

Then he raised bleary eyes to me and croaked, "You need not call for an undertaker, lad. I am not dying. Not yet." He licked his lips, staggering to his feet. "God's teeth," he said, swaying as he struggled to catch his bearings. "How do they brew their ale in these parts? I feel as if I've licked Satan's arsehole."

I eyed him. "You didn't even finish it. Look: Half that jug has spilt. . . . The ale," I whispered. As he blinked uncomprehendingly, I knelt by the pool of liquid under the jug, dipping my fingertip in the pool and bringing it to my nose. The smell hit me like a mallet: the distinct trace of almonds.

I wiped my hand on my breeches, plunged back in time to a chamber in Whitehall, where I held my dying squire in my arms and smelled the same sickly scent on the seal of a note he had inadvertently opened.

"You've been poisoned. This ale is tainted."

He grunted, swerved back around to spew again. "Get me water. I need water. . . ."

I ran back out to the trough, rinsing the pitcher thoroughly several times before I returned with it full. He seized it, emptying water into his mouth and then doubling over to throw it all up. "You need a physic," I said, even as I gripped my dagger's hilt at my belt and felt the burning need to bury it into the heart of whoever had done this. More poison, just like the box sent to Elizabeth and the letter that killed Peregrine: The stranger stalking me had made his intent clear. He wanted me alone and cornered, at his mercy. He was nearby, watching us.

Shelton mumbled, "The last thing I need is a physic bleeding me with leeches," and by sheer force of will, he lurched to the stall where Cerberus, sensing his master's distress, tugged at his tether. "I'll be fine," he said as he comforted his steed. "Give me a few minutes to clear my head. It's pounding like a thousand poleaxing imps." He suddenly guffawed—a hoarse rattle. "I feel like I did when that mob in the Tower went over me with their pikes."

"But, the poison: It could still be inside you—"

"Do not tell me what to do," he snarled. "I am still your elder, boy. I told you to let me be a moment. Go see to your beast before he breaks down that stall gate."

I knew better than to argue, slipping into Cinnabar's stall to stroke his ears and neck until he settled down. His trough was almost empty. As I looked about for feed, it occurred to me that I had not seen Raff this morning.

"Where is the boy?" I asked. Shelton was murmuring to Cerberus and did not look up at me as he replied, "He never came back last night. I sat up, waiting for him until that capon went cold, but he never showed. He must have other places to sleep."

"You did not see him all night?"

"That's what I said, isn't it?" Shelton pointed past the stall. "There's a bag of feed over there and some sour apple rinds."

The bag was only half full, the feed moldering, crawling with mites. "We should graze them," I said, grimacing. "God save us, this is a horrid place. I cannot wait to get—"

The clatter of hooves outside interrupted me. I stalked out to find Lord Vaughan and Gomfrey seated on two mares with ribs poking under their hides. The horses here didn't appear to be faring any better than the household; all of a sudden, my rage over the attempt on Shelton and certainty that I was being misled, coupled with my growing fear that the stranger could strike again at any moment, sharpened my voice. "My lord, this is an outrage!"

Lord Vaughan turned in his saddle with a startled expression. Before he could say a word, I strode up to him. "First, you ride out without waiting for me, though I specifically told you I wished to see the spot where the disappearances took place. Then I come to the stable to find my horses unfed and your idiot groom nowhere in sight. And to top matters off, my manservant almost—" I curbed my tongue, stopping myself as I remembered Agnes's words.

They do not want you to know what goes on under this roof.

Lord Vaughan regarded me. In the daylight, he looked even more gaunt and hollow-eyed, his grief like a pall cast over him. I could not help but pity him. Yet as much as I wanted to believe that a man so broken by his son's death would never countenance evil done against my servant or me, I could not trust him or anyone else in this manor.

"Well?" I stood with my hands on my hips, ignoring the granite-eyed steward staring at me from his lord's side.

"I . . . I beg your forgiveness," said Lord Vaughan, haltingly. "I tend to rise very early and thought it best to go with Gomfrey first, to ascertain the precise location where Lady Parry and

Master Godwin vanished—or rather, where her horse was found. The first time I went with Her Majesty's men, my son and wife were gravely ill; and I was not myself. I feared I might have forgotten. It's not marked, you see. . . ."

His explanation faded into uncomfortable silence. He did not need to elaborate further. He had no doubt nursed a dependency for wine even before his son's demise; with Henry now lying cold in the little mausoleum, he was drowning himself in it.

I understood grief. I had nearly lost my own reason because of it. Softening my voice, I asked, "Did you find it?"

He nodded. "It is closer than I first thought; less than an hour's ride. I came to fetch you."

I gave terse assent. "We ride alone. Have Gomfrey attend to my manservant, who's taken ill." Turning around, I marched into the stables to saddle Cinnabar. "You will not say a word," I warned Shelton, where he stood clutching the side of a stall. "You must stay here and recover."

Chapter Fifteen

Despite the circumstances, I was glad to have Lord Vaughan to myself. My own experience had taught me that sorrow can unlock our hearts, letting loose our deepest emotions—the hatred, fears, and regrets we hide even from ourselves.

I intended to use his grief against him. I had no compunction now, not after what had occurred. Someone in his household must know what had happened to Lady Parry. Agnes had accused all of them but I was not about to accept her word. I would question and eliminate them one by one, until I found my culprit. God help them if they tried to hide the truth from me.

The mastiff Bardolf loped behind us. I kept glancing over my shoulder at him, thinking such a large beast could not possibly keep up with us. But he was tireless; of all the animals in Vaughan Hall, he didn't seem malnourished at all, muscles rippling under his gleaming black coat, ropes of saliva hanging from his jaws as he remained steadfast at our horses' heels.

I would not wish to find myself in a confrontation with him. As we rode through forlorn Withernsea onto the open road that stretched to York, I said abruptly, "How long is it since you and Lady Philippa were wed?"

He appeared startled by my question. "Philippa is my second wife. I was married once before, but she died of the Sweat in 1539. I wed Philippa three years later."

Interesting. "Did you have a son before Henry?"

He frowned. "Why do you ask?"

"No particular reason. Only that Raff . . . well, I wonder why you employ him. Has he no family in the village, or is he a foundling you took in?"

He remained silent for such a long moment that I thought he would fail to answer. When he finally did, his voice was subdued. "Raff is my child, if that is what you imply. I made a mistake. One of our servant girls: a foolish indiscretion on my part. It meant nothing, only she got with child and abandoned him afterward. I had not the heart to send him away."

"Yet your wife despises him. Surely, that must have caused conflict."

He sighed. "It brought her no joy, but once she bore Henry, she tolerated Raff because we had a son of our own. Abigail, our second child, was born the following year."

"How old was Henry?" I did not want to salt his wound but it was necessary. If I could break apart his grief, he might let slip what I needed to know. Of everyone in the Vaughan household, after Mistress Harper (whom I now suspected was terrified), Lord Vaughan seemed the most tenderhearted. No man who mourned as he did could be without a conscience.

"Seven." His voice was almost inaudible. "He would have turned eight this year."

I paused to do quick sums in my head. If he had married

Philippa in forty-two and Henry had been seven when he'd died, it had taken her eight years to conceive—an inordinate delay for any marriage. If my estimation of Raff's age was more or less correct, then he must have been born *after* she wed Lord Vaughan, but two or three years before she herself had a son. If it had taken her so long to get pregnant, might there have been another child in between, an infant son named Hugh who died? It would explain her hatred of her husband's by-blow. Raff would have been a constant reminder of her husband's infidelity and her loss.

Without warning he said, "I don't understand why you're asking me this. Surely my marriage and failure as a husband are irrelevant to the task at hand?"

"Forgive me, but I must request your indulgence. I seek only to establish the mood of your household upon Lady Parry's departure." This time, I did not care to soften my words. "I have the impression she left precipitously. Your steward told me she was determined to take to the road with the crippled tutor even after he warned her of the risks. Yet she went anyway, leaving behind a sick child, and by all accounts, your wife, as well. You are Lady Parry's kinsman; why did you not detain her or at least ensure she had more suitable accompaniment? Had she waited only a few days more, the queen's escort would have arrived."

He avoided my gaze, causing me to sit upright on my saddle, intent on him. God's teeth, he *knew* something. I was not fishing in murky waters.

"Lord Vaughan," I said sternly, "if you have something to say, now would be the time. Her Majesty will not abide prevarication, and my own patience is starting to wear thin."

His jaw worked, as if he were uncertain of how much to

reveal. At length, he said, "My aunt and my wife disliked each other. Philippa can be difficult. She and Blanche did not agree on much." His shoulders sagged. Without further hesitation, it came pouring out of him. "God save me, I tried to persuade my aunt to stay until we could make proper arrangements. But she and my wife had argued grievously over Henry's care. It had reached a point where neither of them was willing to concede. Philippa had recovered by then; at first, it seemed that Henry was also on the mend, but then he took a turn for the worse and Blanche wanted us to send for a physician. She said he might die otherwise." As he held back tears, his voice tightened. "She was right, of course, but Philippa wouldn't hear of it. She told Blanche she knew best how to tend her son and ordered Blanche out of his room. My aunt told me she could not be party to Henry's certain death and would go to York on her own, if need be, to bring back a physician."

"Then, she wasn't planning to return to London? She went with the tutor to York to fetch a physician."

"Yes." He lowered his face. "And I let her go, because Philippa was irate that I had dared allow my aunt to supplant her own charge and wouldn't hear of me going as well. Master Godwin offered to accompany her; I reasoned he would provide sufficient protection. I didn't truly want to leave my son, sick as he was, but I swear to you, I thought they'd return in a day or so!" He looked up at me, guilt carving furrows on his face. "I didn't think this—this terrible nightmare would befall us."

I let a few moments pass so he could compose himself. Once I felt he had, I said, "Tell me why your wife and Lady Parry disliked each other."

"I have. I told you, they argued over Henry and—"

"No," I interrupted. "Such enmity cannot happen over-
night, that Lady Parry would ride off against all advice to the
contrary. In times of crisis, women set pettiness aside, particularly when a child's life is at stake. Something other than a
disagreement over Henry must have caused this rift between
them. What was it?"

He looked haggard now, twice his age. I had finally fit the
key into the lock but I did not enjoy turning it. Then he whispered, "It was because of . . . her."

My heart clenched in my chest. "Who?"

"Our new queen." He paused. "Philippa despised Lady Parry's
devotion to her. Philippa and her family, you see, they are . . ."

"I know. You are all papists."

He nodded. "Philippa's father and brother participated in the
Pilgrimage of Grace. Indeed, Lord Hussey and his son so ar-
dently upheld the rebellion to stop the king from tearing down
the monasteries that they died in York by royal command—
hung, disemboweled, and quartered like criminals. Lady Hussey
eventually perished of grief, while Philippa and her three sisters
lost everything, their family's estate forfeited by attainder of treason. That is why Philippa accepted my proposal. She had no
choice. One of her sisters, Lady Browne, had been attempting to
arrange a minor post for Philippa in the household of Lady
Mary, who later became our queen. I knew Lady Browne's husband from my own infrequent travels to London—he, too, is a
cloth merchant—and he arranged my meeting with Philippa."

Philippa's sister had tried to find a post in Mary's household;
Lady Vaughan's family had known our late queen, like Sybilla
Darrier. . . .

Trepidation filled me as he went on. "You must understand,

all of us who revere the true faith dwelled in terror. The king had destroyed everything sacrosanct to us; it was as if a curse had befallen the realm. Philippa was nineteen when we wed, but she never forgave what her family had suffered nor that because of it she was left impoverished, without a place at court. Even though she did not love me, I was willing to marry her. I always lived a quiet life; I am of good but not noble birth. My kin are not court people. My great-grandfather was born here in Yorkshire; he became a landowner after establishing himself in wool trade and acquiring Vaughan Hall. To Philippa, I was little more than a commoner. Looking back now, I fear she was right. The enclosure of monastic lands decimated me; my holdings could not compete."

"Does your wife—did she ever mention a family called Darrier?" I had to pull the words out of my throat. "In specific, a woman named Sybilla Darrier who served Queen Mary and whose father and brothers also died in the Pilgrimage of Grace? Has anyone in your household, including this Master Godwin, ever mentioned her?"

He frowned. To my frustration, I could tell at once he had never heard the name before.

"Certainly not Master Godwin," he said. "Philippa might, but she never talks of the past. After her sister failed to secure her a post at court, she urged Philippa to accept my proposal but Philippa herself—she acts as though her father and brother never existed, though I know she carries them in her heart. What I know of her trials, I learned because her sister's husband told me."

Yet it was entirely possible that Lady Browne had in fact known Sybilla. I recalled Sybilla telling me about her own father and brother's death, which had precipitated her, her mother's, and her sisters' escape to Brussels, where they met Renard, the scheming Imperial ambassador. He had placed Sybilla as his spy in Mary's service. It was an undeniable connection that I would be a fool to ignore.

Was this stranger I sought part of a circle of secret papists, bent of vengeance because of Elizabeth's accession?

"Here." Lord Vaughan reined to a halt. We had reached a crossroads of sorts, the road dividing into the main one leading to the City of York and the other toward the west. It was a bleak place, windswept and rugged, scattered with jagged boulders. "We found her horse here. It was in a sorry state. I had to put it down later, as it had gone lame."

I looked about, holding down my cap with one hand as Cinnabar took advantage of our inactivity to munch on a dry patch of grass. The wind was rising, flecked with snow, the sky blackening at its edges. A storm approached. We had to return to the hall soon.

"I don't know where the actual incident took place," said Lord Vaughan sadly. "The horse could have wandered from the site. It was in a pitiful state after being outside all night."

"But we know Lady Parry never reached York," I said. "Nor did she arrive in London with Master Godwin, whose horse, unlike hers, was never found." I did not add that I was beginning to harbor dark suspicion of this mysterious tutor sent at Lady Browne's recommendation. There were no bodies. Was Godwin involved in the abduction, despite his outward appearance of gentility? Was he the stranger?

Thunder rumbled overhead. Bardolf lifted his hind leg to urinate on a rock. Nothing I saw gave any indication of what

Lady Parry and the tutor had encountered, other than the fact that the very isolation had ensured there would be no witnesses. If there had been a struggle, it might have been visible, the land being as parched as it was, but miles stretched between here and York where a corpse might be dumped to rot.

My heart sank. The only benefit I had reaped from the excursion was the information imparted by Lord Vaughan, which in no manner provided any reassurance.

I was as far as I could be from the protection of Elizabeth and the court, and even as I stumbled around in search of clues, the stranger stalking me could be preparing his next move.

As soon as we returned to the manor, I led Cinnabar into the stables to unsaddle and rub him down. I found Shelton nursing his headache but otherwise looking better than when I left him. He had been offered food, which he declined, he told me, because his stomach felt like "the very pits of hell." Gomfrey had also done his stiff best to appear both concerned and solicitous.

"That steward doesn't care if I live or die," Shelton remarked, with a spark of his old spirit that gave me comfort. "He makes my own time as the Dudley steward look like a bleeding saint's. Nothing worse than a man who thinks he's better than his position in life."

"True," I said, and I told him what I had learned, admitting in frustration that I was no closer to finding Lady Parry. "But I'm going to do everything I can. That wench Agnes told me last night that no one here could be trusted, so I will question her first. What about Raff?"

Shelton eyed me. "No sight of him. And you'll have a time questioning the wench, as well. It seems she too has disappeared. Gomfrey told me she vanished in the night."

Throwing my horse brush aside, I whirled about and strode to the manor.

The kitchens were in an uproar, Mistress Harper with her head in her hands weeping as Gomfrey issued a stern barrage of orders. He glanced up coldly as I barged in. "Master Prescott, his lordship is with her ladyship in the solar. You can wait in the hall. We've had a most distressing morning and—"

"Where is Agnes?" I demanded, cutting him off. "I am told she has vanished."

Gomfrey blinked. "I would not say that. But she has apparently absconded. It is hardly your concern. Mistress Harper and I will contend with it."

"First Lady Parry and the tutor disappear, then Raff, and now Agnes?" I retorted. "You have not made much of an example of contending with anything thus far."

Gomfrey said tightly, "Begging your pardon, Master Prescott, but Raff has not disappeared. The boy has a habit of running off. He can be gone for hours, days, even. He is wild as a beast and about as unreliable. Had you inquired, I would have told you as much. I am quite certain he is somewhere about the manor and will appear in due time, as he always does."

Mistress Harper moaned, looking ready to collapse as she wrung her apron between her hands. "All this work: whatever shall I do? Agnes knew how much I needed her; I don't understand how she could do this, leave without a word or even her wages."

"She left without pay?" I said. "In the middle of the night, with her fear of sprites and the roke outside? Impossible."

"I can assure you," Gomfrey replied, "it is not. Agnes was born in Withernsea. She knows the path home very well indeed, as she went there often to visit her mother and—"

"I saw her last night," I said. His entire being stiffened, even as Mistress Harper gave a small gasp of dismay. "She came into my chamber to bring candles and a pitcher of water for the morning. We spoke briefly before she heard Mistress Harper call for her. I can assure you, Master Gomfrey, she showed me no inclination of leaving this manor."

"Is this true?" Gomfrey directed his question at the housekeeper, to my disbelief.

"Do you doubt my word?" I demanded, enraged; but Mistress Harper nodded. "Yes, it's true. I did call for Agnes. The fire needed kindling, and my hands are not what they were after a long day of cooking. I found her upstairs; she told me herself she was tending to Master Prescott. She came back to the kitchens with me, stoked the fire, and then, we . . . we said our goodnight." Her voice quavered with shame, as well it should have. If the housekeeper drank herself to sleep every night, she would have no idea if Agnes had tiptoed home or fallen off the cliff.

"You should not have withheld this from me," scolded Gomfrey. "I am the head steward: Every incident in the household, no matter how trivial, must be reported to me. Nevertheless, regardless of where she was *before* she left, the fact remains that Agnes is no longer here and now it is incumbent upon me to find a suitable replacement from the village." He turned to me. "Master Prescott," he said icily, "if you please? Mistress Harper has a great deal of work to attend to, if you wish to dine tonight."

I looked again at Mistress Harper, who was dabbing her apron at her eyes and avoiding my gaze as she shuffled to her kitchen block.

Reluctantly, I followed Gomfrey. The instant we were in the inner quadrangle, I said to him, "You will not question my honor again. It seems you need reminding of who I am."

"Oh, I know who you are." His tone adopted a contemptuous edge. "You have made your importance quite clear to everyone, but that does not mean I need oblige you. Lest *you* need reminding, Master Prescott, you are not my lord." He inclined his head. "Now, if you'll excuse me, I must make my way to the village. We cannot be without a maidservant."

As he moved to the hall, I called out, "Who is Hugh?"

He paused, just as Agnes had done when I asked her. Then he said, "I have no idea whom you refer to. By your leave, Master Prescott, I bid you a good afternoon."

I returned to the kitchens. Mistress Harper gave me a weary look. "I cannot hear more questions," she said. "I have so much to do with Agnes gone. You heard what Gomfrey said."

I echoed the steward's words to me: "Gomfrey is not your lord."

She sighed. "But he is. He answers to her ladyship and oversees my charge. We are—or we were—but three servants, with poor Raff tending to the stables and gates. My lady allows Gomfrey full rein over this house. I am not surprised Agnes left, to tell the truth. Gomfrey was always chastising her for her laziness, and after that situation with the tutor—" She ran her hand over her face. "There I go again, saying things I shouldn't. I beg you, do not press me anymore."

"What situation with the tutor?" I moved closer, lowering my voice. "Mistress Harper, I know something happened in this house to send Lady Parry fleeing from it. No one is telling me the truth but I *will* find it anyway. Now, what is this about Agnes and Master Godwin?"

If possible, she appeared even more distressed. After gnawing at her lower lip for several moments, she finally said, "Agnes . . . she was never content. Were it not so difficult to find help in these parts, what with our distance from any city and their lordship's impoverishment, she would already have lost her post. When Master Godwin arrived, she . . ."

"Made advances to him?" I suggested.

Mistress Harper did not appear surprised at my assumption. "Yes. She said she would make him fall in love with her, because he was crippled, and who else would deign to look at him? Oh, she thought herself so sly. And Master Godwin—well, bad leg or not, he's still a man, is he not, and he reacted to her as such, or thus she claimed. She talked about him all the time, about how they would marry and move to London, where he'd find himself a position teaching a nobleman's brood and she would serve a true lady in style." She waved her hand dismissively. "Full of fancies Agnes was, as if she were born to velvet. I did not believe a word of it; I rather thought he would eventually ruin her in the way men do and she'd end up with nothing for her troubles but a belly and scolding from her ladyship. Another bastard in the house would not be to my lady's liking, not after Raff."

"And then what happened?"

"The fever." She sighed. "Master Henry and her ladyship fell ill. After that, every one of us was up at all hours of the day and night, tending to them. Then Lady Parry came. We'd had no advance word of her arrival, but she put the nail in Agnes's hope. When Master Godwin offered to escort Lady Parry, Agnes was fit to be tied, though Lady Parry is a matron of a certain age—oh, it was horrid to hear, the way Agnes carried on. She cared nothing that Lady Parry vanished or Master Henry died; she ranted that Master Godwin had gone and forsaken her, and now what was she to do, left here to scrub her fingers raw until the end of her days? As I said, she never was content. The more she thought she could get, the more she wanted."

I felt a surge of triumph. Finally, I had something: Agnes and Godwin had been involved. While it did not clarify much, it did thicken the stew, as my Alice would have said.

"Did the tutor love her? Do you think he'd have done as she claimed if he had returned?"

"I surely could not say. Agnes lied about everything, from how much work she did to whether the sun was out. It was her way. I doubt he saw her as more than a pastime. He was educated, a man of letters from London. Agnes could barely spell her own name. What can two such persons possibly have in common, I ask you, save for a romp in the hayloft on Saturday?"

I found myself smiling. She did indeed remind me of Alice.

"Mistress Harper, does the name Hugh mean anything to you?"

Her brow creased. Then, to my disappointment, she said, "I can't say that it does."

"Thank you for obliging me," I said. "I will not trouble you further."

As I turned to depart, she added suddenly, "I thought Agnes tried the same with you. From the moment you set foot in this house, she was aflutter. She must have thought, here you were, another man from London, and from court no less: her second chance. When she told me she was in your chamber last night, I assumed . . . That is why I did not tell Gomfrey. None of my business what people do after the candles are snuffed."

"I appreciate your discretion but I assure you, nothing untoward happened between Agnes and me. As you can imagine, we have nothing in common."

Except, I thought as I left the housekeeper to her work, the fact that three persons had disappeared from Vaughan Hall—and Agnes was now one of them.

Chapter Sixteen

𝕴 went upstairs to my chamber to inspect my saddlebag. My coin pouch was gone. It had not contained enough to forge a new life, especially if one hankered for London, but perhaps it seemed so to Agnes. Or perhaps she had been so frightened by my questions that she decided to take what she could and leave rather than be exposed, lest her liaison with Godwin came to light.

Whichever the case, I had been robbed and after only two days here, it felt as if I'd been immured in Vaughan Hall for a hundred years. I longed for this thankless errand to end; I had to stop myself from marching to Lady Vaughan's chamber to question her. She had eyes and ears; she ruled the house with an iron gauntlet, and Godwin had been educating her children. I found it almost impossible to believe she had not at least suspected her maidservant was a slattern who had cast eyes at Godwin, given her sensitivity toward her own husband's indiscretion. But I would see her that night in the hall, no doubt, and ask her then. I also planned to question her about her argument with Lady Parry.

Outside, virulent storm clouds piled on the horizon. The wind moaned and rattled something, a loose weathervane or chimney cap. As I paced the narrow confine of my chamber, hearing the occasional spatter of rain mixed with sleet striking the high windowpane, I decided I should check on Shelton before it grew too inclement to venture outdoors. While I was at it, I would pass by the family cemetery to determine if one of the headstones contained the name Hugh, though I was beginning to question my own obsession. Raff had probably said a name that meant nothing. Still, I could not get it out of my head as I made my way back down the staircase, through the desolate hall and empty passageway to the postern door to the garden.

The wind assaulted me. I walked toward the cemetery with my face down and cloak flapping. Only when I was among the somewhat sheltered gnarled copse of trees did I notice a little figure huddled by the mausoleum. Slowing my approach to avoid frightening her, I heard her gasp when a sudden gust tore her snood from her head and little Abigail Vaughan leapt up to bound after it as it reeled and somersaulted, buoyed by the wind, toward the cliff edge.

I dashed after her, catching her in mid-stride. Her fair hair whipped about her face; turning mournful eyes that seemed to me much older than her mere six years, she said, "Oh, no. It is lost. My snood is gone. Just like my brother."

"There, now." I took her in my arms away from the cliff. "It's but a snood."

"But my lady mother will be angry," she said. "She told me I must be very careful with my things because she can't afford to replace them whenever I lose or soil them."

I let her down. I had no experience with young children, but she seemed to me a sad waif in her sodden gown and cloak, her hair tangled in braids. She was also shivering; by the looks of it, she had been outside for too long.

"You shouldn't be alone," I said gently. "It's starting to storm and the wind can be dangerous. What if it lifted you up and carried you away like your snood?"

She raked her foot back and forth on the ground. "Nobody would mind," she muttered. "They loved my brother best."

"I think your father would mind. He would miss you very much, I suspect."

Her solemn eyes lifted to contemplate me. "Yes, but he misses Henry more. I can tell. He cries a lot when he thinks no one is looking and he drinks too much. My lady mother shouts at him all the time. She says she should never have married him."

My heart went out to her. Girls were rarely prized like boys, for sons inherited while daughters wed and became their husband's chattel. I wondered what would happen to Abigail. Her circumstances were hardly conducive to a decent marriage, let alone personal happiness. Once again, anger at Lady Vaughan gripped me. Was the woman so callous that she would leave her own daughter to wander about like this, mourning her brother and subjected to cruel remarks not meant for her ears?

"Your mother is grieving," I said, trying to reassure her. "People sometimes say terrible things when they are hurting."

She turned wistful, gazing at the mausoleum. "I miss Henry. He always played with me. Now, he's not here and there's no one to play with us."

"Us?" I crouched down beside her. "Who else do you play with besides Henry?"

She shrugged. "We used to play with Raff, until Master

Godwin came to teach us and our lady mother said we couldn't play with him anymore. She hates Raff, too. She says he's a . . . a bastard?" Her brow crinkled. "Is that the right word?"

I nodded. "It is. But it's not a nice thing to call someone. Did Master Godwin like Raff? Was he kind to him?"

Her frown deepened. "Raff was afraid of him."

"He was? Why do you think he was afraid?"

She hunched her shoulders. "Master Godwin hit him once across the head and said he was a cur. After that, Raff kept away from him." She brightened with that unexpected urge to share that children display. "Henry and I would play games with Raff and his friend. It was fun."

"Friend?" My breath turned shallow. "He has a friend?"

"Oh, yes, but I'm not supposed to tell. We promised Raff, Henry and me. It's a secret."

"I can keep a secret," I said. Around us, the storm gathered force, the intermittent rain and flurries of snow starting to fall steadily. I had to pry this from her before I was obliged to bring her inside; I was surprised no one had come looking for her, but they would soon enough. "I know several secrets myself," I added. "In fact, just between you and me"—I hushed my voice in a way that I sensed she would respond to—"I am also a secret."

She giggled. "You are not! I can see you, so you cannot be a secret. Raff's friend is secret because you can't see him."

"Oh? Is he . . . invisible?"

Abigail nodded, leaning to me. She smelled of wet earth and damp wool. "He hides in the tunnels under the manor. He lives over there." She pointed past my head. I turned to look; she was indicating the squat watchtower on the western side of the manor.

"In the tower? Raff's friend lives all alone up there?"

"Yes." She clasped her hands in eager delight that she could confide something she had once shared with her brother. "He's shy. Raff says he cannot be seen by anyone because he's afraid the evil king will kill him." She sighed. "I can't visit him now that Henry is gone."

"You could take me." I wanted to grab her by the hand and force her to lead me there that instant. I would have thought it a mere child's tale, make-believe to pass the time in this forsaken place, were it not that from what I knew of him, I doubted Raff could have concocted such a story on his own. He surely was illiterate; and who would have cared enough about him to dandle him on his lap and recite such a fanciful fable?

Abigail said emphatically, "I cannot take you. The tunnels scare me. It's dark and there are too many spiders." She shuddered. "Ugh. I hate spiders."

"Me, too. I do not like spiders or the dark. But if we go together, we won't be afraid."

"No. I cannot." Her face shuttered again. "I am cold. Can I go inside now?"

"Yes, of course." Coming to my feet, I forced out a smile. "Let me take you."

"You don't have to." She pulled her cloak about her. "I know the way. The postern door is over there." Turning around to leave, she paused. She cast a shy look at me. "His name is Hugh. Please, if you go visit him try not to scare him. He's very shy."

Tugging at her damp skirts sticking to her legs, she scrambled through the cemetery to the manor, leaving me standing there under the rain, my cap dripping about my ears.

I had finally discovered the secret of Vaughan Hall.

A child was hidden in the tower.

* * *

could not wait to tell Shelton, but when I arrived at the stables, drenched to my very skin, I found him seated on the hay pile, nursing his stomach. To my surprise, the mastiff Bardolf lolled next to him with an adoring look on his massive face.

"Raff hasn't come back yet?" I asked, and Shelton grimaced.

"No, he hasn't. And lest you are wondering, I am feeling much better."

"I am sorry." I sat beside him, told him what I had learned. When I finished, he gave me a skeptical arch of his brow. "Children make up tales. It's hardly proof of anything untoward."

"Do you not see?" I said, as Bardolf thumped his tail under Shelton's caress. "She said the friend's name is Hugh. He lives in the tower. How can that not be proof?"

Shelton belched. He may have been feeling better but he did not look it. "I don't see how a children's game can tell us about whatever mishap happened to Lady Parry." He tried to shake his head but it evidently still hurt, for he winced. "You have your answer. Hugh is a make-believe friend. He's not real, while what happened to Lady Parry is quite a different matter." He let out a troubled sigh. "Call the spade by its name, lad."

"What does that mean?"

"That Lady Parry is dead." He held up his hand to cut off my protest. "Be reasonable. I know this place seems like a far corner of hell—and after what happened to me, I share your opinion— but is it not more likely she and this Godwin went to fetch a physician and were ambushed by brigands? The entire realm fell apart after Mary took the throne—not that it was safe to begin with. I think they fell afoul of men like those who came after us and we shall never know what happened to them. I think it is time for us to leave. There is nothing left for us to do here except kick up our heels."

I started to come to my feet in furious incredulity, until Bardolf, sensing my abrupt move, growled. "The beast has a liking for me," remarked Shelton. "He hasn't left my side since you came back. At least something here cares if I puke or die."

I bunched my fists at my sides. "What about that hooded rider we both saw on the horizon or the message that wretch imparted before he died? What about the attempt on the queen, the notes, and now this, your own near death? Someone *must* be behind this!"

"Why?" His quiet question made me even angrier. He was only speaking his mind, and much as I wanted to refute or deny him, he was making more sense than I cared to admit. "Maybe you only want to believe there is some plot because she put you to this errand. She asked you to help her, and you—as you have from the day you met her—feel obliged to fulfill her request at any cost. No," he said gruffly, again overriding my protest. "I know you're going to say that I never cared for her, and you would be right. Queen or not, Elizabeth attracts trouble wherever she goes. She is not like you and me, lad. She is a Tudor."

"I too share her blood," I retorted, stung by his words that reminded me uncomfortably of what Kate had said before I left court. "Have you forgotten it?"

"I could never forget it. You are her kin and you must be loyal. I admire you for it. But this isn't like those other times when you helped her. People have accidents; they die or disappear. Ale gets fouled; thieves assault travelers; assassins try to poison queens. It happens, but it does not mean anyone here hides a secret. It does not mean . . ." His voice faltered.

"Say it," I whispered.

"It does not mean Lady Parry's disappearance has to do with Sybilla." He went silent, watching me as I gritted my teeth.

"You think I am imagining it," I said at length. "You think I've spun a delusion to deal with my guilt because I failed to capture her before she leapt off the bridge."

"I think despite everything, you have a passion for her you cannot escape. You want this to be a plot so you can avenge what she did to you and Peregrine, though you know as well as I do that while you hunt a ghost, whoever seeks harm on the queen remains at large and you are no closer than you ever were to apprehending him. You should be at court, working together with Cecil and the others to find him, not wasting time here searching for secrets that do not exist."

I turned away. "I'll see that food brought to you. You must rest and regain your strength."

Shelton grunted, but he did not try to argue or call me back.

Once he had spoken the truth as he saw it, he invariably stood by it.

T he storm erupted with a torrential downpour and iron clashing of thunder.

Inside the manor, I ate alone in the hall, served a trencher of cold remnants from the previous night's feast by downcast Mis-

tress Harper, who informed me Master Gomfrey had not returned yet from Withernsea and his search for a replacement
for Agnes. Lord Vaughan and her ladyship, she added, had elected
to remain in their rooms.

This parsimonious display had a deliberation to it that outraged me. I was being treated like a troublesome errand boy,
forced to idle while they hid away in the hope I would grow tired,
throw up my hands, and leave. I ate what I could, drank my fill
of gritty well water (I wouldn't touch a cup of wine or ale), and
then climbed the stairs to my chamber, where I found myself
deliberating what I had learned thus far, as well as Shelton's unwelcome advice.

Was there a child hidden in the tower? Or had Abigail merely
imparted a game she had made up with two older boys? Maybe
she was confused, and Henry had devised the tale of Hugh, an
invisible friend. It made perfect sense, far more so than concealing a child; but something in my gut told me it was not so simple. There was a mystery here in Vaughan Hall. I *knew* it. It was
right under my nose and it all somehow connected to the stranger,
who in turn had a connection to the past. I must resolve it. Lady
Parry's very life could depend on it.

I lay back, pillowing my hands, staring up at the timber-
beamed ceiling. I played the events again, backward in my head.
The discoveries I had made since arriving here, about Lady
Vaughan's familial past and possible link to Sybilla, who had also
suffered losses during the Pilgrimage of Grace; the attack on the
road by those ruffians and the stranger watching us; and further
back, to the opening of the gifts in Elizabeth's apartments and the
horrifying death of her spaniel. I saw Kate once more, terrified

with the glove in her hand as I searched the upended box for clues. I dwelled on the note in cipher, sent to Dudley's seer, and Elizabeth's subsequent summons and the tattered message she had shown me.

You must pay for the sin.

Leaping up, I paced the room. What did it mean? What sin did this stranger seek to avenge and what link did he have to the woman everyone believed was dead and Vaughan Hall? I raked my hands through my hair. At my bedside, the tallow started to gutter. These seemingly disparate incidents must hold something in common. How could they not?

But, I suddenly thought, what if Shelton was right? Did I hunt a ghost from my past even as a murderer stalked the queen, and Lady Parry and Godwin lay in a wood somewhere, pecked over by crows?

The very possibility was chilling. It took a few moments to realize the tallow had gone out but when I turned to strike flint to it, I realized a vague glow still illuminated the room. Looking upward to the arrow-slit window, I saw muted light refracting off the thick pane, distorting it so that it flickered into my room like an eerie nimbus.

I was not tall and the window slit proved too high for me. Dragging the clothes chest to the wall, I perched on tiptoes, straining to look out. I grasped the latch and yanked it, but years of sea salt and grit had sealed it shut. Cursing, I went to fetch my poniard to dig into the crevices about its edges, not thinking of how I would explain the blade gouges in the stone, until I heard the latch pop and I yanked the leaded pane ajar. Gripping the sill with my hands, I pulled myself upward with my feet dangling, to peer through the slivered opening.

I found myself staring through rain and fog at the tower of the manor—a toadstool silhouette I could barely discern.

Faint light wavered there.

In the uppermost part of the tower, flame glowed.

I did not hesitate. Pulling on my soiled travel clothes, I cracked open the door, wincing as its hinges creaked. I peered into the corridor. No one was about. Easing my way toward the staircase, I no longer cared if the storm raged or was teeming with goblins. Someone was indeed in that tower and I must find out whom.

A growl froze me in my tracks. In the penumbra, I saw Bardolf, poised like a sentinel at the landing of the stairs. I did not move. He growled again, with a menace that I knew I should heed. I started to shift backward when he bounded toward me with heart-stopping swiftness.

I ripped my dagger from its sheath, braced for his assault. He came within inches of me, his breath rank and meaty. I liked dogs; I did not want to kill one, especially not the lord's pet. Bardolf lowered his ogre-like head to sniff my boots. I half expected his jaws to chomp on my foot, forcing me to plunge my blade between his shoulders, but after a thorough examination of the smells impregnated in my boot, he looked up, drooling, and nudged me with his snout.

"There now," I whispered. "Good boy." I did not dare touch him back, but he seemed assured that I posed no threat and let me move past him. I heard him padding behind me, a heavy clicking of nails on the floorboards, and though I would have preferred he remained where he was, I figured having him at my side as I went about my business might serve me well. He would certainly alert me to anyone, or anything, that lurked in the night.

I could not leave by the main entrance. A heavy iron bar had been lowered across the double doors, which I would have to lift, making enough noise to wake the entire house. Turning past the empty hall, I tried to remember the way Agnes had led me from the kitchens, thinking there must be access to the tower from the inner quadrangle. Abigail had spoken of tunnels, but I had no idea where to find them, even if I were inclined to go looking for underground passages in the middle of the night.

Electing to use the same corridor to the chapel, I proceeded cautiously, moving through deep shadow. I could barely see anything before me, but Bardolf's assured pace at my heels seemed to indicate I moved in a direction familiar to him. Surely, he must require some means to get outside to relieve himself; I could not fathom fastidious Lady Vaughan tolerating dog piss in her rushes, and soon enough, to my relief, colorless illumination beckoned—a postern door left ajar to the quadrangle, the same one through which Agnes had brought me from the root cellar.

I stepped into a clammy netherworld. The rain had ebbed, summoning in its wake a shroud of fog tainted by brine, muffling sounds, and shapes. I now understood Gomfrey hadn't sought to intimidate me. In such a dense miasma, it would be all too easy to lose my way and end up tumbling into a void to my demise. Pausing to take stock of my surroundings and allow my eyes to adjust to the gloom, I picked my path across the quadrangle. Things I had not noticed in my haste to escape from the root cellar with Agnes now loomed like fragments of petrified monsters—a broken coach, half capsized, with wheels sunk in hardened mud; barrels heaped in a haphazard pyramid; a makeshift awning over a stall for repairing objects. My heels crunched upon a soggy mixture of old gravel, sand, and dirt pooled on flagstone; I could barely hear my own footsteps but in my heightened awareness, I imagined they echoed like a giant's.

Bardolf dashed ahead. I clamped down on my cry to stop him as he vanished into the murky night, and I came to a halt, anticipating a sudden scuffle. When nothing happened, I moved on, nearing the tower, which grew larger and more forbidding than it seemed from a distance. All of a sudden, I was before it, staring at its rounded stone ribs, up to that single glowing window tucked under a decrepit peaked roof.

In the dripping silence, I thought I heard weeping. I paused, shutting out every other sense to amplify it. It was too faint to establish a definitive gender; but it sounded to me like a child, and as I made my way around the tower until I reached the adjoining manor wall, moving away from the window, the weeping faded. I knew then that I had definitely not imagined it. But when I rushed back to the spot, it was gone. So was the faint light, as if it had never been.

I started back around the tower, seeking an entrance until I located a door, square-cut and inset high above me, accessed by a shattered wooden staircase that clung like a cobweb to the tower side. The tower must have once functioned as refuge against a siege; but it had long since fallen into disrepair. The steps hung rotted, skeletal. Even if I could leap up and grab hold of the bottom rung, it would not support me. The entire dilapidated structure would crumble under my weight and send me crashing to injury or death.

I heard Bardolf return, his panting labored. He slipped past me to sniff at the ground. He paused, lifting his leg and jettisoning urine, and started snuffling once more.

"You make a fine watchdog," I muttered. Thunder grumbled in the distance. The rain resumed, not as hard as before but enough to make me wish I had not forgotten my cap. It was the bane of my life, this penchant for not having a cap at the most inopportune times, and I started to chuckle under my breath, thinking this was a fine to-do, roaming about at night in a storm, seeing strange lights and hearing disembodied cries from a tower which no doubt had stood deserted for ages.

Bardolf barked. I hushed him before I peered at where he stood, his stance alert, his tongue hanging out. He barked again. Lurching forward, I saw what lay directly under his paws.

A small trapdoor almost embedded in the quadrangle stone.

I leaned over to grab hold of its rusted handle. It was wet and slipped in my hand; I tugged at it until I felt my shoulders and arms burn. As I thought I would have to find another way inside—or better yet, relinquish my absurd notions and return to the manor and rest, so I'd be better equipped to deal with the lord and lady come morning—I heard the voice again. Only this time as I paused, crouched over the trapdoor, it came from above me: a chanting of sorts, like a child singing a defiant lullaby.

Bardolf's ears perked. He too looked up, whining in his throat.

"You heard it, boy?" I said and he turned expectantly as if to urge me to hurry up with whatever I was doing. I raced back to the sagging awning over the stall with its utensils. Everything was rusty, decayed to near uselessness. A bellow of frustration lodged in my throat. Was there nothing in the entire manor that actually functioned as it should? Finally, after scavenging near the heaped barrels, I located an old shovel. It was hardly in better shape than anything else but I splashed through pools of mud back to the trapdoor, lodging the shovel under its handle and hauling upward with all my might.

I was breathless now with exertion, sweat sliding down my back to mingle with the rain and adding to the chill of my sodden clothes. I was going to catch a fever, sure as night; and if anyone came upon me with a shovel trying to dislodge a trapdoor they were going to think me mad, as well. Still, I tried again, pushing the chipped shovel farther under the handle. Looking at Bardolf, who had sat in apparent content to watch, impervious to the rain beading his coat, I pressed down hard until I heard my own gasp of pain escape me.

The shovel's wooden handle broke, the ruptured part I held splintering and slicing my palm. With a curse, I flung the handle aside, sucking at the blood, when I saw I had cracked open the door just enough to see a crevice of darkness underneath it.

I went to my hands and knees, ignoring the dirt crusting my wound as I scraped and dug with the broken shovel around the door. After what felt like an hour of exhausting labor, I tried the handle again. It gave way a bit more, but still not enough. And the smell that wafted from within that small opening was putrid, making me think of dead things and compelling me to dig again, removing layers of caked dirt and moss even as the dreadful thought began to occur to me that a decomposing body might lie under here—Lady Parry's own, perhaps.

The next time I grabbed the handle, I managed to pull the door enough to get my hand and arm through. I encountered empty space, cool and damp. It must be a root cellar like the one near the garden postern, where those barricaded in the tower would have stored their foodstuffs. There was a broken bolt on the door's underside, too, which I felt with my fingers. It no longer worked, the passage of time and nature having sealed it to the door.

I went back to excavating, stopping only until I had to sit back on my heels, covered head to toe in grime. I had propped the door halfway open. I yanked at the handle again. The trapdoor finally gave way with a reluctant groan.

Bardolf was up, poking his nose eagerly into the opening. I had no idea what was down there and started to reach for his collar to detain him when he plunged inside with a joyous bark.

Dogs have a sense of danger, and he had not seemed perturbed in the least. Squeezing through the opening, which was wide enough for a basket but not much more, I dropped onto narrow steps leading into utter blackness, as if I were about to descend into a bottomless pit.

Above me, the tower was silent.

Whoever was up there knew someone else was here.

Ugh! I hate spiders. Abigail's words returned to me as I crept down the stairs. I was woefully unprepared; I didn't have a torch or even a stub of candle to light my path, even if I'd managed to keep the flint dry in the downpour, and my feet sloshed in my boots, making slurping sounds as I brushed against walls and careened around, expecting to stumble upon a corpse. The smell was dreadful, invading every part of me, yet as I forced myself to breathe through my mouth to mitigate the worst of it, I began to realize it was not the stench of decomposition but rather of human excrement. Perhaps the manor's latrines emptied near here, and with the rain, filth had seeped up through the ground into the cellar. I could not determine if the floor was wet, given my already sopping state, but I did not bump into anything else and slowly managed to make my way toward a lighter square of black in the overall black space.

It was a low archway, which I hit hard enough with my forehead to see a burst of stars. Ducking down, I passed under it into a bare chamber no larger than a shed. To my left rose another flight of narrow steps like a spine from the inside wall. It was still too dark, but Bardolf was nowhere in sight, so I assumed he had climbed the staircase. Taking the steps two by two without looking down, for there was no balustrade and I nursed a queasy dislike of heights, I kept my gaze fixed upward; the stairs wound to what seemed the very top of the tower. Then I reached a landing and door; withdrawing my dagger from my boot, I tried the latch, and the door swung open onto another chamber, larger than the one at the foot of the stairs, but still cramped. A poorly mortared arrow slit in the far wall allowed the night to seep through it, along with enough light to illuminate the room and show there was nothing inside it.

I returned to the stairs. The silence proved unnerving. I could hear my own heart beating fast in my ears and the drip-drip of my wet cloak on the stone behind me. It probably was neither wise nor safe to have come here without my sword, but I steeled my nerve with the reassurance that Bardolf had not barked again or made any indication from above that there would be trouble. He must know whoever was singing, and I doubted Gomfrey or Lord Vaughan would be huddled inside this tower crying and reciting children's songs during a storm.

It had to be Hugh, the mysterious secret friend. The Vaughans had deceived me. There was a boy hidden in their tower for some inexplicable reason—a child with whom Raff and their own son and daughter had played with, but whom they had not wanted me to discover. The explanation would come later. I would wring it from their throats if need be, but for now I was anxious to prove I wasn't teetering on the edge of insanity, that I had been right in assuming there was indeed a secret hidden here; and if the Vaughans had lied about it, how could I trust that they told the truth about Lady Parry?

I reached another door, which stood ajar. Light glimmered inside from a lantern or candle. I had not imagined it. I had to pause, ease the clench in my chest.

Please, try not to scare him. He's very shy.

If he was only a child, he would indeed be scared. Left here alone, he would be terrified to see me swagger in, smothered in dirt, like a fiend out of a nightmare. My attempts to brush the mud from my face were ineffective—I needed a thorough soaking in water and soap—but I did so anyway, even running my hands down my now-ruined tunic before I moved over the threshold.

Bardolf was lying on the stone floor, his tail wagging as he saw me standing there. My gaze took in everything at once—a large circular chamber, perched atop the tower under the peaked eaves, with a sagging cot in a corner, a tousled blanket over it, and a crooked stool and fruit crate upended on its side next to it. A wood trencher and askew lantern were on the crate, but the wick inside the lantern burned low, so that the light flickered and spluttered.

I did not see anyone. Taking another step inside, keeping one eye on Bardolf, I looked around. The chamber was the width of the tower's circumference, the main room where the inhabitants would have tried to survive an attack on the manor. There was no place to hide.

Then I returned my gaze to the bed. The blanket was more than rumpled. As I stared at it, I saw a slight rise and fall, a quiver of substance under the bunched fabric.

Someone was hiding under it.

"I'm not going to hurt you," I said softly, treading carefully to the bed, keeping the door behind me in case he bolted up and tried to escape. "I'm a friend. Abigail told me about you. I know you are Raff's secret friend. I'm here to see you safe." Even as I spoke in a manner I might have used to coax a potentially feral creature, I had no inkling the child could understand me, though he had played with the others and surely had some ability to communicate.

Coming to a halt, I saw the form under the blanket tremble, coiled upon itself in a knot.

I reached out to pull aside the blanket. A mop of ginger-colored hair showed; the sheen of tear-stained cheeks. I saw hands covering a face pressed into hunched knees.

"Hugh?" I whispered.

Taut silence fell. The boy stirred.

"You . . . you know my friend?" he asked, and Raff lifted his face to mine.

Chapter Seventeen

𝕴 could not speak for a bewildered moment. Raff regarded me with a plaintive, frightened cast in his eyes, and there was a quality to the light in the room, a subtle trace of shadow upon his face, that jolted me. He suddenly looked shockingly familiar.

"I don't know Hugh," I finally said, and as I heard the disappointment in my voice, I realized it should not matter. He was still a child, who had been cowering here over a day now. Someone in the house must have frightened him, sent him fleeing with an earful of threats and the order to hide from me. I stepped back a bit, to show him I meant no harm, and he sat up warily, eyeing me as if I might thrash him at any moment.

"Is your friend Hugh around here?" I asked, thinking perhaps the other child had also fled and was hiding somewhere in this tower.

He murmured, "Hugh always hides. He doesn't like strangers."

"Where does he like to hide?"

"He's . . ." Raff did not seem to know how to explain. "He is here," he finally said. "But he still hides." He looked down at his bare feet. A vein in his temple twitched.

Raff's friend is secret because you can't see him.

I suddenly wondered at my own confusion. Hugh must be a figment of Raff's imagination. The boy was undoubtedly strange but far from stupid. He had conjured an invisible playmate, as any boy in his situation would—to keep loneliness and fear at bay, to deflect the rejection and insults. He reminded me of myself at his age, with nowhere to belong, nothing to call his own, only I had had Alice. Until she left me, she had always been there to remind me that I meant something to someone in this unforgiving world.

"When the nice lady visits," Raff finally said cautiously, "she always tells Hugh to hide until she can come for him."

"Who is the nice lady?" I kneeled before him, without touching him. His hands were clasped in his lap; he had well-formed hands, marred with nicks and scrapes from his chores, but with long, slim fingers. "Are you speaking of Lady Parry?" I was guessing, but he started, looking at me again. "Do you know her, too?"

I nodded. "She is my friend. Might you or Hugh know where she is?"

He shook his head. "I don't know. Lady Vaughan made her go away. Lady Parry told Hugh to wait for her. But she never came back."

Lady Parry knew about Hugh? My confusion returned. It must have shown on my face, for with unexpected resolve Raff said, "Lady Parry says Hugh is special. She gave him a gift." Climbing off the cot, he pushed past me to tug the cot away from the wall. Crouching down, I heard him scratching and peeped under the cot to see him prying a loose paving stone from the floor. He reached inside a hole and withdrew something. "See?"

I took the object, wrapped in a worn blue cloth bag. Untying its frayed cords, I upended it into my palm. A tarnished silver ring fell out, with an impressive cabochon sapphire embedded in it. "Where did you get this?" I asked, bemused.

With a patient sigh, Raff replied, "I told you. Lady Parry gave it to Hugh," and he ran his fingertip along the ring's edge. I heard a tiny click; the stone embedded in the ring popped up via an ingenious lever, revealing a miniature painted on its silver-backed underside.

It took me a moment to see what it was: a slender figure dressed in a red-gold gown, holding a book. Disbelief exploded inside me. I had seen a larger version of this very portrait hanging in Hatfield's hall; I recognized the parted hair under the pearled hood, the narrow, almost elfin face, the enigmatic eyes—

"Dear God," I heard myself whisper. "This is Elizabeth."

Raff cocked his head. "The lady in the ring is called Elizabeth?"

I dragged my gaze to him. How had I not seen it before? In the shifting interplay of shadow and light cast by the ebbing lantern, his eyes were just like hers—a mercurial sable gold like a lion's, so that at certain angles they appeared almost black, their slant more exaggerated in him but as heavy-lidded as hers. And his hands: He had her long, slim hands. . . .

My entire world capsized. I collapsed against the cot as if my bones had turned to liquid, my hand clutching the ring. I kept looking down at her tiny painted figure, a duplicate of a portrait she once told me had been painted when she was only fourteen years old.

"The nice lady," I whispered. "Lady Parry, she—she brought Hugh this?"

He nodded. "Hugh likes to look at it when he is alone. But it is a secret." He smiled. "I know how to keep secrets. Lady Parry told me to hide the ring for Hugh. She told me I must keep the ring and Hugh hidden at all times."

When the nice lady visits she always tells Hugh to hide until she can come for him.

I was having trouble breathing. Hugh was Raff.

And Raff . . . he must be Elizabeth's son.

Outside the tower, the wind keened. I had not heard it swooping about the eaves, so stunned by the revelation that everything beyond it ceased to exist. But as the sounds returned to me—rain shattering against the walls, the sizzle of the dying wick, and the soft, watchful panting of Bardolf on the floor—the danger of my predicament overcame me.

Lady Parry had disappeared because of this boy. He was the secret of Vaughan Hall.

I had to get him away from here.

Raff sensed my sudden disquiet. He backed away, toward Bardolf, who rose to his questing hand. I detected no aggression in the dog's stance but I knew that if I tried to harm the boy in any way Bardolf would probably defend him.

"We must leave now," I said to Raff. "Can you do that with me?"

He went pale. "I cannot leave. Lady Parry says I live here. This is my home."

"What about Hugh? Doesn't he want to meet the lady in the ring? Her name is Elizabeth and I know her. She is also my friend. Can you ask Hugh if he will leave with me?"

The boy went still. It was the confirmation I needed, if I still harbored any doubt. Shattered by everything that had been done to him, Raff had devised an alternate self, a secret named Hugh, someone who could be his companion and whom he could share with the other children—an imaginary friend who was, in fact, all too real.

"We can bring the lady in the ring with us." I returned the ring to its bag, showed it to him, and then carefully inserted it into the inner pocket of my cloak. "See? She'll be safe here."

Raff remained immobile, his hand on Bardolf. I was dreading the thought of seizing him against his will, if I could even manage it without fending off the mastiff, when, to my immense relief, he nodded. He still seemed uncertain but no longer afraid.

"Hugh wants to go."

He turned to the door. Bardolf stretched out his front legs, emitting an enormous yawn that gave me a full view of the bone-crushing size of his maw, and padded after the boy. Raff looked at me from the door. "Are you coming?"

Jerking forward, I took him by the hand.

He was frightened of the storage room. He refused to go near it and wanted to bring me the other way, through another opening, which I had failed to notice in the wall of the lower chamber—a ragged hole that must lead into the tunnels Abigail had mentioned. Raff must have come in and out of the tower through those tunnels, but I had only to look at the open-

ing to know I would never get through it. Though I was not a
large man, it was too small for anyone bigger than Raff—which
explained why no one else used it save for him and the Vaughan
children.

Only after I reassured him that Bardolf had been in the storage room and look, he wasn't scared, did Raff allow me to take
him in my arms, wrap my cloak about him, and bring him up
the stairs through the trapdoor.

The rain pelted. With him against me, I staggered and stumbled through the quadrangle to the kitchens. Here, he stiffened
again, saying anxiously, "I am not allowed anywhere in the
house. Lady Vaughan says stable boys do not sleep indoors."

"Lady Vaughan is asleep," I said. "Close your eyes." I felt him
settle his cheek against my shoulder. The ferocious need to protect him gave me strength as I tiptoed into the fire-lit kitchens,
Bardolf behind. Unhooking the key to the root cellar, I unlocked
the door and moved into the passage through which Agnes had
brought me, praying the other trapdoor in the cellar would require the same key. Setting Raff down, I unlocked it with a sigh
of relief and we dashed up the steps into the garden.

He refused to let me pick him up again. He seemed relieved
now that we were outside the manor, and as I led him toward the
stable block, he asked, "Where are we going?"

"Far away," I told him. "You will go with my manservant,
Scarcliff. He looks like an ogre but he is strong and brave. He
will protect Hugh almost as well as you have."

Raff quavered, "He . . . he will not hurt me like Master
Godwin? He kicked me when he saw me playing with Master
Henry. He said I should be drowned."

"I promise you he's not anything like Master Godwin." Raff's words clarified why he had fled to the tower. The crippled tutor had mistreated him and Shelton's limp must have been noticeable to his keen eyes. He had associated it with the previous abuse inflicted on him.

In the stables, Shelton slumbered. I shook his shoulder, waking him. He blinked groggily, his one eye widening when he saw Raff behind me with the dog. "So, you found the dimwit," he croaked. "Where was he hiding?"

"Never mind that. You must get up. I need you to take him away."

"Away?" Shelton righted himself on his elbows. "Are you mad? It's storming like a witch's cauldron out there. I'm not going anywhere until you tell me why you want me to—"

"Shelton." The harshness in my voice stopped him. "Listen to me: This boy is why I was sent here. He is the reason Lady Parry came and, I think, why she disappeared. I do not have time to explain it to you. *We* do not have time. He is in danger. Now, get Cerberus ready."

He did not hesitate, reaching for his boots. "Where should I take him?"

I paused, considering. "Not to London. Take him to Hatfield. Elizabeth's governess, Mistress Ashley, is there; tell her who you are and that I sent you with the boy to seek refuge. She'll know why," I added grimly. "I've a feeling she's always known, just as Lady Parry did."

"Hatfield it is." He was already on his feet, towering over Raff as he bent his maimed features to him. "Can you ride a horse, boy?"

Raff shook his head. "Not one like yours."

"No matter," said Shelton. "I'll put you on the saddle croup. You hold on tight, you hear me? It's quite a fall if you don't."

Within minutes, he had saddled Cerberus and led him out of the stall. Cinnabar neighed. After I tucked the blanket Shelton had been lying on over Raff, I took up the saddlebag with Shelton's belongings and handed it to him. "I don't have any coin. That wench Agnes stole my purse. She had another key to my chamber, it seems."

He chuckled. "You never were much good with money or caps." He patted the saddlebag. "Not to fret. I've a little coin Nan gave me, in case we ran out of ale."

"Shelton," I said, "you must guard him with your life."

"Aye, I understand." He strapped on his broadsword and beckoned Raff, who went to him with the blanket clutched about him. He hoisted the boy onto the saddle, then used the block to heave himself up and, clicking his tongue, rode Cerberus out without looking back.

I stood under the rain, watching them canter to the manor gates and into the swirling dark. Not until they had vanished from view did I turn back to the manor.

It was time to tear out the heart of the mystery in Vaughan Hall.

As I walked back to the garden trapdoor, I prepared for my next move. I would not confront the Vaughans until morning; I needed enough time to elapse for Shelton to be well on his way to Hertfordshire and for Gomfrey to return from the village. The steward had a role in this; whether directly or as a witness, he was astute enough to have sensed Raff was no ordinary bastard. He might even know where Lady Parry had been taken or who Godwin truly was.

My attention fixated on the tutor. Lady Vaughan said he had been with the family only six months yet had made a previous trip to London to place an order for books. Like everything in this wretched place, the truth was more obscure. Lady Parry had not traveled here solely to tend to the sick in the house, I suspected, but to ensure Raff did not fall ill, perhaps even to take him to safety from the fever. She must have been appalled to discover him toiling in the stables and at the gates, sleeping wherever he could, treated worse than the family dog.

You must pay for the sin.

I had not been wrong. All the events that had transpired were part of a vendetta against Elizabeth, whose sin this stranger I sought had somehow discovered. Was the stranger Godwin, who had worked in this very house? Lord Vaughan had lied when he claimed the boy was his, which indicated that at least he, if not his wife, knew whose son they sheltered. Had the tutor found out and seized Lady Parry because of it? If so, I might still hold out hope that she was alive, for whatever Godwin planned, he had not taken Raff. Perhaps he had tried but the boy had evaded him as he had me, hiding away to avoid being captured.

I did not know, but Raff had clearly learned how to fend for himself. If he were indeed about ten years old, Elizabeth would have only been sixteen when she bore him. It must have happened after her father King Henry's death, during the reign of her brother. In those years, I still dwelled in Dudley Castle, unaware of events at court, but I could imagine the terror Elizabeth must have felt. She may have been the king's sister but she was still the daughter of Anne Boleyn, who had been beheaded for treason and adultery. Both Lady Parry and Mistress Ashley had served Elizabeth since her childhood; they must have connived to have her deliver her babe in secret and selected this remote manor to hide him, far from prying eyes. Where better than among Lady Parry's kin, where Elizabeth could keep watch through her trusted servant?

If Lady Parry had not been there to fight for me . . . I might not have lived to see this day.

Yes, I had no doubt both Lady Parry and Ashley were complicit. As astonishing as it seemed, it also did not escape me that Raff's situation had unsettling echoes of my own. Here I was, a secret Tudor, sent unknowingly to find another like me. It must be why Elizabeth had selected me for this assignation, though she did not know who I truly was. Lady Parry's disappearance had caused her great distress not only for the lady herself, but for the child she had come to see. Elizabeth could not have risked sending anyone else to Vaughan Hall but me, because I was the only one who would keep her secret. Once again, she had misled me by withholding the truth, but I found that I could not blame her. How could she have confessed something so dangerous, so damning, in midst of the court, with ears at every door, with everyone around her watching and waiting to catch her in some inadvertent admission?

These thoughts had me in such turmoil, I did not realize I was no longer alone until I entered the kitchens, replaced the key, and turned to find Mistress Harper. She kneaded her skirts, her face marked by the crease of her bedsheets, her bonnet askew on her head as she said tremulously, "You should not have done it. You should have left good enough alone."

I took an enraged step toward her. "It is *they* who should not have—" I started to retort and then the blow came from behind, a hammer upon my nape. I felt its impact shudder through me, the pain like a hot sun, so intense it scorched everything black.

After that, I felt nothing more.

Chapter Eighteen

He must be killed! He knows everything. He has spirited that bastard away and as soon as he leaves us, he will report it all—to *her*. He will be our ruin!"

The shrill voice reached me through a head-thudding stupor. I felt, as Shelton had aptly described it, as if a thousand imps wielded poleaxes in my temples, and when I attempted to open my eyes, the light blinded me.

Light. There was sunlight. It was day.

I tried to struggle but could not move my arms or legs. For a horrified moment, I feared my injury had rendered me immobile for the rest of my life. I had heard of blows to the head that left a man unconscious until he came to, only to discover himself trapped inside a useless body.

Forcing one eye open, I stared downward. I sat on a chair, my ankles bound. The pounding in my head did not permit me to look around, but the burning ache across my chest indicated I had been tied, my arms restrained behind me and fastened at the wrists.

Shadows darkened my vision. I blinked repeatedly, unable to

~open my other eye. Then, as my surroundings floated slowly into view, I saw the long table before me.

I was in the manor hall.

"This has to end, Philippa," said a weary voice that belonged to Lord Vaughan, though I heard him as if he spoke through a hollow tube. "We cannot go on like this. He knows, yes, but we'll only bring more trouble upon our heads if we harm him."

"More trouble?" A shrill laugh erupted from Lady Vaughan. "You do not know anything! You have not seen how they can gut a man while he hangs from a rope, throw him like a slab of beef onto a block, and yank out his entrails while he still lives. But I have. I know how long they can make the agony last, and I assure you, husband, you are not fit for such martyrdom."

A teary sniffling reached me. I strained to detect from whence it came when I heard Lady Vaughan snap, "Stop mewling, girl. You brought this on yourself! I told you to get him on his back, pleasure him until he slept, then steal his purse and bring it to me, not run off to that miserable hamlet. Had you done as you were told, you'd not be in this position."

Agnes lifted terrified protest. "But, he didn't want me! He questioned me. He—he threatened me! What was I to do—" A stinging slap cut off her wail.

"Shut up." Lady Vaughan's skirts brushed against my legs. I felt them as she passed by, thank God. I was not injured to the point of being paralyzed, only immobilized by my restraints.

"Enough." Lord Vaughan's voice slashed through Agnes's piteous sobbing. "Gomfrey found her, didn't he? He brought her back. There is no need to strike her."

"Oh?" retorted Lady Vaughan. "She defied my orders. She was going to run off to York, or even London, perhaps, with his coin in her bodice and quite a tale to sell. She must go into the sea with him. She is no use to us now."

Agnes wailed. I heard the staccato clatter of heels on the floor, a sudden gasp that was not the maidservant's, then Lord Vaughan's trembling voice: "I said, enough. I will not be party to such infamy. We are not murderers. It is over, Philippa. Do you hear me? *Over.*"

As Lady Vaughan cried, "He'll see us to the gallows!" Lord Vaughan ordered, "Gomfrey, release him."

The steward stepped from somewhere behind me; as he came around with a dagger to kneel at my feet and cut loose the ropes of my ankles, I glared at him.

He recoiled. "He's awake!" He scuttled backward on his knees, his cowardice giving me a savage rush of satisfaction. Had my leg been loose, I would have kicked him.

"You'd best learn to crawl," I rasped. "You'll be doing a lot of it by the time I'm through with you."

Lady Vaughan stood as though petrified, clasping her wrist where her husband must have grabbed her, Agnes huddled beside her, bound to a stool. Lord Vaughan stood a few paces from them; as his dark-circled eyes met mine, I saw the desperate toll that years of hiding Elizabeth's secret had wreaked on him.

His look of defeat urged me to move. A drunkard, grief-stricken over his son, he had let matters come to such a pass that they had assaulted the queen's own man. I was by no means safe, despite his effort to subdue his wife.

"He—he heard us," said Lady Vaughan. "Blessed Virgin, he heard everything." She barked at Gomfrey: "Kill him now."

I lunged forward, pulling my chair with me against the floor. "Do it and you shall indeed perish on the gallows. The queen will send others, should I fail to return. She will send her own guard and then, by God, she'll raze this manor to the ground for what you have done!"

Lord Vaughan stood utterly still. His wife pushed past him, stalking up to me. Her expression twisted, that trace of faded beauty I had marked when we first met vanquished by the ravenous hatred consuming her. "You think your heretic queen will save you?" she spat. "You think she'll send her yeomen and lords of the Privy Council to bring us to task?" Her eyes narrowed. "I think not. She sent you here with only a manservant; she may have told you she sought Lady Parry but she lied." She paused, taking in my silence. "Your queen never dispatched an escort to fetch Lady Parry back. That note we found on the saddle: My lord husband sent it to her along with a letter, assuring her that her secret was safe. I rather think she will welcome your disappearance, as well. She never wanted her wanton error revealed."

The icy meaning of her words sank into me like teeth. "You are wrong," I whispered. "That child, he means everything to her."

"Oh?" She smiled with a callous disregard that made me want to throw myself at her throat. "He might have once, but not now. She knows well how every Catholic in this realm believes her illegitimate. She will be fortunate to see her own coronation, much less live out the year. Should it come to light she hid away a bastard, they will take her down like wolves. They'll tear her apart and put her cousin, our rightful queen, Mary of Scots, in her place."

"You will die for this," I told her, but she did not flinch.

"No," she said. "It is you who shall die."

The resolve in her voice made me struggle against my tethers, yanking furiously at the ropes even as she reached out her hand to Gomfrey. "Your knife."

Still crouched on the floor, the steward extended the blade to her, as Agnes yowled in the background. Anticipation suffused Lady Vaughan's face. I braced for her thrust even as I strained to break free. I would die fighting for my last breath.

She did not hear her husband come from behind her, the candlestick he swiped from the table aimed at her head. He brought it down with a sickening crack. Her eyes flared. She swayed, the dagger dropping from her fingers. She started to turn around, exposing to me the wound on the back of her head, then she toppled into Lord Vaughan's arms.

As he sank to the floor with her, he said, "Have mercy on us," and started to weep.

Gomfrey cut my restraints. Shoving him aside, I staggered to my feet and looked down at the lord of the manor with his dead wife in his arms, crying as he buried his face in her bloodied hair. I said hoarsely to the steward, "Untie the girl."

While Gomfrey hastened to free Agnes, I leaned against the table. My legs threatened to buckle under me, but a cautious probing of my own nape detected only a painful knot. My left eye was swollen shut, no doubt blackened from my fall to the kitchen floor, which was why I was having such trouble opening it. Otherwise, though battered and bruised, I would survive.

Mistress Harper emerged tentatively from the doorway leading to the kitchens. She gasped when she saw the scene before her and rushed to Agnes, who sat limp on the stool, her bindings strewn at her feet as she moaned.

"See to her," I heard myself say. My voice was flat.

"Yes, at once," Mistress Harper quavered. She dragged Agnes to her feet, one arm about the girl's waist. Turning to Gomfrey, who had regained something of his impassive demeanor, I ordered, "Fetch my belongings from my chamber and bring them here."

With a terse turn of his heel, he left to do my bidding. A servant to his marrow, he knew better than to challenge me now that the edifice of lies his master and mistress had built had come tumbling down about their collective ears.

I sidestepped Lady Vaughan's body.

I could not find it in myself to care that she was dead.

An hour later, after I washed myself with a pitcher Mistress Harper brought me, changed into my court doublet, hose, and breeches, and stuffed my filth-stiffened clothes into my bag, I returned to the hall. Pale and still sniffling, Agnes had my cloak; it was then that I belatedly remembered Raff's ring. I snatched my cloak from her, probing the inner pocket. When I felt its small bulk there, I waved her aside and turned to find Lord Vaughan waiting.

He had had his wife's corpse taken away. Bardolf reclined at his feet and little Abigail sat beside him, ashen with fright. Before I could utter a word, Lord Vaughan said, "I will tell you everything. I swear it on my daughter's soul. Only, I beg you"—his voice fractured—"do not arrest me. I am all my daughter has left."

I hardened my reply, though I had already determined it was

not my role to condemn him. "Your only hope is that you with-hold nothing more. When was Raff brought to you?"

"In the winter of 1548," he replied in a thread of a voice. "My aunt, Lady Parry . . . she came here with him at night. Philippa had not been able to conceive. After everything she had suf-fered, she thought God was punishing her. When Lady Parry arrived with a man unknown to us and the babe in her arms, we thought God himself had answered our prayers. We were assured the child was healthy; all we need do was care for him as if he were our own. My aunt promised us we would lack for nothing; she gave us a sum of money and said we had only to send word to her using a cipher provided by the man with her, one Master Parry, though he bore no relation to us. She did not say whose child it was and I did not ask. But I knew. I knew al-most at once."

Master Parry was Elizabeth's treasurer, whom I had met at Hatfield and whom she had told me to contact should I need money. The plot to hide her child had indeed originated from deep within her most intimate ranks.

"How did you know?" I drew a chair up beside him. Abigail pressed her face into her father's doublet as Lord Vaughan ca-ressed her hair. He then called for Mistress Harper, who hastened in. "Please," he said, "take my daughter to her room." Abigail tried to resist, clinging to her father until Mistress Harper managed to coax her away. As she left clutching the woman's hand, I felt a deep sorrow for her. She had lost her brother and seen her own father murder her mother, albeit to protect me. She would never forget it, marked by the tragedy in her home.

"I may look like a country fool," Lord Vaughan said once we

were alone, "but even I had heard the rumors during one of my trips to London, something about the princess and the king's younger uncle, Admiral Seymour, who had wed King Henry's widow, Kate Parr. It was said there had been flagrant behavior: an incident of the widow Parr restraining the princess in the garden while Seymour cut her dress to shreds, and other more disturbing tales of him bursting into the princess's bedchamber when she was abed, near-naked himself, while all her ladies watched. The widow queen finally sent the princess away to a manor in Cheshunt. Her own brother King Edward forbade Elizabeth to set foot in court. And then," he added, lowering his voice, "the arrests came."

"Admiral Seymour," I said, thinking quickly of what I knew. "He was arrested by his brother, Lord Somerset, was he not? He was tried and executed for treason."

Lord Vaughan sighed. "He was, indeed. I remember it well because the princess was also questioned and several of her servants, including Master Parry, sent to the Tower for a time. The Admiral was condemned of plotting to marry her, but she denied any knowledge of it. Shortly thereafter our payments for Raff's upkeep ceased."

"You had payments?" I thought Elizabeth had indeed risked her life by hiding away her son. If Seymour was Raff's father and the child's existence discovered, it would have made her appear guilty in Seymour's plot. She could have bowed her head to the sword like her mother before her. Had she, in her youthful exuberance, consented to Seymour's advances? Or had something more sinister occurred under his roof, a violation of a girl by a man who was supposed to be her guardian, the husband of her stepmother, the widowed queen?

"Yes," said Lord Vaughan. "For almost a year, payments came quarterly, issued through a solicitor in York, a client of Master Parry's. I had to travel there to receive them. Sometime following Seymour's execution, the payments stopped. I made inquiry but the solicitor had no explanation to offer. Then he disappeared. Gone abroad, I was told. I wrote several times to my aunt, using Parry's cipher. On a few occasions she came to visit and left a small jewel or purse of coin but never enough to see to our needs and by then my own livelihood was suffering."

"Did you ever try to contact the princess directly?" I asked.

"Never. I am a loyal subject, as I assured you. I never shared Philippa's belief that the Tudors were accursed for breaking with Rome or imposing heresy on us. I am of the old faith but no traitor. I kept my head down and trusted that in time, the monies due would be sent."

"But they never were?" His account fitted with what I knew of the manner in which Elizabeth had lived toward the end of her brother's reign. As young Edward began to sicken, those who ruled in his name harbored constant fear of a revolt and did their utmost to subdue both Elizabeth and her sister Mary by keeping them impoverished and far from court.

"It was as though Raff had been forgotten," Lord Vaughan went on, "and once Philippa gave birth to our children she began to nurture this hatred of him. We had seen by then that while he was indeed robust—he almost never had an ailment—he was . . . unusual. Not simple, but not normal, either. Philippa did not want him near her; she believed he would curse our children. We engaged nursemaids from the village when he was a babe, but once he grew old enough, Philippa refused him any affection. She could not abide kindness shown to him. Her loathing of him grew until I thought she might have seen him dead had I not been here to protect him."

"Protect him?" My voice was sharp. "You call what he has endured *protection?*"

"I did what I could," he said sadly. "I know it was not enough, but as the years passed, Raff became something we feared, a child that must be kept secret, though we had never asked for him. Philippa kept saying we should give him to a farmer far away, to rid ourselves of the obligation; but how could I allow that, given who he was? I insisted that he must be educated and be raised with our own children."

"You speak as if your wife had no idea of whose child she spoke of."

He hesitated for a moment. "Perhaps in some part of her, she did," he said at length. The admission seemed to pain him. "I never told her of my suspicions but I think she shared them, only she found it easier to deny. She finally accused me of having been unfaithful with some doxy during one of my trips to London and then, having entrusted the child to my aunt, concocting a scheme to hide the fact that Raff was mine. She was so vehement; she relished making me feel guilty and I let her. I thought it better for her to blame me instead of the boy."

I leaned back in my chair. The hall was dimming, the afternoon fading toward early winter dusk. "She certainly knew who Raff was today," I reminded him. "She admitted as much and implied he had been deliberately abandoned here, among other things."

"Yes. She changed her tune after the tutor arrived," he said.

A shiver went through me. "Why? Did Godwin know about Raff?"

"He never mentioned it, if he did. Indeed, he seemed to despise and disregard the boy as much as Philippa did."

"Can you describe him to me?" I leaned toward him again, intent now on this revelation that the tutor's appearance had altered the situation in the household.

"He was . . ." Lord Vaughan considered, his hand trembling slightly as he smoothed the blood-spotted front of his doublet. "How shall I put it? You could not find a more diffident man, almost submissive. He always wore black and he spoke softly, so you had to pay close attention to what he said. Yet he had this air of sophistication, which he used to great effect. He entranced Philippa. He was comely, if too thin and pale, and despite his crippled leg, elegant of movement. He did not seem to me like a man who must earn his board teaching children, but then, as Philippa often said, I should know more than most to which depths people could fall."

"What did she mean by that?" I said. "What depths did she refer to?"

"I suppose the fact that she too had fallen, marrying beneath her rank." A bitter smile twisted his mouth, betraying that while he might never admit it aloud, he too had suffered for his choice of a spouse. "She never let me forget that had the circumstances been different, I would not have won her hand. In any event, she declared Godwin a gentleman, like those she had met growing up in her father's house, of good breeding and position, who had, like her, lost much in the upheaval following King Henry's break with Rome."

"Was Godwin papist, too?"

Vaughan assented. "He attended mass with us, so, yes, he must have been." His voice hardened a fraction. "I began to think my wife was in love with him. To hear her speak, you would think Godwin could do no wrong; it was he, in fact, who suggested Raff was no longer a suitable companion for our children and must be put to work instead. He told Philippa the boy was simple, hopeless at his lessons; that he ran off and hid for hours, and was leading our children astray. Philippa was adamant that Raff tend the stables. We had so few servants as it was and so much work to maintain the very roof over our heads . . ." He avoided my stare, his face visibly affected by his recollection. "Regardless, I carry the blame, for I did not argue against it. She would hear nothing in his defense and Raff—he had such fear of Godwin. He avoided the tutor at any cost."

"So, you let your wife and a hireling dictate the rule of your house," I said, disgusted by his weakness, even as I was now certain Master Godwin had had far more sinister intent that Lord Vaughan could ever have suspected.

"Not entirely," he started to say. Then he paused. "Master Godwin worked for meager pay," he explained. "We could hardly afford a tutor in the situation we were in, and Philippa was constantly fretting that he might seek a better position, though he told her he was content with a room and his books. I reasoned, as he was crippled, he must have had difficulties securing posts in the city—Londoners being what they are—and Raff preferred to be outside; he loved the animals, often bedding in the stables of his own accord. Bardolf followed him everywhere, and he had a sure hand with the horses, almost a talent for sensing if they were hurt or ill. He was more himself with the beasts than with any of us, and didn't seem to mind."

I had no doubt Raff had welcomed it, anything to escape Lady Vaughan and the tutor. I kept the thought to myself, however, for there remained a final piece to the mystery I needed to resolve. "You did not like or trust Master Godwin yet you allowed him to accompany Lady Parry to fetch the physician for your son. I must confess that I find that strange. Why would you entrust your aunt's safety to the very man whom you believed your wife conspired with?"

"What I told you about that day is the truth," he insisted. "No, I did not care for Godwin. How could I? No man cares to see his wife beholden to another, but he taught our children well and never showed us any disrespect. York is but a day away. My son was dying. Godwin offered to be of service, and with my aunt so determined, it seemed the only way. I did send that note we found on her horse to court. It was the first time I had dared write to the queen. Philippa was irate; the fact that Godwin had also vanished, along with Henry's death—she wanted us to hide any evidence of Lady Parry's visit and report that my aunt had never arrived here. I refused. I told her we must welcome any assistance Her Grace could provide. But no one came until you."

I believed him. I saw it in his eyes, the anguished candor. He had killed his own wife to stop her from destroying whatever was left of his life; he had done it for Abigail, more than to save me, but he had not willingly dispatched Lady Parry to her fate. Yet perhaps his wife had; perhaps she and Godwin had been planning something nefarious that Lady Parry's unexpected arrival had interrupted. Perhaps the very reason for her rift with Lady Philippa had arisen because Lady Parry had suspected her and Godwin and confronted them. I might never discover their intent now. Philippa Vaughan was dead, and though I had found Raff, I was no closer to discovering the whereabouts of Lady Parry or the tutor, though now I believed at least one of them was alive. Godwin's horse had never been found. What if he had taken Lady Parry after they left the manor? If so, he could be the stranger who had sent the poisoned box to the queen and stalked me on the journey here.

Nevertheless, in order to satisfy or refute my suspicions, I had to return to court. I had to expose my own self and wait for him to strike. He had had plenty of time and opportunity to come for me here, and thus far, he had kept his distance since the incident on the road. Whatever he planned, I had the disquieting sense that he wanted me back in London.

"This cipher you were provided to correspond with Lady Parry: Do you still have it?"

Lord Vaughan gave me a startled look. "I . . . I fear not." As he saw me frown, he added, "I wanted to employ it to compose my letter to the queen, but when I went to find it, I realized it was gone."

Chapter Nineteen

𝕴 immediately had Vaughan search his study—a mess of documents and estate paperwork strewn everywhere in the chasm that had opened around him since his son's death. Following several hours of futile exploration, he failed to unearth the cipher. He was deeply apologetic, almost distraught as he told me he had always stored it with the bundle of letters from his aunt. He showed me the letters, wrapped in faded ribbon and kept in the back of a desk drawer.

"It was here," he said. "I swear to you; it's been here for years, ever since Raff came to us. I used it various times to read the letters my aunt sent. I don't understand how I could lose it."

"You did not lose it," I replied. "Godwin took it from you."

His face blanched. I did not explain further, striding back into the hall to prepare my departure. Though I could not condone what Lord Vaughan had let happen, upon my return to court I would do everything I could to shield him from Elizabeth's wrath. He was misguided and craven, enslaved to drink and his wife's caprice, but he was not cruel. He had no doubt been the sole bulwark between Raff and Lady Vaughan. If only for that, he deserved mercy. He could not have known that in hiring Godwin, he had admitted a viper into his house. That cipher he believed lost was the key to the letter in the poisoned box. Godwin had stolen and used it. He was indeed the stranger behind Lady Parry's abduction and the attempt on the queen; he was the man I hunted. I had to find him before he found me.

I departed Vaughan Hall under the cover of night. As I rode away, Bardolf stood at the gates and lifted a mournful howl.

As Cinnabar was eager to stretch his legs after too many days in the stable, I gave him rein, galloping through Withernsea with the promise that I would never see that dismal village again. In my cloak pocket, I carried Raff's ring.

I barely stopped until I reached London, pausing only to rest for a few hours and fill both my belly and that of my horse in whatever ramshackle inn I found, before pushing onward, almost past endurance. Steady snowfall fell as I neared the city. Upon reaching the gates, the church bells tolled for evensong, a cacophony of sonorous clangs that warmed my icy feet and hands. Home, I thought. I was home at last; and with this thought, a smile cracked my dry lips. Not long ago, London had been a wasteland of terror and sorrow for me, but now as I rode through the crowded streets to Whitehall, I remembered that I had not yet visited the churchyard near the Tower, where Peregrine lay buried. I must go there once this assignation was over, to pay my respects and tell him that I would never stop mourning or missing him and I had found another boy who needed me—forsaken, often scared yet never defeated, a child like each of us had been.

I showed my safe conduct signed by the queen to sentinels

posted outside the palace. Increased security was evident every-where I looked, guards stationed at the foot of every staircase and by every exit. I led Cinnabar across the inner courtyard to the stable block, where I brushed him down and saw him safely in his stall, then paused at the water trough to gaze into the near-frozen water.

My reflection was dim but I saw enough of my appearance to realize I would never get past the guards encircling Elizabeth's apartments. I should have made my way to my chamber in the palace and at least attempted to make myself more presentable.

I did not. Hurrying up the staircase, I strode through the tapestried labyrinth of passages where few courtiers lingered; it was that rare hour between royal appearances, if Elizabeth had even been making them—too late for her daily stroll in the gal-lery and too early for her repast in the hall. It suited me fine; I would prefer not to contend with anyone outside her immedi-ate circle. With any luck, Cecil and her councilors would be at various tasks, scheming over their papers, so she and I could speak alone.

In my mind, I braced myself. I had thought of little else during the journey back, reciting words that varied between accusatory and reproachful. She had sent me to Vaughan Hall without the truth, as Kate had warned. Once again, she had relied on my loyalty to play on my emotion and see to it that I left without being fully aware of what lay at stake. I knew she could not have told me here, in this place of subterfuge, with every room in-fested with ear holes; but she still should have imparted more than she had. All I could reason was that she had feared telling me her secret. She must not have slept easy all these years, bur-dened by the sacrifice she had made, but she had still sent Lady

Parry to Vaughan Hall. Only weeks on her throne, one of her first acts had centered on Raff. I must at least allow her an explanation.

I ran my hands over my soiled doublet, adjusting my belt and eyeing my mud-spattered boots as I neared the archway to her apartments. As I had anticipated, guards were there, sprawled in the alcove, caps at their sides as they played dice with the relaxed demeanors of men with too much time on their hands. The sight relieved me. Evidently, there had been no other attempts on the queen thus far or Cecil would never have tolerated such insouciance.

As they saw me approach they scrambled to their feet, grabbing for their pikes to face me. I was about to reach into my doublet for my safe conduct when a voice from behind me called, "Halt!" and I turned to see men striding toward me with grim visages.

At their head was Robert Dudley.

I cursed under my breath. I should have expected this. I made a pact with him only to vanish without a word; he had no doubt been seething. He would now harass me, try to impede my meeting with Elizabeth, but I would not allow it. I had had enough of his insufferable arrogance.

Lifting my chin as he came before me, his nostrils flared under his fine chiseled nose, I said, "My lord, I am honored by your welcome."

His mouth curled; with a teeth-baring smile, he hissed, "Honored? You thieving cur: The honor is all mine." Without removing his virulent stare from me, he ordered, "Take him," and the men behind him—guards in breastplates and oiled cloaks—surrounded me.

I forced myself to remain calm. "You are about to make a grave mistake. I bring urgent news for Her Majesty and she will not be pleased—"

He leaned to me, exuding the costly scent of ambergris from his bejeweled damask. "You are correct. Her Majesty is indeed far from pleased. Dee deciphered the letter we found in the box. Do you know what it said?"

I went still. "I surely do not."

His smile widened. "Oh, I think you do. I think you know very well. Royal blood, indeed." As he started to step back, to lift his gloved hand to issue another command to the guards, I said angrily, "I am the queen's man. You must free me at once. I must warn her. I demand to see Her Majesty this instant."

Dudley shot out his fist, slamming it into my face and reeling me backward against the guards. "You will demand nothing, traitor. We now know what you have been about all along. You seek the queen's demise for your own miserable ends. You shall never see or speak to her again." He barked at the guards: "He is to be taken to the Tower."

I started yelling as they dragged me down the gallery, kicking and struggling, blood from my split lip seeping into my mouth. My cries reverberated. "I must see her! *Elizabeth!*"

But as they hauled me away with Dudley at their heels, the wide-eyed sentinels at her door remained in place. No one emerged from her apartments, though I could hear Urian barking from behind her closed doors. No one came to see what was happening.

Elizabeth did not appear.

*   *   *

A barge waited at Whitehall's water stairs. The tide ran low, and as they shoved me into the barge under the canopy, pikes aimed and ready to skewer if I attempted to escape, Dudley sat on the bench before me and instructed the wherry men to bring us to the Tower's water gate.

Traitor's Gate.

You seek the queen's demise for your own miserable ends . . .

I found myself trembling, watching the city slip past as we sailed down the Thames, the streets bustling with pedestrians, the facades of taverns and inns and shops crowded against one another. Snow drifted down about us in swirling flurries; as we neared the Bridge, I tried to brace myself with my feet against the barge's sides, as we gathered speed from the water funneling through the arches and careened through, jolting and swaying, pitched almost vertical in the foaming rush.

The wherry men were experienced, using their wide oars to maneuver past the whirlpools in the wake of the Bridge. Bile soured my mouth as I looked around at the stone span resting like a calcified dragon across the river with its cluster of painted buildings and massive opposing gates, their tops spiked with poles bearing the tar-boiled heads of traitors.

What had the letter in the box revealed? Whatever it was, I could have no doubt that I was in serious peril—called a traitor and sent to the Tower.

Royal blood, indeed.

Suddenly, I felt a sick drop in the pit of my stomach. It seemed impossible. *Who* could have known? Cecil knew about me, of course; he had known about the royal blood in my veins long before I did but he would never have confessed it after all this time, lest it roused Elizabeth's fury that he had kept it from her and he too ended up imprisoned. No, Cecil would not have dared. Who else? Think, I told myself, as panic engulfed me. Who else?

I froze. I had told Queen Mary. During my last assignation at court, I had gone to her in desperation as she was about to send Elizabeth to her death, to protect the princess and prove my loyalty, citing that the same blood bound all three of us, my mother having been their father's younger sister, after whom Mary herself was named. My revelation had stopped the queen from ordering Elizabeth's execution, if not her imprisonment, but she must have confided my secret to someone else. I dreaded to think it but that someone could be no other than the man who had been at Mary's side since the start of her reign, whispering venom in her ear: the Imperial ambassador, Renard. It explained why he had come after me once Mary ordered me from court, forcing me to flee abroad. I had never known how he knew where to find me, but now it seemed all too clear. Mary had told him of the threat I posed as a possible rival claimant to the throne, and he had decided to put an end to me. Who had he told in turn? He must have sent trusted agents, but had he gone so far as to inform them about me? Could Godwin be one of his agents? Had he enclosed the letter in the poisoned box, his abduction of Lady Parry a lure to bait my trap?

Yes, that had to be it. Nothing else made any sense. I had not been imagining it; the sin he wished to avenge was my own: the sin of my birth. With me in the Tower under suspicion of treason, Godwin could proceed to destroy Elizabeth with impunity, using her son as a pawn.

Though terror smothered my very breath, I forced my words out. "My lord, you must heed me. I tell you, the queen is in grave danger."

Dudley glanced over his shoulder at me from under the shadow of his velvet cap. "I hear only a corpse talking," he said. He turned away, directing the boatmen to bring our vessel into the wide pool lapping at the steps of the water gate. The Tower rose above us, hemmed by its weathered walls, the formidable White Keep looming up from within its center.

The guards secured the barge to the quay; Dudley disembarked and stood watching as the guards started to lift me out, one hand on his hip, snow powdering his broad cloaked shoulders. I shook the guards away, traversing on numb legs the flight of slimed steps and the cloistered passageway leading into the cobblestone courtyard at the heart of the Tower.

The last time I had been here, stalls had festooned this courtyard, vendors allowed inside during the day to sell food and other goods to those who oversaw the administration. There had been an old scaffold, as well; I now darted my gaze to where I remembered seeing it, situated a short walk from the chapel of St. Peter ad Vincula. Many of those who had died here, including Elizabeth's mother, lay entombed before the altar.

The scaffold was gone, the courtyard offering only a view of the sky and no reprieve, devoid of stalls. I was marched to the Beauchamp Tower; as I suddenly recognized the macabre irony of it, I started to struggle until Dudley said, "You should best not fight. She might yet show mercy if you show some dignity. You might get the axe rather than the rope and cleaver, though you hardly deserve it. Besides," he added coldly, "you should be grateful to share the very rooms I once had with my brothers under Queen Mary. Were it up to me, you'd be thrown into the Little Ease with the rats, but she insists you must reside here until she decides your fate."

The room was as I recalled it. More like the inside of an impoverished manor than a cell in the realm's most forbidding fortress, it was vaulted and airy, or as airy as any room in the Tower could be, with musty tapestries on the whitewashed walls, a recessed hearth, and mullioned embrasure offering a circumscribed view of the execution area beyond.

My heels struck echoes on the plank floor. Dudley ordered the guards to release me. After they retreated outside the door, he said, "I believe we left some of our books in the bedchamber, though of course they are not very useful when it comes to reading. As you know, we cut out most of the pages while imprisoned to convey our letters, but feel free to peruse at will. It is not as if you've much else to do."

He turned heel to depart. Without raising my voice, I told him, "Whatever you think I have done, you will condemn her to certain death if I am not allowed to speak to her."

He stiffened. "You are a liar. You have always been a liar. My family should have strangled you for the whelp you are, and spared us the misfortunes you have wrought. You should never have been allowed to live as long as you have."

I did not move. "Tell her he is alive and at Hatfield."

"Who is alive?" he spat. After years of dueling with me, he now believed he had secured my defeat and he sneered as I reached into my cloak. Though the guards had removed my belt with my poniard and sword, I had not otherwise been searched, an oversight in Dudley's gleeful exercise of power. Removing the ring from its bag, I extended it to him. "Show this to her."

Dudley stared at the ring in my palm. If I had not known better, I would have thought he recognized it. Then he let out a cruel laugh. "Is this all you can think of to save your flea-ridden hide, another of your base tricks? I think not. She is no longer prey to your wiles."

"Then you have no reason not to let her judge for herself. If she finds you kept this from her, she will have executed an innocent man who did only as she bade."

I waited, knowing that if he left without taking the ring I would never leave this place alive. Then, to my overwhelming relief, he snatched the ring from me and strode out.

My legs gave way. I crumpled to my knees.

I had entrusted my only hope to my worst foe.

Chapter Twenty

I spent the night curled up on the bed without sheets or coverlet, wrapped in my cloak, listening to the grumbling of the Tower at night: the occasional roar of the aging, wild beasts caged in the menagerie; the tromping of the night watch below the window; and the deafening, dread-filled silence in between.

When dawn's light leaked through the panes, footsteps came at my door and a sullen guard delivered a meal. I regarded the trencher in disgust: moldering bread and a bowl of watery gruel I would not have tossed to a beggar on the street. A flare of irritation caused me to growl, "You call this sustenance? I demand fresh water. Or am I to satiate my thirst with my own piss?"

The guard, one of the many menials who greased the Tower's inner workings, looked taken aback by this display of defiance by a royal prisoner. "I'm not permitted to—" he started to mumble, but I waved him out, furious, overturning the trencher and taking childish satisfaction in the splatter of gruel against the wall.

My fury ebbed as quickly as it had flared. Pacing to the embrasure, I pressed my face against the icy glass. I was trembling. The snow had stopped, leaving melting piles about the courtyard, indented with sodden footprints. As I watched guards and others engaged in the Tower's business come and go, I wondered how long they would keep me here before they led me to my death. I had devoted my life to seeing Elizabeth safe, even when she had trodden a fine line between righteousness and treason herself. I had never questioned her motives—

A sudden gasp curdled my throat.

Elizabeth. She now knew the truth. She knew everything and she wanted me dead. I turned about, the opaque mystery shedding its final layers. The child she had borne and hidden, Lady Parry's disappearance—it was all Elizabeth's doing, because now she was queen and under no circumstances could she allow Raff to endanger her. Had she seized advantage of a terrifying situation to ensure her secret would remain unknown? Had I unwittingly walked into the very snare she had prepared, unaware that another agent, a Spanish agent, also stalked me? If so, if the letter in the poisoned box had indeed betrayed my secret, then like Mary before her, Elizabeth would now see me as a rival, a bastard but still a man, with Tudor blood in his veins.

She would never let me live.

She never tells the entire truth if she can avoid it, and what she does not say often ends up costing someone their life.

God help me, Kate had warned me. Elizabeth was a survivor. She had outlived numerous attempts on her life—tenacious and unrelenting, she had finally gained her throne after years of peril. I had no doubt she would see me dead to protect it.

I rushed to the door then, banging my fists against it, bloodying my knuckles as I shouted myself hoarse for the guard. My fear for Shelton, whom I had sent to Hatfield, and for Raff, too, who did not know who he was, overcame me. When the guard did not come, I reeled from the door to prowl the chamber, desperate now that I had finally uncovered the truth.

After hours of pacing like the caged lions above the Tower gatehouse, I exhausted myself. As dusk once again swallowed the light I fell onto the bed, trying to find some measure of reassurance in the fact that Elizabeth had not ordered me killed outright, grasping onto the faint hope that Cecil might yet intervene. Though I had left court without word, betraying his trust, he valued me enough to instill caution in her.

She might keep me alive. For now.

When the jangle of keys came at the door, turning the lock, I sprang to my feet, edging from the chamber with nothing but my fists to defend me. A cloaked figure appeared, removing her hood to let it crumple about her shoulders as she looked about the room in disbelief.

"Kate!" I had not reached her before she stepped aside and another figure entered, fully hooded and cloaked in black velvet.

Lifting a slim white hand to pull back her hood, Elizabeth revealed her icy countenance.

The moment extended between us, fraught with the memories of our past adventures, with my suspicion of the falsehood I now believed her capable of. She was visibly gaunt, cheekbones incised under her skin. I had been right that she did not rest easy. Already her burden had begun to age her before her time.

"Leave us," she said. Kate retreated from the room. I was alone with the queen and a past we had both tried to conceal.

She did not hesitate. "Is it true?" she asked. "Are you who the letter claims you are?" She did not offer the letter in question and I debated for a moment if I should disabuse her of any notion that we shared the same blood. She had nothing to prove it, as it appeared Cecil had not told her what he knew. But, even as I considered it, I knew the time for lies was past. I would go to my death with the truth on my lips.

"I am." I drew the unlaced edges of my shirt about my throat, feeling vulnerable before her in my sagging breeches and soiled hose, stripped of finery and pretense.

"Why did you not tell me?" She took a single step forward. "Why did you leave it to be discovered thus, in a letter concealed in a box of death intended for me?"

"Would you have believed me?" My question detained her advance. "I saw no reason to tell you. It made no difference. I would have served you, regardless. I have never wanted anything more."

"I find that hard to believe," she said, "given who you are."

"Believe what you will, my lady. What right can I possibly claim?"

"But you—you are my aunt Mary of Suffolk's son! You might have been . . ." Her incredulity faded into the unseen chasm between us. "You should never have kept it from me," she said fiercely. "I gave you refuge. You had my trust yet you thought it wise to tell my own sister, who sought my death, while leaving me in ignorance. Did you not think I deserved to know?"

"Yes," I said softly. "I did. It seems we both hid secrets we should never have kept."

Her mouth pursed. Then she swept past me, her cloak parting over her plain black gown as she gazed out of the embrasure. "When Mary put me in here," she said, "I thought I would die like my mother. I even made plans to summon the swordsman from Calais. And when I was freed, I vowed to never set foot in the Tower again." She gave a hollow laugh. "Yet it seems I must lodge here for my coronation. It is the custom, I am told." She paused. "*If* there is to be a coronation. As matters stand, nothing is certain anymore."

I did not answer, remaining quiet as she composed herself, looking out toward the very site where her mother had perished. Her sigh was subtle, less an exhalation of surrender than one of forthcoming courage for the battle ahead. "What do you want of me?"

Her words took me aback. When I failed to respond, she turned to face me. "Well? That letter was in a cipher devised only for Lady Parry and me. No one else knew of it, yet somehow you discovered it. And you sent Robert to me with the ring. You must want something. Otherwise, why go through the expense of such an elaborate ruse?"

"You—you think *I* am responsible for all this?" I suddenly wanted to burst out laughing at the absurdity of it, when only hours before I had suspected the same of her. Then I saw her face tighten and I added, "I am no traitor. You must know that. Whatever else that letter claims, I never sought your ruin. The last thing I ever wanted is to be who I am."

Her struggle to accept my declaration brought a deep crease to her brow. For her, being who she was superseded everything; she had been born to her destiny, believed in it with fervent single-mindedness. She must have found it nearly impossible to concede that I did not envy or desire it, even though she had now begun to recognize the immense weight it entailed.

"I did what was necessary to keep your sister from killing you," I went on. "I had no choice; she had to know I was more than an intelligencer, that I had personal cause to serve both her and you. The only part I have in any of this is the ring. The boy gave it to me—"

She moved forward so swiftly, she cut off my voice. "Where is he? I will give you whatever you want—a title and castle, enough money to go abroad and live safely. I will see to it personally. You have my word. You can have anything if you only tell me where he is."

Her anguish overpowered her; as I marked the fear she fought against with all her strength, I said quietly, "I told Lord Robert. He is at Hatfield, with the man I believe to be my father."

"Liar!" Her hand flashed out, striking me across my cheek. *"Where is my son?"*

As I stood there, the sting of her palm on my skin, I whispered, "I do not know."

"You . . . you do not *know?*" she echoed, incredulous. "Did you not see him at Vaughan Hall? Did you not just confess you had him taken from there? If you do not know, who does?"

"He is . . . he is not there?" My dismay must have shown on my face, for Elizabeth reeled back, her hand at her mouth. "He—he is not," she whispered, her voice fraying. "I sent a messenger to Hatfield as soon as Robert brought me the ring. Ashley returned word that no one had arrived there. It is the only reason you are not dead. Dear God in Heaven, if he is not at Hatfield where you sent him, where is he? He is an innocent. I only ever wanted to keep him safe! Who has my son?"

In that moment, the briars of deception became terrifyingly clear.

I moved quickly to her. "Elizabeth, you must heed me. If I am to save him, you have to trust that as I would give my life for you, so will I do so for him. This man who has him, who planned all of this—I am the only one who can stop him."

"Man? What man?"

"I do not know him," I said. "I know only his name: Simon Godwin. He served as tutor in the Vaughan household, but he is far more than they suspected. I think—no, I believe—that he is a hireling of Simon Renard's, the Imperial ambassador at your sister's court. Renard discovered the truth about me; your sister must have told him. This gambit Godwin plays is about me, too; he seeks to destroy us both."

"But Renard is gone," she said. "After my sister died, he was recalled to Spain."

"He still could have instructed this man to stay behind to serve as his hound. Renard hunted me when you were under arrest. If your sister confided the truth about me, he would have wanted me dead. Mary was gravely ill; Renard must have feared that as her life weakened, I could emerge as a rival. He could not allow it. He wanted you, and you alone, to inherit the throne. It is part of the gambit." I added grimly, "The vendetta."

"Vendetta? You believe a Spanish agent took Hugh to destroy me?" She uttered her son's real name, the one she had given him, and I ached to hear her despair. "But, why? How did he even know that Hugh existed?"

"He knew because of where you placed the boy," I said, thinking back on the pieces of the mystery that until now I had not fitted into place. "Lady Vaughan's family are papists, survivors of the Pilgrimage of Grace. They were acquainted with members of your sister's court; and Renard knew them. He serves Spain. King Philip may have saved you before—but not to safeguard you. No, he has only ever wanted you in his debt. You told me he does not dare openly challenge you. That day we found the letter in the box, you said he feared the French more because should something befall you, France would champion Mary of Scots in your stead. Has he offered yet to marry you?"

She did not move, did not speak, but as I watched, I saw a tremor pass across her face.

"My lady," I urged, "now is no time for secrecy. Enough we have had already. Has Philip of Spain submitted a proposal of marriage?"

"Yes," she whispered. "He has, but I . . . I did not accept. I told his envoy Feria that I must consider it, that it is too early for such preoccupations."

I nodded. "As Philip expected you would. Yet to counter the French and keep his grip on England, in the end he must have you. Yet now he knows you will eventually refuse, so he must find a way to force your hand. What if he had a secret to wield, something so powerful, so damning, it could destroy you? You are vulnerable; he could threaten you with your own past so you must choose between him or defend yourself at a time when your realm is weak, your rule opposed by papists who see you as a bastard queen. Elizabeth, what if he had your son?"

"Dear God." She went ashen. "He could dethrone me before my reign has begun."

"Precisely. This is Philip's doing. He kept this agent Godwin here to do his bidding. Raff is in peril; Godwin will take him to Spain. You must send word at once to every port, forbidding the departure of any ships bound for the continent. And," I added, "I must be set free."

Her mouth quivered. For a paralyzing moment, I thought she would refuse. She had me captive, a grown man of her Tudor blood destined for the block. She could eliminate the threat I posed to her throne, while the son she'd hidden away remained a secret only a handful of her loyal intimates knew about. Despite all his power, Philip of Spain had no proof; he could never establish that Raff was truly hers. She might survive the storm Philip prepared to unleash; she would never see Raff again, but she still might rule. Only her love for Raff could sway her and I was not certain it would be enough.

She squared her thin shoulders. "Kate! Come at once. Bring his weapons."

Running into the bedchamber, I seized my cloak. When I returned to Elizabeth, she had drawn up her hood. Kate was at her side; her hand briefly touched mine as she gave me my belt with my sword. "I need coin," I said and she fumbled for the purse at her waist. "It's not much," she said.

I pocketed it. "It must suffice." I longed to embrace her. "Take the queen back to Whitehall. Do not leave her for a moment. Shut her up in her rooms and wait until I send word."

"I am still here," said Elizabeth, with a hint of aspersion.

"No, you are not," I replied, turning to her. "You were never here. I am still imprisoned and thus I must remain until I see this matter through. Raff and your realm depend on it."

Chapter Twenty-One

The night fell upon me with snow-flecked wings as I left the Tower and raced toward Dead Man's Lane. Elizabeth and Kate had taken to the river in her private barge to return to Whitehall. Before they left me outside the gate, Kate implored me to stay safe. I would have cherished the moment, as the barge pulled from the quay into the rising tide and I saw how she kept her eyes on me, saying without any words that she had never ceased to love me.

But I could not cherish the memory of her eyes locked on mine, not yet. Something had happened to Shelton and I prayed as I plunged into the warren of slush-filled streets that he had managed to make his way to Nan. I did not expect to find Raff there; yet as I reached the Griffin and banged on the door, staring up to the shuttered window on the second story where they kept their lodgings, I hoped I was wrong. Shelton still had formidable strength; despite his physical shortcomings, he would have fought for the boy. Perhaps he had. Perhaps he had slain Renard's hireling and had brought Raff here to hide until I could come for him.

The door was unbolted from within. I pushed my way inside. The main room was shuttered, stools stacked on the tables. As I heard a scuffle behind me and spun about with my sword unsheathed, Thom flattened himself at the wall. His hands came up to ward off my blow.

I lowered my sword. "Where are they? Quick, lad, there's no time."

"Upstairs," he gulped. "The master . . . he is gravely wounded. He—"

I did not tarry for his explanation and pounded up the staircase. I took it all in at once: the tallow lamp burning on the table, illuminating the small tidy room, and the cushioned settle upon which Shelton lay, his massive scarred chest exposed, his face pale and eye closed, as Nan looked up at me, her hands hovering above the blood-soaked bandage wrapped about his midriff. His loyal dog, Crum, lay at his feet.

"You promised," she said, as though she had been chanting recriminations in anticipation of my arrival. "You promised you wouldn't let him come to any harm. Look at him now." She paused then, regarding me. "Though you don't look to have fared any better," she muttered, referring to my swollen lip, blackened eye, and overall dishevelment.

Her voice caused Shelton to crack open his eye. He did not appear to recognize me at first, but as I neared the settle, he croaked in a near-inaudible voice, "Don't let her nag you. My Nan frets too much. As I told her, I am not dead yet."

I sank beside him. "What happened?"

He shook his head slightly. "I never saw it coming. He struck me so fast. We were on the road. The boy and I were so tired, he fell asleep against me . . . I was pulling the blanket over him when that villain rode out of nowhere. His steel was in me before I could react." His face contorted. "I tried, lad, but I was in such pain . . . I fell from Cerberus and the boy, he started to tumble with me. The rogue snatched him from my hands. It was over in an instant."

"He rode all the way here like this," added Nan. "Rode to our very door on that horse of his, bleeding and with every stray cur in the city lapping at his heels. He wanted me to go to the palace, to beg audience with the queen." She glared. "As if she or any of her noble lords would heed the likes of me; they'd have tossed me in the Fleet, and then where would he be, eh, his stomach putrid from the wound and only little Thom down-stairs to call for his winding sheet."

"You did the right thing," I said, without looking away from Shelton. "They never would have listened." I searched his face. "Did you see who it was?"

He closed his eye. "It was too dark . . ." He paused. "But as he rode off, he said something to me. He said, 'If you want to save the boy, you must meet him on the bridge.'"

I went still. Then, without warning, rage surged in me. I had been right from the start.

"You must rest." I touched Shelton's hand. His fingers clutched mine. "He is alive," he said. "As they rode away, I could hear the boy sobbing. He was scared but he was alive."

"Do not worry, I will find him." I rose from my haunches. As I swerved to return downstairs, already intent on my next move, Nan grasped me by my arm. "If something should happen to you, it will surely kill him. Whatever you do, remember he lives for you. He's only held out this long because you mean every-thing to him."

I leaned to her, kissed her flushed cheek. "I don't intend to die any more than he does. Just make sure he keeps waiting for me until I get back."

As I stepped off the bottom rung of the stairs into the tavern, a cloaked figure seated with its back to me rose and turned. I saw Thom squatting in a corner, his eyes huge.

"It would appear we are destined to be together through fair or foul," Dudley drawled. He wore a fitted leather doublet, padded breeches tucked into thigh-high riding boots, a sword hanging in an ornamented scabbard at his side, and fringed gauntlets on his hands, as though he were about to embark on a court progress.

"Remove yourself." I made to stride past him when he blocked my passage.

"The queen has commanded it," he said. "She has ordered me to protect you."

"I don't need your protection. What I do, I must do alone."

He chuckled. Not in an overtly insulting manner, which in and of itself was surprising enough, but it was his next words that prevented my lunge at his throat: "She says I am to accord you the respect I would grant her own person." He spoke as if he were yanking his words out from between his teeth. "She must favor you, indeed. She would not have you undertake this venture unguarded. If you do not allow me to accompany you, then I am to trail behind you like a lackey. It seems that now, Prescott, I must serve you."

"You do not understand," I said. "If we are seen, it could threaten the very life of—" I stopped myself in time, but he leaned close to me in a repulsive gesture of confidence.

"Her changeling?" he said. "Do not look so aghast. I have

known about him for quite some time. She once asked me to sell off some of my lands to help her gather coin for his upkeep. She confides in me. As I told you once before, she loves me as much as I love her."

"But you love yourself still more." I moved around him. "Accompany me if you must, but you must do exactly as I say."

Outside, I found his horse and my Cinnabar tethered, guarded by a burly yeoman of the guard. I had an impulse to declare that we might as well gather up the royal pennants and trumpets in parade but I curbed my tongue. "Ride ahead," I instructed Dudley. "Take your guard with you and make as if to cross the bridge to Southwark. Only someone with your credentials can persuade the sentries to unlock the gate. I will follow once the gate is open."

With a scowl, Dudley motioned to the guard and began to ride to the bridge. I waited until they had distanced themselves before I called for Thom, who came out running.

"Take care of my horse." Handing over Cinnabar's reins, I dashed into the shadows of Dead Man's Lane, racing toward the reunion that had long awaited me.

If you want to save the boy, you must meet him on the bridge.

The last time I had been on London Bridge, I was chasing the woman who betrayed me. It had been crowded that evening, groups of travelers, ox-driven wagons, livestock, and men on horseback waiting in line to embark upon the narrow roadway threading between the clustered shops and other establishments. Tonight it was quiet, a halo of torchlight and candles winking in windows over it. Many of the bridge's residents never left—lusting, toiling, brawling, and dying on that stone span connecting London with bawdy Southwark. I could discern faint voices drifting in the chill air: a sing-along from one of the illicit drinking holes that thrived after hours, though the law forbade the sale of alcohol on the bridge, the risk of a drunkenly fueled conflagration being far too great.

Pausing near a landing quay to gaze toward that overladen structure silhouetted against the midnight sky, the river's swelling tide barreling with deadly force through its twenty close-set piers that made crossing under it an often lethal enterprise, I wondered if I was going straight to my death. I took a moment to breathe, pushing aside my lifelong aversion of deep water to imagine Dudley's reaction when I failed to join him at the gate. Let him loiter there keeping the sentries occupied while I embarked on this far more dangerous route.

I whistled. Within seconds, one of the boatmen who plied the Thames for a living neared the water steps. "Going to Southwark, are ye?" he asked. He was a shrunken, hunched figure, clothed in bits of rags and frost-eaten wool, his gnarled hands, swollen from gripping an oar, tucked into mittens with the tips cut off. "Best hurry. The tide will not wait."

I dangled Kate's pouch. "Can you get me to the bridge? If you can, all this is yours."

His filmy eyes fixed on the purse, even as he cackled. "Too late for that. No one can shoot the bridge at this hour. You must wait. Why not spend some of your coin in Southwark? Plenty of pretty lasses there to entertain a fine gentleman—and lads, too, if that's to your taste. Then I'll fetch you tomorrow and we can go to the bridge."

"It must be tonight. Can you do it?"

He stuck out his lower lip, considering. "You set me on a fool's errand," he muttered.

"Indeed." Handing him the pouch, I clambered into his boat. Water sloshed in the curved keel. I lifted my booted feet, resisting the nausea that assailed me as the boatman maneuvered into the swift Thames, separating us from the embankment until we became a speck in a vast churning soup, where fragments of broken branches, garbage, and occasional bloated things bobbed and careened past us. With my hands clutching the edges of the knotty bench, I prepared.

Godwin had not killed Shelton because he wanted him to impart his message. It gave me no comfort, though it proved I had not been wrong in my initial fears. Whoever Godwin was, he must have a connection to Sybilla. Luring me to the bridge was a deliberate ploy, as the only place where I could search for him was the very house where I last confronted her, engaging in the struggle that resulted in her fall. Only the thought that he had not come after me directly imparted some relief. It betrayed weakness, perhaps because his crippled leg made him no match for me in a sword fight. He had relied on subterfuge in the Vaughan household, winning Lady Philippa to his side even as he pilfered Lord Vaughan's cipher to read the letters to and from Lady Parry. Nevertheless, despite his cunning, either he had not uncovered Raff's identity or he had failed to apprehend the boy at the manor. He instead seized Lady Parry, sending the poisoned box upon my arrival at court with the letter inside it, denouncing me in a cipher intended to confound. He had not wanted me arrested, not then; he had known Elizabeth would dispatch me to search for Lady Parry and he was at the ready, hiring those ruffians to impart his cryptic message, the same one he had left under Lady Parry's saddle for the queen.

You must pay for the sin.

It was a masterful gambit, chilling in its tenacity. Even now, he had anticipated that I would find some way to persuade Elizabeth to release me from the Tower.

What dark end did he seek?

I had no other answer than vengeance for Sybilla. Godwin had been watching us all along, poisoning Shelton's ale to goad me. I should never have sent Shelton away with Raff; in my confusion, I had revealed the very secret Godwin had been unable to procure. If my suspicions were correct, he had powerful protection, too, through his master King Philip. Spain's wealth could secure him safe passage from England. Even if Elizabeth's orders to halt the ships reached her ports in time, a man like Godwin would have other means of escape.

I had to find him first.

I looked ahead as the bridge came closer, deafened by the roar of the river gushing through its silted and debris-laden piers. Somehow, I had to access it without using the gateways, locate the house without him realizing I approached. It was crucial that I not provide any more advance warning, for he already knew I would accept his invitation.

The boatman paddled to one side, evading the river's pull. "I won't go any closer," he yelled over his shoulder at me. "The tide will swamp my boat."

We had neared the sterling at the base of one of the massive piers. Unsteadily, I unlocked my grip on my seat to peer over the boat's side and gauge the distance. It was not too far to swim, were I not burdened by weapons. I espied moss-licked stairs carved into the side of the pier, leading up to the bridge and some type of opening. Residents must use those stairs to come down and fish at low tide; bundles of nets lay heaped on the sterling itself. Yes, that was a way in, but the more I contemplated it, the more I realized I would be mad to attempt it.

I would have to access the bridge from the Southwark gate, even if I had already given away my purse and had nothing to bribe the sentries. Turning about, I saw the boatman was trying to say something. He lifted his voice—"Sit your arse down!"—but as I started to move back to the bench, the boat pitched with violent suddenness in an unexpected surge of the tide.

With a horrified cry, I lost my balance, pitching backward into the water.

It was a dark cauldron. All my air evaporated from me in a gasp; as I gulped in brackish salt of the sea and accompanying filth tossed into the Thames every hour of every day, I flailed, kicking frantically. As I surfaced, panting, my clothing and weaponry weighing like armor, I saw the boatman rowing furiously away. He was not going to risk himself by trying to save me, not after I had paid him and fallen in because of my own clumsiness.

Besides, there was no way for him to save me. The river already propelled me toward the pier. I fought against it with every muscle, knowing that if this relentless torrent yanked me under, I was doomed. There was no shore nearby to swim to, only steep embankments flooded by the influx of the tide. I would drown.

My only hope was to reach the bridge and somehow get myself out. But it was becoming increasingly difficult to remain afloat. The cold water stole through me; if I continued to thrash,

I would exhaust my strength. Unclasping my cloak, I let it sink below me. I told myself to loosen my limbs, keep my head above water, and let the tide bring me close. Yet as it did, alarm fired my veins, for the sterling appeared enormous, built to withstand the river and protect the piers.

Still, I made a move toward it. Better to risk death by bashing against it than end up sucked under the bridge. I felt something tangle about my calves; as I reached down, submerging my head, my fingers strained, snagging on a net. I flung my head up, blinking water from my eyes. The bridge filled my entire being. I looked further to where the waterline lapped. There: a rusted hook attached to the net and embedded in the sterling. Breathing fast to quicken my blood, as Walsingham had taught me during those excruciating exercises in Brussels, I yanked on the net and employed it to drag myself closer.

The river pummeled me. I concentrated only on paddling forward, grasping section by section of net, until I was reaching out with one trembling hand to take the hook. Sharp pain sliced my palm. I cursed, swallowing more water, coughing and sputtering as I tightened my grip and with my other hand withdrew my poniard from its soaked sheath at my belt to slash the net enveloping my legs. I might cut myself, too, but every moment I tarried was one less I had to live.

Grasping the hook, I scrabbled up the sterling's tiered side, my sodden boots slipping and catching on its roughened edge. There was a terrifying moment when I faltered and started to fall backward. With shoulder-searing effort, I heaved and collapsed, faceup, pooled in water, my belt with the sword in its scabbard snarled about my waist, digging into my ribs.

I gazed at the bridge's underside as cold settled into my

marrow. Within minutes, my teeth stared to chatter and I knew I had to move before I congealed where I lay. Hoisting myself to my feet, every part of me numb—which was a blessing, given how bruised I must be from the ordeal—I limped to the steps. The flight was narrow, none too safe, rising upward without any balustrade. Adjusting my belt, I climbed. Once I reached the top, I did not look down the dizzying drop to the river below, using my poniard to probe the wood beaming set into the stone framework for an opening. I eventually found it, pushing up a small trapdoor. Peering through it, I gazed upon the miniature city swathed in snow upon the bridge.

I saw no one abroad but could hear people within candle- and tallow-lit homes, the clatter of cutlery and occasional voice reprimanding a child. Unlike London itself, where night released a horde from its underworld—beggars, vagrants, and others taking to the streets along with packs of feral dogs—here a sense of calm prevailed, with hourly patrols from the northern and southern gates maintaining uneasy order. Fear of fire was always present. With so many buildings, some over six stories tall and all crammed together, an errant spark from a poorly tended hearth or toppled lantern could result in a holocaust that would ravage the only means of ground transport across the Thames.

I ducked into a nearby doorway, removing my boots and emptying them of water as best as I could. I could smell the river on me, a pungent stench. From where I stood, I could not see the gatehouse where Dudley waited, my view blocked by the folly of Nonesuch Palace, a gilded edifice whose jutting palisades straddled the bridge. But I was not far from Sybilla's house and I crept toward it, keeping under eaves and hanging signs, unsure of when the patrols would next make their rounds.

Passing shuttered windows and doors behind which riotous laughter and the banging of fists on tables betrayed an illicit tavern, I kept watch for stray curs. I saw only a few, snuffling over piles of refuse; as I slipped past them, one lifted its muzzle, eyes opaque in the moonless night. It bared its teeth but made no move toward me.

The darkness turned the multitude of structures indistinguishable, balconies and walkways like webbing over the road, the passage ahead an endless tunnel. I could hear my boots slosh as I walked; nearing the closed haberdashery and doorway to the house, I paused to catch my breath. I had forgotten in my stealth how cold I truly was. Now the chill returned, making me shiver uncontrollably. I was in no state to contend with a Spanish agent, crippled or not.

Taking brief reprieve by the haberdashery, I surveyed the small upper-story window inset like a scar in the house's façade. There was no sign of habitation, no flicker of candlelight. Yet he must be here, waiting. He had to know I would come.

I had no other choice but to enter. Setting my fingers on the latch, I slowly turned it. The door opened on well-oiled hinges.

My time of reckoning was at hand.

Chapter Twenty-Two

The parlor on the ground floor was empty and glacial as a tomb. Before me, a flight of rickety stairs led to the second floor. Standing still, the dripping of my clothes muted on the warped plank floor, I strained to hear any sounds. When I did not, I drew out my wet sword, wiped the blade on my breeches, and began to take the stairs, wincing at each groan and protest of the weathered treads, aware that I was announcing my presence as brazenly as if I had barged in shouting with Dudley and his guard at my back.

The door to the room was ajar, its contents shrouded by gloom—the cot and corner desk, a chair pushed against a peeling wall. It was as though nothing had transpired here, as if time had stood still between that moment years ago, when Sybilla had lunged at me with her blade drawn, and now, as I braced again for her assault, my breath coming fast and shallow, my sword held so tight that its pommel gouged my wounded palm.

There was no swift move in my direction, no rearing shadow. As I stepped over the threshold, swiping my blade, my vision began to adjust and I saw evidence of recent occupation: a pitcher on the desk, a tarnished platter and wood bowl. I blinked, my eyes burning from exposure to the vile river, and then I heard a muffled gasp.

Whirling around, I cried, "Show yourself!" As my voice echoed, the gasp became louder, a desperate wrenching sound. The chair facing the wall rocked slightly. I approached it with my heart in my throat; using my blade, I hooked the back of the chair. It was heavy and tall; as another sob issued from it I yanked it around to find a woman in a soiled gown bound to the seat, mouth gagged and unkempt tresses falling over her face. I recognized her at once.

"My lady Parry," I breathed and I spun around again, thinking someone crept up behind me. When I saw we were alone, I pulled out the rag stuffed in her mouth. The crevices at either side of her lips were torn, jagged with scabs. Lady Parry had never been robust, and weeks of captivity had reduced her to colorless skin and bone. As she sagged in the chair, tears seeping down her sunken cheeks, I knelt before her and sawed at the ropes. Her skirts had protected her legs to some measure, but her wrists were raw from chaffing.

"My lady, please look at me," I said gently. She had not seen who I was; as terror flared in her eyes, I said quickly, "It's Master Prescott, the queen's man. I am here to see you safe."

She whimpered, reached out an imploring hand.

"Can you stand?" I started to assist her but she shook her head. She was too weak. "I must send someone for you," I said. "The person who did this: Where is he?"

She shook her head again, seemingly unable to formulate words. Then she clutched at my sleeve, her fingers sharp as bird claws. "The child," she whispered. A desperate sob escaped her. "I tried to resist . . ."

"Where is he?" My voice rose in urgency. "Where did he take him?"

Lowering her face, she began to sob. "The saint's crypt . . . You must save him."

I raced back down the stairs into the street, my heels pounding on the roadway as I ran to the northern gatehouse. Dudley and his guard had already come through the gate; standing by his horse with reins in hand, Dudley whirled on me. "How dare you make me wait like a menial—"

"Lady Parry," I interrupted. "She is here! She needs help."

To his credit, Dudley reacted at once. "Where?" he barked as the guard drew his sword.

Breathless, I explained the house's location; as the guard raced toward it, Dudley took in my sodden appearance. "Did you swim here?"

I grimaced. "That is of no consequence. Where is the saint's crypt?"

He frowned.

"The crypt," I said. "Quickly, man, before it is too late! The boy is there."

Dudley looked utterly bewildered. Just as I was about to stride past him to ask the wide-eyed sentries watching us from the gate, he exclaimed, "The crypt of Thomas Becket. It is by the ninth pier, toward the middle of the bridge. Pilgrims used to stop there on their way into the city, but it was closed after the break with Rome— Damn you, Prescott. Wait for me!"

I shoved him aside and vaulted onto his horse, swerving it about. Digging my heels into it, I galloped away, Dudley's cries for me to halt swallowed by the swirling snow in the air.

The clangor of hooves echoed in my ears as I rode to the

chapel. A group of drunken men staggered from one of the drinking holes; they wagged fists at me as I plowed through their midst, narrowly missing them as they threw themselves out of my way.

The chapel sat huddled over the pier: an egglike structure with pointed spires and arched stained-glass windows, with delicate stone tracery and figures of saints and disembodied crowned heads carved over its portico. A crenellated turret faced the street on the bridge; the chapel itself clung to the side of the pier and stood on the sterling below. I heard the river funneling through the pier as I leapt from Dudley's horse and yanked out my sword.

Behind me, the horse was breathing hard from our brief but intense ride; the roar of the river below dampened all other sounds. Approaching the chapel's double doors within the portico, I braced myself. I had never been inside this place, had no idea what to expect. But the message was clear enough: This was a sacred house of worship, dedicated to a bishop who'd been canonized after he was murdered for defying his sovereign, his chapel shuttered since King Henry confiscated the Church's wealth. Here, the sins of the past were symbolized by a sacrosanct place that had been defiled by Elizabeth's own father.

Though not a gesture I often indulged, I crossed myself and then pushed on the door. It was locked. Rounding the chapel, I searched for another entrance. Godwin had brought Raff here, so he must want me to enter; it was the final stage in his plan but he was not going to facilitate my entry. He knew I would be armed, ready to do whatever was required to save Raff. He had to challenge me first, sap my strength. Then, only then, would he engage.

Pressed against the side of the bridge, I espied a broken window-pane in the lower set of windows. It was hardly large enough for a child, let alone a man, and too high to reach. I gauged the chapel wall. A residue of moss from the ever-encroaching damp of the Thames coated the exterior. Enterprising bridge-dwellers had exploited the chapel's neglect to remove pieces of the outer stonework themselves, leaving a patchwork of misshapen holes. Could I climb up?

Sheathing my sword, I took hold of the stone wedges and fitted the tips of my boots into the crevices and indents; the mortar joining the stones was crumbly, wet from the recent snowfall. As I dug in, I was able to widen some of the holes, enough to gain precarious foothold.

Pressed flat against the chapel, my fingers clinging to the shallow indents around the stones, I began to ascend, resisting the flare of pain in my battered body, summoning my reserves of strength until I was close enough to the broken window to grasp its sill. Slivers of broken glass razed my fingers; my gauntlets were gone, lost during my fight to survive the river. Clenching my teeth, I hoisted myself upward and closed my eyes, then used the hilt of my poniard to smash at the glass, wincing as it shattered and fell in a shower of colored shards, widening the aperture. I felt a piercing slice across my brow, the warm spurt of blood. With a final thrust of my legs, I rammed myself bodily through the window, breaking the leading, and with a gasp tumbled through it into a void.

It was not a long fall but it had enough impact to knock the air from me. I lay stunned, panting and staring up at the criss-crossed stone vaults above.

Staggering to my feet, I saw that I stood on a black-and-white tile floor, smeared with dust and grime. I swiped my sleeve across my brow, spraying scarlet droplets. The cut on my brow was probably not deep but it stung horribly. Wiping blood from my eyes, I looked around.

The chapel had been lovely once, adorned with all the incense-fragrant trappings of a faith that relied on glorious manifestations of wealth to exalt its fervor, but not much remained of its glory now. Submerged in shadow interspersed by shifting opalescence filtering through the stained-glass windows, the chapel of St. Thomas stood barren. Gaping tombs in the walls, intended for wealthy patrons entitled to rest here for eternity, were ransacked. As I moved to the altar, I nearly tripped over a skeleton in rotting velvet tumbled across the floor, the upended slab of a nearby sarcophagus broken in half. Thieves had come inside, scavenging whatever could be taken in the wake of Queen Mary's death.

Nearing the apse, where a faded fresco high above was barely discernible, I caught sight of an open entryway to the side. Faint illumination issued from within. With my dagger in hand, I approached cautiously, straining to hear anything that might precede an impending attack. Past the threshold, a staircase led down into darkness, a moldering scent wafting from the unseen space below. A torch sputtered in a sconce at the top of the stairs—a courtesy, I thought grimly, or a distraction? I seized it anyway, using it to light my way as I crept down the stairs.

The crypt opened before me. It too was vaulted, though here the ceiling was lower—an enclosed but surprisingly large space, permeated by damp but not wet, despite the fact that this part of the chapel sat on the river and the Thames's high tide would brim at its very skirts.

A sinking in my stomach overcame me as I lifted the torch higher.

The crypt was empty.

"Where are you?" I heard myself whisper. "Miserable villain, show yourself."

An odd clicking sound reached me, echoing into the crypt. I spun about, the torch wavering in my hand, casting erratic light and causing shadows to leap across the far walls.

A figure appeared from a distant doorway, coming slowly, the tapping of its cane on the stone floor reverberating in my ears. I edged backward as it shrugged aside the dark, resolving into a figure in a black doublet, breeches, and hose, legs sheathed in boots. Only as I stared did I see its left leg twisted inward.

It was the tutor Godwin—yet as he neared, to my simultaneous shock and horror, I saw that it was not.

"At long last," said Sybilla Darrier. Her husky voice clutched me like a talon. "You have passed every test. Impressive." She halted a short distance away, leaning on her cane. I had to lift the torch again, to avoid the flame blinding me, though I exposed my torso to her.

Her face wavered in the light, marked by those indigo eyes even more pronounced now in her near-waxen visage. She was still beautiful, even if I would never have recognized her had I passed her on the street, her once-lush blond hair shorn close to her skull, her cheekbones angular, her loss of flesh adding to her illusion. I realized now what had eluded me: She *was* Godwin. She had deceived us all, passing for a slender, strange young man who had seduced Agnes and Lady Philippa, hoodwinking Lord Vaughan and everyone else in the manor.

There was no other Spanish agent. It had always been her.

"Where is the boy?" My voice was calm, though I still was having trouble reconciling myself to what I saw, my entire being breaking out in cold sweat, the pounding of my heart making it feel as if it might burst from my chest. I was face-to-face with the very woman who had haunted my dreams, whose betrayal I agonized over and death I had so fervently wanted to believe and deny.

She canted her head, as if in puzzlement. "Boy?"

"Yes." I leveled my blade at her. "You took him. Where is he?"

"Are you so eager to conclude our game? We have only just started. You must have questions only I can answer."

"No game. No questions. It is over. If I must, I will kill you myself. *Where is he?*"

"You will kill me?" Her mockery rang out. It made the hairs on my nape stand on end, for it was still her laughter, still imbued with all its seductive power. "Have you not heard? I am already dead. I have been dead for years." Clenching her cane with her left hand, she spread her right arm wide. "Go on, then. Kill me. Only this time," she said, her voice lowering, "make sure you do not fail."

I met her eyes. "Tell me. What must I do to save him?"

"Not so fast. As you can see, I am not the opponent I used to be. You took that from me."

"I won," I said, fighting back the urge to lunge at her and finish it. "If you had had your way, you would not have hesitated to see me to my grave."

"I did try. But I concede your victory. I conceded it on this very bridge, the day I leapt from your pursuit. I could have fought you to the death. Instead, I let you save your princess."

"You did not concede. You never will. You and your master,

Philip of Spain—you will do everything you can to see her topple from her throne."

She chuckled. "Yes, I believe we understand each other. Yet I so enjoyed our time together. . . ." She let her innuendo charge the air with the memory of our shared passion and loss. "Did you think of me at all, during those years you hid abroad? Did you ever wonder if they dragged the river to find me, the woman whose skin you coveted? Because I thought of you when I made it to shore, my leg shattered, near-dead from the cold. I thought of you when the boatman who found me took pity and for the few coins in my cloak brought me to Renard. I thought of you every hour of every day in the months it took me to learn to walk again."

"You knew," I said, trembling. "Renard . . . he was the one who told you about me."

"He did. Oh, you were careless. You confided in Mary—and she was distraught. She dared not kill her sister now, not with you waiting in the wings, another threat. Eventually, she went to Renard. You are fortunate indeed that Cecil had contacts at court to warn him and knew the time had come to send you away. Renard's men lost track of you in the swarm of refugees escaping Mary's persecution, but I knew it was a matter of time before you would return. You never could stray far from Elizabeth's side. And time was all I needed."

Hoisting the torch into a bracket in the pillar beside me, I sheathed my poniard at my belt and withdrew my sword. The damp hiss of its release brought a smile to her lips. I realized that I should not indulge her in meaningless confessions; I had the advantage. She was crippled; she could not fight me physically, not as she once had. But she had Raff; I could not risk killing her until I established where he was. Once I did, she would not leave this crypt alive. I had longed for this hour from the moment she plunged from the bridge: to see her again, to have all my questions answered. But like everything else between us, her truth was twisted, monstrous.

"How did you find him?" I asked.

"How else? Elizabeth herself led us to him. After Mary released her from the Tower, she had her lover Dudley sell off some of her lands. Philip ordered her watched closely in case she betrayed herself—as she did. Even under house arrest, she did not cease to scheme and entrusted the funds from those lands to her Lady Parry."

"You followed Lady Parry . . . ?"

"Alas," she sighed, "I could not, for I was still too weak. But Renard had her messenger followed and once he deduced where the money was being sent, he had the man intercepted. The funds were lost. Elizabeth must have been beside herself but she could not risk sending money again, not until she took the throne. In the meantime, Renard made inquiries. When he learned Lady Vaughan had a sister in London, it was almost too easy. The queen was dying; Renard could not hide me anymore, for he received word of his recall to Spain. Seeing as Lady Vaughan's family had suffered as mine had, a discreet recommendation was all it took. Lady Browne referred me to Vaughan Hall. Thus did I become Master Godwin."

"But you did not find the child, though he was there all the time."

Triumph colored her voice. "Oh, I found him."

For a moment, I was too stunned to speak. Then I breathed: "The box of gloves—you sent it to rouse my suspicion, using the same poison that killed my squire. You taunted *me*."

"As I said, you passed every test. You suspected from the start, did you not? How it must have tormented you, the fear I might still be alive. You must have thought you were going mad."

Without answering, I passed my gaze over her. A pulse beat at the base of her throat, visible under the lacings of her collar. I also noticed something else: The tips of her boots were shiny in the torchlight. Wet. She had been outside.

"Let the child go," I said. "He is not to blame for our sins."

"Do you think I ever cared about him? He is the bastard son of a bastard queen: He means nothing to me. Had you not tried to save him, he would still be mucking out stables. I only took Lady Parry to ensure Elizabeth would send you to investigate; I knew she would, for whom else could she trust with her misdeeds? You were always her most loyal creature."

"You lie." I clenched my sword in my fist, resisting the urge to ram it into her. "You left a letter in that box telling her who I was. You wanted me dead."

"It was a test, another part of the game! My letter was in her own cipher; it was a challenge to see how long it would take before she realized it, but I never doubted you would find her secret first. She was never as clever as you. Now, you are revealed for who you are and as soon as you deliver her bastard to her, she will see you to your death." Her voice drove at me, harsh and unrelenting. "Do you know how many believe she is the by-blow of an incestuous whore, with no right to wear the crown? Her own sister Mary believed it. Yes, Mary thought Elizabeth was not her sister at all. But you—*you* are the son of a Tudor princess. Mary believed your claim, as did Renard. You will come with me to Spain, where King Philip can exalt you as this realm's rightful sovereign. He will build an armada for you, take this land by force, and set you in her place. You will be king." She paused. "If you refuse, the boy dies."

I held on to every shred of will to contain the fury cresting inside me, the savage need to rent her apart, to bathe myself in her blood. I had told Elizabeth the truth; Philip had indeed sought to use a secret against her, but I had been wrong in my assumption that it was Raff.

I was the secret. I was the weapon.

"And if I do not accept?" I said. "No matter what Philip does, he cannot force me."

"Now, who is the one who lies? You cannot deny your fate. I have seen how much you hunger for it; I have tasted it. It is the very reason you survive." Anticipation turned her features taut. "Follow your destiny, Brendan," she said, and time swirled, collapsing, returning me to that night when she appeared in my chamber at Whitehall, ensorceling me with her touch, with her mesmerizing beauty. I had thought lust had been my downfall, but now I understood it was more ominous: Sybilla embodied the very self I fought against, the temptation of what I could become if I surrendered to my own desires. "Follow me," she said, "and take what is yours."

I let her promise seep within me, as remorseless as it was intoxicating. She was right. I was a Tudor. How could I resist, with a kingdom within my grasp, an untried queen to depose, and Spain's might at my back? I would be king. I would rule.

Then the moment began to unspool, and as her eyes turned black and I realized she had suspected all along what my choice would be, I whispered: "You must see me dead first," and she flung up her arm, smashing her cane into my face.

Blood sprayed from my nose. Pain shot through my cheeks, blinding me as I thrust my sword. Swerving with astonishing speed despite her leg, she evaded my blade, which sliced past her, shredding her doublet. With a snarl in her throat, she rushed at me and I saw in her hand the blade she had concealed—a thin rapier yanked from within the cane. As I pivoted, lifting my sword, our blades struck, the impact shuddering through me. She had not lost her skill; the time spent healing her shattered body had lent her extraordinary virtuosity, so that she came at me with ease, her mouth parted, barely a labored breath escaping her as I rallied to defend myself.

Around us, the clang of our blades sparked echoes against the stone vaults. She was maneuvering me to a wall, where she could entrap me. Ducking around a pilaster, I slashed back and forth, keeping her at bay as I raced to the small postern door behind her, through which she had entered the crypt. She was at my heels; as I felt her rapier slash into my shoulder, she said through her teeth, "Loyalty was always your fatal weakness," and I yanked at the door, releasing the roar of the river beyond, its spume and soaking damp.

My sword slipped from my grip. Agony lanced from my shoulder to my wrist. I vaguely heard my sword clatter behind me as I staggered from her advance onto the slippery waterlogged sterling, struggling to stay upright. Out of the corner of my eye, I caught sight of a small vessel moored to the chapel's quay; within it, a bundled sack of cloth writhed as the current raged past, setting the small boat to tugging at its tether. Soon, the rope holding it would snap and the vessel with Raff inside it would be swept to its doom in the voracious whirlpools under the bridge.

I spun around to face her, my blood-drenched sword hand whipping my poniard from my belt. With an inchoate roar, I flung myself at her to ram my blade into her gut, even if it meant I would in turn impale myself on her sword. We would die together, locked in hatred.

A sudden hiss punctuated the air. She went still. A gasp escaped her lips.

Everything slowed to a crawl: her figure immobile, my poniard still in my hand as her eyes flared wide. Crimson bubbled from her lips. Her blade clattered to her feet as she began to keel, her twisted leg splaying. In a haze, I saw the fletched bolt protruding from between her shoulders and looked past her to a figure behind her in the doorway, crossbow lifted.

Meeting my stare, Dudley pulled back the mechanism and fit another bolt into it.

I was next. Before me, Sybilla crumpled to her knees. Dudley fired again. The bolt slammed into her, blood gushing from her mouth. She collapsed facedown, a dark pool spreading around her as her body twitched and went still.

The world capsized. Voices echoed; there was a clamor of footsteps, hands hauling me up. The searing pain in my shoulder numbed my senses. I could feel blood soaking my doublet, streaming down my chest; as Dudley shouted at someone behind him, "Quick, he needs a physician!" I struggled to resist, clutching at his sleeve to whisper, "The boy is in the boat . . ."

It was the last thing I remembered saying before oblivion engulfed me.

Chapter Twenty-Three

Will he live?" The queen's voice reached me as if from across a great distance. Something cold nuzzled my hand. Slowly, I opened my eyes. A burst of light blinded me. I groaned, shifting my head on the pillows. A cool hand touched my brow, pressing upon it.

"The fever is gone," I heard Kate say. "I think the worst of it has passed."

"Thank God." A rustle of skirts approached. Turning my head, I saw Elizabeth's face wavering above me, pallid and hollowed, but quiet fortitude in her eyes. "You are like a cat, my friend. But I fear you have used up the last of your nine lives."

I tried to speak, untangling my knotted voice from my throat. "Raff . . . is he . . . ?"

She nodded. "He is safe. No"—she held up her hand as I struggled to rise—"you must rest. There will be plenty of time for questions later." She moved away, murmuring to Kate. The queen's hound Urian whined, stuck his muzzle into my hand again. I stroked him with my fingertips, feeling the burning ache in my shoulder. My nose felt twice its normal size, too, and throbbed like a tiny anvil striking a forge. I could not keep my eyes open. As I let them close once more, sleep sneaking upon me even as I tried to resist, Kate set a warm compress on my nose and I heard her say softly, "You're going to look like your father."

A few days later, I could finally sit upright. I was in a chamber in the palace, with walnut-paneled walls and a mullioned bay. Kate came and went, tending to me, sitting on a stool at my side and patiently unwinding the soiled bandages on my shoulder to check the tender wound. I winced as she applied her homemade herbal salve, less at its acrid smell than the burn it caused.

"I know it hurts," she said. "But you narrowly escaped corruption setting in. The wound cut almost to the bone. We thought you would die from the fever. You must let it heal, Brendan. You have to endure it. You want to keep use of your sword arm, don't you?"

I had to chuckle, though any movement made me want to shout in pain. She went quiet, replacing the bandage with her eyes averted.

"Kate," I said.

She paused. When she eventually lifted her gaze, it was somber. "No," she said. "I don't need to hear it. I . . . I do not want to know. It is over. You saved the queen once again."

"But I must tell you." I reached for her hand, holding it fast. "I made a mistake. I . . . I am the reason this happened. But I never loved her, not as I love you. Something else drove me; desire, yes, but also hatred. So much hatred. She showed me a vision of who I might be, if I ever allowed myself. She made me almost think that I . . ." My voice faded into silence. "I would have sooner died than hurt you," I whispered. "You must know that."

She did not speak, looking down at our entwined fingers.

"I should have told you," I went on. "I lied to you. I know you can never forgive me, but I . . . I regret it. All of it. I love you. I always will, no matter what."

When she finally looked up, her eyes shone with tears. In a quavering voice, she said, "I know that." She withdrew her hand, stood, and took the pile of reeking bandages heaped in a basin by the bedside. "I forgive you," she said and she turned heel, before I could speak again.

It took weeks before I could stand, and when I did, I swayed like a newborn foal, weak and ungainly, struggling to get my bearings. I persisted nevertheless, walking a little more each day, and soon I managed to tread across the room and back, albeit with a stiffness that Elizabeth's personal physician, Dr. Butts, assured me would ebb in time.

"You look as if you'd been in battle," he sniffed, examining the lattice of contusions from my struggle in the Thames, which covered most of my body in yellowed welts. "I've never seen a man take such a beating. And this cut on your brow: I fear you will have a scar."

I looked over his head to where Kate stood. We had not spoken again of my betrayal. She had said she did not want to know more, and I must respect it. Yet I had the sense she had known from the start that my withdrawal from her and decision to remain abroad, without word, had been prompted as much by guilt as the peril we faced. I resigned myself to our estrangement; I did not deserve her, and though she came to tend me every day, she remained aloof.

But as I now let her assist me to dress—she had seen me naked before and I was in no position to insist on modesty—tying up my hose and tugging on my boots, as I couldn't yet find much strength in my shoulder, I wanted to implore her forgiveness once more.

She let me clumsily haul myself upright before she said, "Her Majesty wants you to attend her coronation. She delayed it until January, so you would have sufficient time to recover. Cecil tried to dissuade her, but she would not hear of it."

"Then I must attend," I said.

Kate nodded, offering me her arm. "Before you do, she wishes to see you."

It felt strange moving through court, passing courtiers who stopped to stare and then, as we moved past, to whisper. I had always lived my life in the background, avoiding notice. Now, it seemed as if everyone knew me, though of course it was not so. My assignment had been clandestine, like my previous ones; the courtiers simply remarked on the sight of a man grown thin from enforced seclusion, his doublet hanging like someone else's on his frame as he leaned on the arm of a lady in waiting. The novelty of it was the only thing that attracted their attention. Within days, if not hours, they would forget it when another novelty arose.

At the entrance to her apartments, I found Cecil waiting. He glowered at the sight of me. Before he could remonstrate, I said, "I had no choice. She asked me. How could I refuse?"

"No one said you had to refuse," he replied, his pale blue eyes sparking. "But you might have at least left word. Walsingham searched London from attic to cellar for you."

Naturally, I wanted to say, no doubt with a warrant for my arrest; but Cecil preempted me with unexpected deference: "You served her well, indeed," and he led us into Elizabeth's rooms.

She stood by the window, clad in azure velvet, regal in her poise as she turned at my approach, her red-gold hair coiled at her nape, her long, slim fingers speckled with rings. She looked better, I noted, still too lean, but then she never did seem to put on flesh, her appetite subsumed by restlessness. As I made to bow, she said, "No ceremony." She flicked her hand at Cecil and Kate, who retreated to leave us alone.

"Does he know?" I asked.

"Do you think me a fool?" She stepped to me. "Cecil believes you helped bring down a Spanish assassin intent on my demise. He may suspect more, but he will never ask. To do so would compromise him beyond his abilities."

She did not need to elaborate. Cecil was busy rounding up royal suitors for a virgin queen; the revelation that she was not would indeed complicate his task.

"Robert does, though," she added, "as I believe he told you. He took Hugh from the boat and brought him here to me." She motioned to a chair. "You grow pale. You may sit."

"By your leave, I would prefer to stand. I've been resting long enough."

She frowned. "Is this the time to question me?"

"Not anymore. I think we confided all that needed to be said in the Tower."

"So you will ask nothing more?" She sounded doubtful. "You intend to let this matter between us rest?"

"I also hid a secret," I replied. "I believe that entitles you to have yours."

A small laugh escaped her. It lit up her face, reminding me of the fallible young woman she still was, only twenty-five, with a divided realm she must make her own. She moved to the door to her bedchamber, rapped on it with her knuckles. When it opened, Lady Parry emerged. Clinging to her hand was a sturdy figure with fresh-cropped, dark red-gold hair.

I staggered to one knee. He let out a cry, running into my arms. I did not feel the pain, then, ignoring the sharp stab in my shoulder and throbbing of my bruises as he clung to me.

"I knew you would come," he said, his voice muffled against my doublet. "You are my friend."

"Yes, I am." A lump formed in my chest. I gazed up at Elizabeth. She stood silent but her expression filled with a gratitude that told me more than any words. With a smile, Lady Parry nodded at me. She was still pale and thin from her trials but also clearly on the mend.

"He must be kept from court," Elizabeth said. "I never had a childhood or youth; he must not suffer the same." She bit her lower lip, watching her son in my arms. "I want you and Kate to raise him at Hatfield."

"Hatfield," echoed Raff brightly. "The pretty lady says Hatfield is my home."

I met Elizabeth's eyes. "It would mean . . ."

She nodded. "It would, but his safety is everything. Besides, I have Cecil and Walsingham to protect me now. You have done enough—more than enough, some might say."

"And Kate . . . ?" I was having trouble speaking, every word sticking to the roof of my mouth. She offered me the one thing I never expected: the choice to leave the court, to retire and care for her child, to enjoy as much of an ordinary life as a man like me could hope for. I would never have imagined it; I had thought instead to request her leave to return abroad, an agent in Cecil's service, far from the memory of what I had lost.

"I should think you will need to ask her," said Elizabeth. "But if I know Kate, I am certain of her answer." She tugged one of her ruby rings from her fingers. "You will need this," she added, with a wry smile. "Maidens like to be properly enticed."

I bent my face, kissing Raff's forehead. He beamed at me. "I'll see you very soon," I promised, and he nodded, returning to Lady Parry, who led him away.

After I took the ring from her, Elizabeth regarded me with unvoiced sadness.

This time, I bowed low. She was, after all, my queen.

I found Kate alone in the anteroom, waiting. She rose quickly from her stool in a soft fall of skirts. "Cecil left to attend to plans for the coronation," she said, clasping her hands before her stomacher. "He told me he would speak with you later. Did she . . . ?" Her voice faltered; I knew in that instant that Elizabeth had confided in her about the child.

"She did." I stepped to her. "Kate, can you forgive me?"

"I told you that I already have." She tried to remain composed, as if the fragility between us might crumble anew. "I must ask your forgiveness, too. The way I treated you when you arrived at court . . . I had no right."

I laughed, startling her. "Oh, you had every right." I withdrew Elizabeth's ring from my doublet. "Kate Stafford, though I am surely the most undeserving of men, will you be my wife? Will you come away with me and never look back?"

She looked down at the ring, tears starting in her eyes. Then, with a trembling breath, she whispered, "Yes. I will, Brendan Prescott, most undeserving of men that you are."

I gathered her in my arms, setting my lips on hers with a sigh.

At last, I knew where I belonged.

On January 15, 1559, the date designated by Dudley's astrologer Dee as the most auspicious, we gathered in Westminster Abbey among a horde of dignitaries, nobles, and officials, while outside in the snow-strewn streets, the crowds shouted their approval as bells clamored and the new queen of England made her procession from the Tower.

The pew selected for us was not close to where her throne waited, but it did not matter. When she reached the Abbey to a deafening blast of trumpets, ablaze in cloth of gold trimmed in ermine, her hair loose upon her shoulders and mantle carried by noblewomen, she was all any of us could see, her stately walk down the aisle as we dropped into obeisance bringing a surge of pride and joy to my heart.

She kept her chin up and gaze level, never once acknowledging those around her, as if it were only her and that empty throne in private consummation; but I saw her tremble faintly and recognized, as few could, her awareness of what it had cost her to attain this glory. Now, she must prove worthy of it. Elizabeth I's reign had only just begun.

As she knelt at the altar for her ceremonial anointing and the trumpets blared again, Kate slipped her hand in mine. I turned to her. Though a queen took the throne that day, my eyes remained fixed on the woman with whom I would spend the rest of my life.

Dudley came to me during the banquet in Westminster Palace. The cavernous hall had become an arbor, silken greenery slung from the high eaves and tapestries hugging the ancient, damp-streaked walls. I was not sure how I felt, watching his damask swagger and envy-provoking proximity to the queen, flaunting before all the high favor in which she held him. Around us, conversation and wine flowed, Elizabeth at the high dais sampling an endless round of dishes before the pages circulated them among her guests.

All of a sudden, he was at my side. "Prescott," he said, "a moment alone, if you would?"

Kate gave me quick assent, and so I left my seat to follow him. He led me from the hall, past nobles already scheming in various alcoves, down the corridors where the chill of the day congealed into frigid night, until we reached an empty enclosed courtyard, the star-speckled sky above us outlined by Westminster's barbed silhouette.

Without preamble he said, "I wish to suggest a truce."

He stood with one hand on his hip, magnificent as only he could be, the jeweled gleam of Elizabeth's favor draped upon his shoulders. His dark eyes flared when I did not answer. "Do you not agree? You intend to hold enmity against me forever?"

"My lord," I said, "the enmity is also yours. You would have seen me to my death."

He clenched his jaw. At length, he said, "I only followed her command."

"As you always do," I replied, though I already recognized that this lifelong quarrel between us must end. He was the man Elizabeth had chosen to love; I did not agree with it and probably never would, but I could not fight it anymore. Moreover, how could I judge, after I too had succumbed to destructive passion? Only those who suffered it could learn to overcome it.

"She intervened," Dudley said, and if I had not known him as well as I did, I might have thought he attempted an apology. "I took that ring to her as you bade. She went to see you. She believed whatever it was you told her." His voice hardened. "You can consider yourself safe now. She will not let anyone, including me, harm you again."

I resisted a smile. Elizabeth might love him, shared her secret with him, but she had not confessed everything. She knew Dudley could never be trusted with the truth of who I was.

He eyed me, pawing the ground with the tip of his boot. "Well? I propose a truce, not a friendship. I hear you will depart court anyway, to retire to Hatfield and tend a garden. I see no reason why we cannot agree to dislike each other from a distance. Not to mention, I spared you from that she-wolf, when I might have killed you as well and claimed she did it."

"Yes," I agreed quietly. "That you did."

He wrenched off one of his cordovan leather gloves, extending his hand to me. As I reached out to take it, he suddenly grasped me, yanking me close. "That evidence against me you said you had," he breathed. "I trust it too will be forgotten?"

I drew back. "Naturally, my lord," I replied and I turned heel, leaving him to scowl.

It was also wise to let him believe I still had something to hold over his head.

Before we departed for Hatfield, Kate and I went to the grave-yard by the Tower to pay our respects to Peregrine. The mound of earth was hoar-frosted now, a simple stone crucifix set at its tip the only indication that a beloved friend lay there. We held hands and said a prayer for his departed soul, Kate struggling to contain her tears.

We then rode to the Griffin, where we found Archie on the mend, though his wound had been even worse than mine, and his recovery not as swift. Still, he lumbered about the tavern, grumbling of how Nan kept fussing over him until he thought he might go mad. Kate persuaded him to let her assess his injury and apply her special herbal salve. While she did, Nan and I shared a tankard and I told her the queen had granted me a pension and retirement from service.

"Only a pension?" she exclaimed. "She owes you a title and deed of land to go with it, after everything you endured for her sake!"

"She would have given it, had I asked," I said. "I did not. I never needed much."

Nan harrumphed. "More's the fool who refuses what could be taken." Nevertheless, she was ecstatic that Kate and I planned to wed and would reside in Hertfordshire, far from London. "We'll come to visit as soon as he is well. You must not marry until we do," she added, with an emphatic wag of her finger. "We must be present to witness the ceremony."

"I am well now, woman," Archie declared, shrugging on his shirt as Kate hid her grin and left a jar of her salve on the side table. "This girl can work miracles with her touch. Look: I am ten years younger already."

Nan rolled her eyes, beckoning Kate. "I have some fresh-baked pies you can take with you on your journey." Together, they went into the kitchen.

Shelton gave me a pensive look. "Are you happy, lad?"

"I am," I said. "Or at least, I plan to be."

"Well? Which is it?"

"Both." I looked away as I spoke. He said gently, "It will not be easy, staying away from her. It is all you have done these past seven years—protect and defend her. You might get bored after a while with all that country air and lovemaking."

"Good!" I laughed. "I hope so. You must also visit us often. I . . . I need my father, now that I have found him."

He grunted, only now he was the one to avert his face. "Yes, well, we'll see that we do, eh?" He paused, returning his gaze to me. "The lad. Is he . . . ?"

I nodded. "He will live with us. He is at Hatfield already. He does not understand what happened to him; only that it was terrifying and now he is safe."

"Innocence," grinned Shelton. "It is a rare gift. Only children and beasts have it."

Kate called from the kitchen: "Brendan, it's starting to snow. We should be on our way."

I rose and helped Shelton upstairs. As I began to step away, he grabbed me in his burly embrace. "Be well, my son," he said, his voice rough. "You deserve happiness. Love and cherish Kate, and the lad, too. And let queen and kingdom shift for themselves."

I held him tight. "You, too. Take care of that wound. Do not overexert yourself."

We parted abruptly, as men do, Shelton saying he must rest a while as I took the stairs back down to find Kate in her cloak, a covered basket of Nan's pies on her arm. Nan wept unabashedly as she kissed us good-bye, promising to come and see us soon. I knew they would, but as we went outside to untether our horses and I helped Kate mount before I clambered awkwardly onto Cinnabar, I was stricken with sudden melancholy.

"He is not a young man," Kate reassured me. "But his injury will heal in time."

I nodded, taking one last lingering gaze at the tavern before I turned to her.

"Come, my love. Let us go home."

Author's Note

𝕴 am indebted as always to my agent, Jennifer Weltz, who continues to champion my work with enthusiasm and expert guidance, as well as to her colleagues at the Jean V. Naggar Literary Agency, Inc. I am also grateful to my editor, Charlie Spicer; assistant editor April Osborn; copy editor Eva Talmadge; and the creative team at St. Martin's Press. In the United Kingdom, my editor, Suzie Dooré, and her team at Hodder & Stoughton publish me with vigor and I am so appreciative for their support, especially to Suzie for her keen editorial skills. I also wish to give thanks to my friend Linda Dolan, who read an early draft of this book and provided suggestions for improvement, as well as my friend Sarah Johnson, who is always there to talk me through the shoals of my profession and read portions of my works in progress.

At home, my partner supports and encourages me, taking care of everyday details that I neglect in my preoccupation with writing. I am indeed blessed to have him. My cats, Chu and Mommy, have endeavored to fill the void left by the loss of my beloved corgi, Paris, and bring me joy, laughter, and love every day, reminding me that tuna time, naps, and belly rubs are not optional.

Independent bookstores are my heroes; in this increasingly complex era of digital revolution and entertainment choices, they continue to promote the importance of the printed word. I especially wish to thank Bookshop West Portal and Orinda Books for handselling my books, recommending me to book groups, and supporting local authors.

In that vein, I am also grateful to all the bloggers who participate in my virtual tours, as well as those who discover my books and take the time to review or mention them.

My author friends, in particular M. J. Rose, Margaret George, Donna Morin, and Michelle Moran, keep me sane when it all starts to feel overwhelming, sharing this often perplexing path of being a fellow writer with me, with all its myriad ups and downs.

Last, but never least, I thank you, my reader. Your e-mails, social media messages, comments on book-related sites, and ongoing support mean so much to me. Without a reader, a writer's words are mute. You give them voice. I hope to entertain you for many years to come.

Rescue work is my passion. Every day in the United States, over ten thousand homeless animals die because of irresponsible breeding and ownership. I will continue to fight against shelter euthanasia and for the rights of animals who cannot defend themselves.

To learn more about my work and schedule book group chats with me, please visit: www.cwgortner.com.

Reading Group Questions

1. *The Tudor Vendetta* takes place in the first few months of Elizabeth I's accession to the throne. What did you discover about the country she first inherited? What were some of the challenges she faced? How does England at the start of her reign differ from her later years?

2. Religious conflict in England is a strong motivator for certain characters. How did Catholics feel about Elizabeth Tudor's right to rule? Do you see any parallels in today's religious divides?

3. Brendan Prescott is Elizabeth I's private spy. In this novel, he must make difficult choices that change his perception of the queen he serves. What are some of the decisions he faces? How do you think you may have acted if you were in his shoes?

4. Secrets are the underlying theme of this series. Do you find the secrets credible?

5. What are your perceptions of Philippa Vaughan? Do you understand her reasons for her actions? What does her character tell us about the roles of women in the Tudor world?

6. Brendan's relationship with Elizabeth is one of both confidant and pawn. Do you agree with how Elizabeth treats him? What are your impressions of his loyalty to the queen? Do you think he likes her?

7. Yorkshire, London Bridge, and the Tower are sites featured in this novel. What did you learn about how common people lived? What are some of the differences they faced compared to those who lived at court? If you had to choose, where would you prefer to live?

Reading Group Questions

8. Elizabeth Tudor is one of history's most famous queens, but here we see a different side of her. Do you agree with the author's depiction of her? Did you find her sympathetic? Why or why not?

9. During the course of the novel, there are many twists and turns. Which was most unexpected for you?

10. Who was your favorite character in the book and why?